Praise for Betty Rowlands' previous
Melissa Craig Mysteries:

A LITTLE GENTLE SLEUTHING

'A first novel by a clearly gifted and knowledgeable
writer, never less than engaging and readable'
Financial Times

'In her first crime novel, Betty Rowlands creates a
fine new heroine'
Scotland on Sunday

FINISHING TOUCH

'Gently old fashioned whodunnit, riddled with
lurking anguish'
The Times

'Melissa Craig, the canny and vigorous crime
novelist who is the protagonist of the novels of
Betty Rowlands, is an engaging, human heroine'
Financial Times

OVER THE EDGE

'An engaging tale, following the style of the best
British whodunnits'
Cotswold Life

'She has the rare skill that grabs the reader's
complete attention at page one and holds it to the
end'
Wootton Bassett Standard

About the author

In 1988 Betty Rowlands won the Sunday Express/ Veuve Clicquot Crime Short Story of the Year Competition. Her success continued with the publication of her three crime novels featuring Melissa Craig, *A Little Gentle Sleuthing*, *Finishing Touch* and *Over the Edge*. As K. E. Rowlands she has written English language courses for foreign executives and has taught business French and English as a foreign language.

She lives in Gloucestershire and has three grown-up children and four grandchildren.

Exhaustive Enquiries

Betty Rowlands

CORONET BOOKS
Hodder and Stoughton

First published in Great Britain in 1993
by Hodder & Stoughton Ltd

First published in paperback in 1994
by Hodder and Stoughton, a division of Hodder Headline PLC

A Coronet paperback

Translation from 'Die Moritat von Mackie Messer'
by Bertolt Brecht
Reproduced by permission of Universal Edition

A CIP catalogue record is available from the British Library

ISBN 0 340 60178 7

Printed and bound in Great Britain by
Cox & Wyman Ltd, Reading, Berkshire

Hodder and Stoughton Ltd
A Division of Hodder Headline PLC
338 Euston Road
London NW1 3BH

EXHAUSTIVE ENQUIRIES

Exhaustive Enquiries

Betty Rowlands

CORONET BOOKS
Hodder and Stoughton

First published in Great Britain in 1993
by Hodder & Stoughton Ltd

First published in paperback in 1994
by Hodder and Stoughton, a division of Hodder Headline PLC

A Coronet paperback

Translation from 'Die Moritat von Mackie Messer'
by Bertolt Brecht
Reproduced by permission of Universal Edition

A CIP catalogue record is available from the British Library

ISBN 0 340 60178 7

Printed and bound in Great Britain by
Cox & Wyman Ltd, Reading, Berkshire

Hodder and Stoughton Ltd
A Division of Hodder Headline PLC
338 Euston Road
London NW1 3BH

EXHAUSTIVE
ENQUIRIES

Chapter One

About the middle of August, Melissa Craig had a telephone call from Joe Martin.

'Just wondering how the new novel's coming along,' he said, his tone deceptively casual. 'How many corpses so far?'

'Three. The latest has been put on ice for a while.'

'You mean he's in the morgue?'

'No, in limbo. I'm working on something else.'

There was a pause, during which Melissa gleefully visualised her agent's brow knotted in disapproval. When she made no attempt to enlighten him, he said stiffly, 'Am I to be told what the "something else" is?'

'Of course, it's not a secret. I'm writing a piece for a local drama group. Their producer is a lecturer at the college where I teach my creative writing class.'

'What sort of piece?' asked Joe suspiciously.

'A pantomime,' said Melissa, wishing she could see his face.

'A *what*?'

'Perhaps "panto*crime*" would be more accurate.' Minor explosions of exasperation fizzled along the wire as Melissa, suppressing with difficulty the laughter in her voice, explained. 'Murderous plots and murky deeds, all in rhyming couplets.'

'What's it in aid of, for God's sake?' spluttered Joe. 'No, don't tell me. The Cotswold Senior Citizens' annual Christmas treat. Or some new fringe activity called "Entertainment for the Feeble-Minded".'

'You shouldn't make fun of the elderly or the handicapped,' reproved Melissa. 'You'll be among their number yourself one day.'

'Thank you for reminding me. Meanwhile, may I remind *you* that you have a deadline?'

'I haven't forgotten. This'll only take a week or two and I'm having a lot of fun with it. I shall return to *Dancing with Death* with renewed enthusiasm.'

'I should hope so.' There was another pause. 'Well, aren't you going to tell me more about your pantocrime?'

'If you really want to know, but I should warn you, there isn't anything in it for you.'

'I guessed as much.'

'Joe, just for once, forget about money. Chloe produces for the Stowbridge Players and she asked me along to one of their readings. Some wealthy eccentric wants an entertainment for the guests at his birthday party and as it happens to coincide with Hallowe'en, they thought they'd make it a spooky murder mystery.'

'And?'

'They'd chosen a piece from some published collection for amateurs but it was pretty turgid. Chloe asked if I could give them some ideas for improving it.'

'If advice was all they wanted . . .' began Joe, but Melissa hadn't finished.

'I suggested that as it was a party and everyone would be half cut by the time they settled down to watch, there was no point in treating it too seriously,' she explained. 'I thought it'd be fun to make a few changes – you know, camp it up a bit – but Chloe was concerned about copyright, so . . .'

'. . . so you undertook to write a completely new script, I suppose? Really, Mel, you might consider your poor starving agent before wasting your valuable time on frivolous causes.'

'Starving be blowed! Last time we met, you looked sleeker than ever. Anyway, I'm really enjoying this.'

'Just the same, if this character's so wealthy, I don't see why he can't pay for his entertainment.'

'But he is paying. He's coughed up several K for lights and sound equipment in Stowbridge Assembly Rooms.'

'Big deal. Who is he, anyway?'

'A chap by the name of Mitchell. Very matey, by all accounts. Likes to be called Mitch.'

'Not Richard Mitchell?' The sudden change of tone conjured up a picture of Joe with head raised, ears pricked and nostrils quivering, like a hunting dog scenting the air. 'Rich Mitch – the one the tabloids call "the barrow-boy millionaire"?'

'What a vulgar way to describe anyone . . .'

'Always hitting the financial headlines . . . owns a string of companies . . . branched out into the hotel business a year or so ago?'

'Could be. Chloe mentioned he owns the Heyshill Manor Hotel, where this thrash is taking place. Gosh, I wonder if it is him!' Melissa, never able to resist an opportunity of teasing Joe, assumed a sultry tone of voice. 'How exciting – I've always wanted to meet a millionaire. Perhaps I can wangle a meeting. They say he's a handsome hunk, too, and still a bachelor . . . mmm!'

'Up to you. I doubt if he'd be your type.' This time there was frost on the line.

'Now, why should you say that? He might be very charming – and he'd be quite a catch, wouldn't he? If I could nobble him, I wouldn't need to write crime novels for a living.' That was a bit cruel, she thought, knowing how Joe felt about her, but it did no harm to remind him now and then that she didn't rate him a potential suitor.

'You be careful,' said Joe in what she thought of as his schoolmaster's voice. 'Where there's that sort of money, there are crooks.'

Melissa burst out laughing. 'Oh Joe, anyone would think he belonged to the Mafia!'

'How do you know he doesn't? Your so-called "pantocrime" might be a set-up for some scam or other.'

9

'Oh, shut up!' It was illogical, of course, but the word 'scam' sent a *frisson* up her spine. 'You know I don't appreciate that sort of joke.'

'Who said I was joking? Just be on your guard, that's all. And remember your deadline.' Before she could think of a riposte, he hung up.

Having handed a script entitled *The Grisly Fate of Ann Bull of Cow Lane, or Innocent Blood Avenged* to a grateful Chloe Anderson, Melissa prepared to resume work on her current novel. The weather, however, was far too pleasant to be wasted at a desk and by ten o'clock each morning she was out of doors, revelling in the blue skies and glowing warmth of the early September days and congratulating herself on having had the good sense and good fortune to leave London and settle in a peaceful Cotswold village.

'How I endured living in town I can't imagine,' she remarked one morning to her artist friend who occupied the cottage adjoining her own. With a contented sigh, she contemplated the multi-hued mass of flowers bordering her little kitchen garden, the ripe fruit on her apple tree and the hawthorn hedge bejewelled with scarlet berries. 'Who'd swap this for traffic fumes and buses thundering past the window?'

Iris Ash, lean as a shoot from a coppiced hazel and brown as a nut, paused in her task of lifting potatoes and wandered across to the fence dividing the two gardens.

'So you opted for combine harvesters and the smell of dung!' With a wry grin, she jerked her head of short, mouse-brown hair in the direction of a heavy machine throbbing and clanking to and fro in a dusty haze on the far side of the valley.

'Oh, you know what I mean,' said Melissa. 'Country noises and smells aren't nearly so bad. And it's such a joy to be able to grow my own vegetables,' she added smugly, throwing a handful of freshly gathered beans into a basket.

'Good crop there,' said Iris, eyeing the heap of long green pods. 'Going to freeze 'em?'

'Not all of them. I promised some to Chloe.'

'Your actress pal? How's the show coming on?'

'First rehearsal this evening. She's invited me along, and guess who'll be there. Rich Mitch in person.'

'Lucky you. Saw his picture in the *Gazette* a few days ago, handing over a cheque for some worthy cause.'

'Yes, I've heard he's a bit of a philanthropist. I've been kidding poor old Joe that I've got designs on him.'

'Watch it!' Iris's grey eyes twinkled. 'The Honourable Penelope de Lavier is about to land him, so I'm told.'

'Iris! I didn't know you read the gossip columns!'

'Got it from a client.' Iris was much in demand as a painter of water-colours of the houses and gardens of local landowners.

'Did you learn anything else?'

Iris raised an eyebrow. 'Why all the interest? Not seriously after him, are you?'

'Don't be wet, Iris, of course I'm not. He's still in his thirties – too young for either of us, I'm afraid. Pity.' Melissa sighed in mock regret. 'He might find a mature lady crime writer more intriguing than some feather-brained deb with shoulder-length legs.'

'Penelope de Lavier is no feather-brain,' declared Iris who, it emerged, had had her ear bent for the better part of an hour by an ambitious, but in this matter disappointed, mother of an eligible daughter. 'Runs the Dizzy Heights boutiques with Lady Charlotte Heighton. Wants finance – plans to get it along with the wedding cake.'

'That rings a bell. Didn't I read something in *The Times* Business Section? They've got plans to open more branches and they're looking for a backer.'

'Not looking any more, according to Lady Vowden,' said Iris with a puckish grin. 'And she says Penny and Charlotte's motto is "finders keepers" so you'd better not be too charming to young Midas or you'll get a knife in your back.'

'Now don't you start! I've had enough dire warnings from

11

Joe about the danger of sinister connections with the underworld.'

'You're cruel to that nice man.' Iris had long expressed the opinion that Melissa should give Joe more encouragement. 'By the way,' she added inconsequentially, in a careless tone that entirely failed to deceive, 'if your thespians want a hand with set designs, I wouldn't mind helping out.'

'And get to meet Rich Mitch at the same time? Iris! Fancy you turning into a gold-digger, at your age!'

Iris was unabashed. 'Seriously. Might lead to a commission to paint his haunted manor.'

'Is it haunted? Chloe never said.'

'Got to be. Built over the remains of a medieval priory. Well, can't stop here gossiping. Want to finish this before lunch.' Iris levered herself away from the fence and reached for her fork. 'By the way, got a spook in this panto thing, haven't you?' She gave a throaty cackle. 'Hope the real ones don't think you're making fun of 'em. Might turn nasty!'

Chapter Two

'This fellow Mitchell is a bit of an oddball,' said Chloe as she parked her elderly Fiesta among the Range Rovers, Porsches and Mercedes in the forecourt of the Heyshill Manor Hotel. 'Insists we have all the rehearsals here, intends to be at every one, wants to speak the prologue himself and brings in some boozy old pal of his Dad's to play the policeman.'

'Wish fulfilment – indulging a lifelong desire to tread the boards?' suggested Melissa.

Chloe shrugged. 'Could be, I suppose. I only hope they've got some talent between them. I thought tycoons gave the orders and then let their minions get on with it.'

'I'm sure a lot of them do, but I suppose some like to know what's going on in their offices. I've heard of heads of corporations wandering round incognito and ringing up branches to check that the receptionist isn't being rude to the customers.'

Chloe grunted. 'That makes sense when they understand the business. I get the impression this character doesn't know a fly tower from a proscenium arch.'

'I shouldn't worry,' chuckled Melissa. 'I doubt if you'll have either in the small function room.'

'Oh, you know what I mean. He's tickled pink with your script, by the way.'

'That's good.'

Chloe heaved her substantial form out of the car and began groping behind her seat. 'Oh blast!' she muttered. 'I forgot the bag of props.'

'What props?'

'The stuff for the prologue – you know, the knife, the gun, the bottle with the label marked "Poison" . . .'

Melissa burst out laughing. 'You've failed the first test, I'm afraid – you'd better collect your cards.'

Chloe's plump face was a study in dismay. 'He'll think I'm hopelessly inefficient,' she wailed.

'Don't admit to forgetting – just say your props person hasn't prepared them yet and he's got to mime. It'll make him feel ever so professional. Come on, it's almost seven o'clock. You'll lose Brownie points for being late.'

'Hope the others are here.' Chloe cast an eye round the gravelled forecourt. 'Oh good, there's Dittany's car – she's bringing some of them.'

'Who?'

'Dittany Blair. Unusual name, isn't it? Some sort of flower, I believe.'

'Rather beautiful. Like this place.' While they were speaking, Melissa had been admiring the broad façade of the ancient manor house, its walls of honey-coloured Cotswold stone made golden by the evening light. 'Iris hinted that it has quite a history.'

'So I believe. The main part of the building's Jacobean but the site is much older. It's been added to, of course, and modernised. The new conference wing is at the back, out of sight.'

'I'll bet it costs a fortune to stay here.'

The oak-beamed reception hall was thickly carpeted, the atmosphere a subtle blend of pot-pourri, wax polish and general opulence. A gilded basket of bronze chrysanthemums stood on a marble column and the walls were hung with pictures of horses and hounds racing across fields and jumping over hedges. Above a stone fireplace, carved with a coat of arms, hung a portrait of a beaming, ruddy-faced gentleman, resplendent in scarlet jacket, black cap and white stock.

'The previous owner, Master of the local hunt,' Chloe informed Melissa.

14

A good-looking blonde woman in an elegant black suit, faultlessly groomed and coiffured, was welcoming a couple who had just arrived. She glanced up as Chloe and Melissa entered, flashed them a brilliant smile and tilted her head over one shoulder.

'Mr Mitchell and his party are here,' she informed them. 'Go straight through.'

'What a gorgeous creature!' whispered Melissa as they made their way along a corridor.

'That's Kim Bellamy, the manager's wife. I met them both last week when I came to look at the room where we're performing this epic. They've been very helpful.'

'They would be, wouldn't they? You're working for their boss,' Melissa pointed out. 'Are those diamonds genuine, do you suppose?'

'They look like the real thing, don't they? They must get jolly good wages – or perhaps she's got a wealthy admirer.'

They passed through a double door marked 'Priory Suite' into a vestibule leading to a kitchen, cloakroom and toilets. Swing doors at the far end were marked 'Conference Room' and as the two women passed through them the faint buzz of a digital watch sounded at the far end of a large, sunny room with panelled walls and mullioned windows.

'That's what I like, good timing!' A youngish man in a well cut slate-blue suit came to meet them. 'Evening, Chloe. This the lady who wrote our script?'

'Melissa, may I introduce . . .' began Chloe, but the attempt at formality was brushed aside.

'Richard Mitchell – call me Mitch.'

'Melissa Craig – call me Mel,' Melissa heard herself say as she took the proffered hand.

His eyes, set in a clean-shaven, tanned face, widened in surprise. '*The* Mel Craig – the crime novelist?' He turned to Chloe. 'You never told me she was that famous!' He pumped Melissa's hand energetically and then released it with a look

15

of deep concern. 'Sorry, don't know me own strength – hope I haven't damaged the writing hand!'

'I don't think you've broken any bones,' said Melissa, flexing her fingers and feigning acute pain.

With great solicitude, he took her hand between both his and massaged it. His skin was warm and dry; she found the contact distinctly agreeable. 'All better now!' he announced, with a pronounced glottal stop and a lop-sided grin that immediately called to mind Joe's reference to the 'barrow-boy millionaire'. With that impish expression and the clipped, metallic London accent, he would have no difficulty charming susceptible housewives into buying double quantities of oranges and bananas.

'Meet me pals,' continued Mitch. 'This is the Hon. Pen.' He took the arm of a slinky brunette who had been hovering at his elbow and now showed her disapproval of his style of introduction by a pout and a flick of theatrically made-up eyes, half hidden behind drooping lids. Mitch responded with an unabashed grin.

'Sorry, duchess!' He assumed the affected accent of a comedian aping the aristocracy. 'I mean, of course, the Honourable Penelope de Lavier. Say "hello" to our script-writer, Pen.'

Penelope held out a limp hand. 'How d'you do?' she drawled. 'I think you're awfully clever.'

'Thank you,' murmured Melissa.

'And this is Will Foley, an old mate of me Dad's from the smoke. Staying down here at his daughter's place for a bit. He's playing the copper in your panto.'

Will had thinning grizzled hair and a steady gaze that reminded Melissa of her friend, Detective Chief Inspector Kenneth Harris. He transferred the drink he was holding to his left hand and took Melissa's right in a firm clasp.

'Nice to meet you, Mel. I like your books.'

'Thank you.'

'Chris Bright's me minder,' Mitch continued. 'Makes sure

I keep all me appointments and don't drive when I'm over the odds.' A stockily built man of about his own age, with shoulders like an American footballer and a pugnacious expression, shook hands and nodded without speaking. 'Well, now you know us all. What happens next, Chloe? Where is everyone?'

'I expect they're waiting in the kitchenette,' said Chloe. 'I told them we'll be using it as a greenroom.'

Mitch's brow puckered. 'Greenroom?'

'Rest room. Where the actors relax when they're not on stage,' Chloe explained. 'Theatre jargon.'

Mitch, apparently unaware of the hint of superiority in her tone, looked impressed. 'You learn something every minute,' he said. 'Did you know that, Pen?'

For the first time, a spark of animation appeared on the chiselled features of the Honourable Penelope and she laid a scarlet-tipped hand on Mitch's arm. 'Of course I did, darling,' she purred. 'I know lots of theatre people.' The look she gave him would have melted Arctic snow and her voice was a mixture of honey and cream as she added, 'We simply must tear ourselves away from business now and again and do some London shows, mustn't we? And there's Stratford just up the road from here – I do so *adore* Shakespeare!'

'She thinks I need educating,' Mitch explained cheerfully to the world at large.

Unseen by Mitch, Chloe telegraphed 'What did I tell you?' to Melissa with an upward roll of her eyes and strode towards a door in the far corner of the room, to the left of the platform which would be serving as a stage. Despite her bulk, she had a graceful, almost regal carriage and she dressed with flair. This evening she was wearing a flowing tobacco-brown dress that flattered her fresh colouring and dramatised her generous but well-proportioned figure.

Mitch's gaze followed her with appreciation and there was admiration in his voice as he remarked, 'Some woman, that!' which evoked a look of disdain from the Honourable Penelope.

Chloe returned with three women and one man, whom she proceeded to introduce to Mitch and his friends. 'Felicity is playing the kitchenmaid who's falsely accused of murder and Norman is her lover, the gamekeeper. Sheila is the heroine's personal maid, in love with the same man but rejected and fiendishly jealous. And this,' she turned to a slender girl with delicate features and smooth, glossy brown hair, 'is Dittany, who's playing the heroine, Ann Bull.'

'And a very beautiful heroine she is, too!' said Mitch as he took Dittany's small hand in his. 'What a smashing name! What does it mean?'

Dittany looked gravely up at him with large, golden-brown eyes. 'It's an aromatic plant that grows in Crete. My father's an amateur botanist so he gave me and my sister floral names.'

'Nice idea,' said Mitch, still holding her hand. 'What's your sister called?'

'Asphodel.' There was a hint of mischief behind the gravity as she added, 'She hates it because she was called "Bog" at school, but I quite like mine.'

If the botanical joke was lost on Mitch, there was no mistaking his enchantment with Dittany. 'It's the loveliest name I've ever heard and it suits you perfectly,' he assured her earnestly.

Penelope jerked impatiently at his arm. 'Darling,' she drawled, 'we're wasting time. I'm sure Chloe is dying to get started.'

'Oh, sure.' Mitch released Dittany's hand, which she had seemed in no hurry to withdraw. He glanced round. 'Hang on a minute – we aren't all here. Where's the two villains?'

'They'll be along presently. I told them we shouldn't be needing them till later,' said Chloe crisply.

Her manner, with its hint of bossiness, drew a little bow of mock deference from Mitch. 'As you say, ma'am! What do we do first?'

'We'll start with a run-through of the prologue – that's you, Mitch – and then do Scene One. Everyone got their scripts?' Heads wagged and scripts were waved in confirmation.

'Right. On stage Mitch, Sheila and Dittany. Mitch, I want you to stand centre front to speak your lines. You'll have a small table with your props and when you've finished I want you to pick it up and exit stage left.'

'Okay. Where's me props?'

'Sorry, they haven't been prepared yet. I thought you wouldn't mind miming, just for this evening.'

'Let's see, what are we talking about?' Ignoring Chloe's suggestion, Mitch consulted his script. 'Oh yeah – the knife, the rope, the gun and the poison. No problem, we can improvise. Sure to be a knife in the kitchen – someone go and look. Give us your tie, Chris, that'll do for a rope. Now, the poison . . .' He looked round for inspiration. 'I know! Pen, chuck us your Mogadons.'

'Oh darling, I do *wish* you wouldn't call them that – you make me sound like a junkie!' protested Penelope.

'Only teasing,' grinned Mitch, but Penelope seemed determined to dispel any misunderstandings.

'They're herbal capsules, to help me relax,' she explained. 'Running a business is *so* stressful nowadays and I simply *hate* the thought of taking drugs.'

'I do so agree with you!' Dittany called enthusiastically from the stage. 'I'm into herbalism as well.'

'Really?' The indifference in Penelope's voice bordered on rudeness but Dittany either did not notice or chose to ignore it.

'Yes, really. Daddy's just published a fascinating book about it. I'll lend it to you if you like.'

'I doubt if I could find time to read it,' said Penelope in the same dismissive tone; then, remembering her society manners, 'Frightfully nice of you to offer.' She rummaged in her handbag and produced a small glass bottle with a bright flower on its label and tossed it to Mitch.

'Ta!' He caught it one-handed and put it on a chair at the front of the stage, together with Chris's tie and the knife that someone had been to fetch. 'I can pretend with the gun.' He aimed two fingers at Chloe like a small boy playing at cops and robbers. 'Bang! D'you want me to start now?'

'Not for the moment. Dittany, will you find a chair and sit at the back of stage right while Mitch does his piece. Sheila, you stand behind her. When he's finished, bring Dittany's chair centre front, sit her down on it and start your business with the brush and comb. Did you bring them, by the way?'

'Here.' Sheila held them aloft.

'Well done. We'll rig up a spotlight for the performance but we won't bother with it for now,' Chloe continued. 'What we'll do is leave the stage in darkness during the prologue, then turn off the spot and fade in the stage light.' She glanced upwards and pulled a face. 'Damn! It's a fluorescent tube – I wanted one with a dimmer. I wonder . . .'

'Get one fixed if you need it,' interrupted Mitch. 'Gotta do it properly.' He turned to his minder. 'See to it, Chris. Chlo'll tell you exactly what she wants.'

'Thanks, that'd be super!' A smile chased away Chloe's earlier condescension. 'Okay, ready everyone?'

Will Foley cleared his throat and held up his empty glass. 'Won't be wanting me for a while, will you?'

'Er, no, not just yet,' said Chloe.

'I'll be in the bar,' said Will and made for the door.

'Don't get pissed!' Mitch called after him. Catching Penelope's disapproving eye, he gave a disarming grin that emphasised the dimples at the corners of his mouth. 'Sorry, Pen! Right, let's get rolling.'

'Isn't there something I can do?' said Penelope peevishly. 'I mean, it's going to be a bit tedious if I have to sit through every rehearsal without some sort of a job.'

Chloe looked taken aback. Plainly, she had not bargained for Penelope's constant presence, but it came as no surprise to Melissa. Mitch was too valuable a quarry – and by all appearances too impressionable – to be allowed out of her sight.

'Er, well, all the parts are cast, I'm afraid,' said Chloe. 'You could take charge of the props, if you really want to help. We'll need a much larger poison bottle with a big label on it . . .'

'With a skull and crossbones,' suggested Mitch.

'. . . and one of those knives with a disappearing point that squirts stage blood all over the place . . .'

Mitch rubbed his hands in glee. 'Great! I've always wanted to play with one of those!'

'Can you manage to organise that?' asked Chloe, ignoring his interruptions.

'Yes, I suppose so.' Penelope's smile was gracious but cool. Remembering Iris's comment about 'finders keepers', Melissa made a mental note to put Chloe in the picture as soon as possible.

'Let's make a start, then,' said Chloe. 'Ready, Mitch?'

'Sure.' Mitch took up his position, cleared his throat, and declaimed the opening lines in traditional pantomime style:

> Good people all, our play tonight
> Tells of that ancient, deadly fight
> For love; a fight that ends in doom,
> Here, within this very room.

Melissa stole a sideways glance at Chloe and saw her eyebrows shoot up in gratified surprise. Mitch, by now fully into the spirit of the thing, embarked on the second stanza, the first two lines of which he delivered in the manner of a school-teacher addressing a class of five-year-olds:

> Among our players, one will die,
> As you shall witness by and by.

For the second couplet, his manner changed again; with rolling eyes and menacing leer, he spoke in a sepulchral growl as he raised each of his 'murder weapons' in turn, miming the appropriate actions:

21

How will the killer take the life?
By rope? By poison? Pistol? Knife?

On the final word, he threw down his script, held the kitchen knife aloft in both hands and, with a shout of maniacal laughter, plunged it into the body of an imaginary victim. There were chuckles from the rest of the cast, but Chris's face registered a comical blend of resignation and embarrassment while Penelope, wearing a detached expression, examined her fingernails.

'Was that okay, then?' asked Mitch, evidently well pleased with himself.

'Super!' called Dittany, upon which his smile became positively blissful.

'That was fine,' said Chloe, 'but don't forget to exit.'

'Eh? Oh, right.' Obediently, Mitch picked up his makeshift props table and moved aside as Sheila and Dittany took up their positions.

'Think he'll do?' whispered Melissa in Chloe's ear.

'He's a natural. I only hope Will's half as good.'

Mitch took a long pull from his tankard of bitter and said, 'What about some incidental music?'

After more than two hours of somewhat ragged rehearsal, Chloe, in response to an appeal from Penelope supported by Mitch, had declared that it wasn't bad for a first run-through and they'd leave it at that for tonight. Now, the entire company, together with their sponsor and his entourage, were relaxing in the small private bar.

Chloe considered Mitch's suggestion. 'We could ask the Music Club if they'd organise a trio or something, I suppose,' she said.

Mitch guffawed. 'I'm not talking about a chamber orchestra! I mean on the joanna, like they had with the old silent movies. Your Music Club got someone who can play that kind of stuff, Chlo? You know, diddle-diddle-dum, diddle-diddle-dum as the crooks are running away, and when the spook appears it goes BOMM, BOMM, BOMM, BOMM . . .'

'Yes, I get the idea.' Chloe joined in the general laughter as Mitch, eyes rolling in mock terror, beat out with both hands a thunderous cadenza that set the drinks dancing on the table.

'I think it'd be super!' Dittany nodded approval over the rim of her glass of orange juice. Her expression of serene gravity was suddenly illuminated by a smile of ineffable sweetness. 'Brilliant!'

Mitch blinked like a man dazzled by sunlight. 'You reckon?' he said. Natural courtesy made him include Chloe in the question but his eyes announced for all the world to see whose approval was the more important to him.

'Oh, yes!' Dittany fairly sparkled with enthusiasm. 'It would fit in so well with the pantomime atmosphere – don't you think so, Melissa?'

'I suppose it would, but perhaps Mitch should talk it over with your producer,' said Melissa in an attempt to give the initiative back to Chloe and at the same time divert Mitch's attention from Dittany. She had observed Penelope's expression during the exchanges and it carried an unmistakable storm warning.

'It's worth thinking about,' said Chloe, with a grateful glance at Melissa. 'We'd have to arrange for a piano to be brought in.'

'No problem. See to it, Chris.'

'Hang on a minute,' said Chloe as Chris reached for his notebook. 'We haven't thought it through yet. We'd need the right sort of piano.'

'Sure,' agreed Mitch. 'One of the old honky-tonk variety. Sort it out with Chris.'

'There's a dreadful old piano in our church hall,' said Melissa. 'I dare say they'd lend it to us if we offered to make a donation to the roof repair fund. Would you like me to have a word with the Rector, Chloe?'

'Thanks. We could talk about it on the way home.' Chloe

pulled a diary from her handbag. 'Now, a date for the next rehearsal. Is this time next week all right for everyone?'

'Next week?' Penelope looked aghast. 'We have to go through this . . . this mummery every week . . . for over a month?'

'You're getting off lightly. If it was a full-length production, we'd be rehearsing for at least a couple of months and it'd be every night for the final week before the show,' Chloe informed her briskly. 'Still, we can probably manage without you for the next couple of times, so long as you're here for the dress rehearsal.'

'There you are, Pen, no problem,' said Mitch, with a bland smile. 'I'll let you know how things are going.'

'Oh, it's all right, darling, I'll come along and keep you company,' purred Penelope, with a change of mood that was plainly an effort. 'But please, take me home now. I need a good night's rest before tomorrow's meeting. We're negotiating with a top designer from Italy,' she informed the assembly, one proprietorial hand on Mitch's arm. 'It's vital for our future strategy that everything goes smoothly, isn't it, darling?'

Mitch finished his beer and stood up. 'You're absolutely right, Pen – business before pleasure.'

It was not the most tactful of remarks and Melissa held her breath for a moment, but the Honourable Penelope had not attended an exclusive finishing school for nothing. With a gracious smile all round, and in the confident manner of one who has been trained to be aware of the effect of her every move, she uncrossed her long, perfect legs, rose to her feet and smoothed the skirt of her saffron-yellow designer suit.

'I just love that colour, it looks marvellous on you!' said Dittany, with a warmth and spontaneity that were obviously genuine.

Penelope responded with a regal inclination of the head. 'Thank you, my dear, how very sweet of you,' she said.

'I'll tell you what,' Dittany went on, either unaware that

she was being patronised or impervious to the fact. 'You shouldn't take too many of those capsules of yours – Daddy says they contain valerian, which tends to make you lethargic. Why don't you try these? They're just as soothing to the nerves and totally harmless.'

Penelope's smile was condescending. 'I'm sure my homeo-pathic consultant wouldn't prescribe anything that wasn't safe,' she said. With barely a glance at the bottle in the palm of Dittany's outstretched hand, she picked up her jacket and held it out to Mitch.

Dittany flushed. 'Oh, I didn't mean to suggest . . .' she began but Penelope ignored her. She snuggled into the jacket, contriving as she did so to brush Mitch's cheek with her hair, and twisted round to shoot him a glance full of promise before picking up her handbag and taking his arm.

'Well, good-night everyone. It's been a totally *fascinating* evening,' she murmured over her shoulder.

'We should be going as well,' said Chloe, standing up. Diaries were put away, drinks finished and chairs pushed back. In the general move towards the door, Melissa noticed the bearded young man who was playing the part of the mur-derer – one of the two who had arrived late and whose name she had failed to catch – take Dittany by the arm and whisper something in her ear. She appeared to give him only half her attention; her eyes were on Mitch and with an impatient shake of the head she hurried to rejoin his group while the man was still speaking. He seemed about to follow and remonstrate, but his companion restrained him.

In the reception hall, Kim Bellamy was seated at a com-puter while a heavily built man in a white dress-shirt with a crimson velvet bow tie studied the screen over her shoulder. They looked up with professional smiles as Mitch and his party appeared.

'Evening, Vic. Evening, Kim!' said Mitch.

'Good evening, Mr Mitchell. Was everything in order?'

'Fine, thanks. We're going to do a spot of work on the light

over the stage and there'll be a piano coming some time.'
He gestured at Chris. 'Mr Bright'll talk to you about it
later.'

'Very good, Mr Mitchell.' Vic's voice was matter-of-fact
but from his slightly bemused expression, Melissa guessed
that he was still not quite accustomed to the eccentricities of
his employer.

Outside, the air was fresh, with a light breeze that set the
trees whispering. A waning moon gave a spectral tinge to the
old house and threw black shadows on the gravel. An owl
hooted near by. Mitch shivered and turned to Dittany, who
was standing beside him.

'Bit parky, innit?' he said.

Dittany pulled her jacket more closely round her slight
frame and looked up at him, her expression solemn. 'Yes, but
it's a beautiful night, don't you think so?'

'Beautiful.' Her head barely came up to his shoulder; as he
looked down at her it seemed to Melissa that he held his
breath for a moment before saying, 'Where d'you work?'

'In the public library at Stowbridge.'

'Oh, do come on, darling. I'm getting frozen!' said
Penelope, tugging at his arm.

Over his shoulder, Mitch called, 'I'll drop in and borrow a
book from you some time!'

Waiting for Chloe to unlock her car, Melissa stood and
watched the dark red Jaguar back out and head for the exit
with Mitch at the wheel. He tooted his horn and gave a cheery
wave; behind him, Chris and Will each raised a hand in salute
but Penelope, in the front passenger seat with her shoulder
inclined towards him, stared straight ahead.

'Well, that was the normal first rehearsal shambles,' said
Chloe cheerfully as she fastened her seat belt. 'I just hope that
friend of Mitch's loosens up a bit.'

'Will Foley? Yes, he is a bit wooden, isn't he?'

'Nerves, I expect. I don't suppose he's done anything like
this before.'

26

'Who's the guy with the beard and the brooding eyes – the one playing the killer?'

'Eric Pollard. He's sweet on Dittany, as you may have noticed.'

'I saw him trying to speak to her just now. She didn't appear to have much time for him.'

Chloe shrugged. 'He's been trying to date her for ages but he isn't getting anywhere.'

'She seems quite smitten with Mitch . . . and vice versa.'

'The Hon. Pen wasn't too pleased about that, either.' Chloe gave a chuckle. 'This could be a lively production!'

Chapter Three

Some three weeks later, Melissa spotted an interesting item in the business columns of *The Times*. Under the heading 'Mitchell Enterprises Enters Fashion Market' was a short paragraph announcing that the company had taken a substantial stake in the Dizzy Heights chain of up-market dress boutiques. She went next door to show the paper to Iris and found her in the kitchen, preparing coffee.

'So, the Hon. Pen made it,' commented Iris, reaching for a second mug. 'Wedding bells next, d'you suppose?'

'I thought you might know that – isn't Lady Vowden keeping you up to date?'

Iris put home-baked cookies on a plate and pushed it towards Melissa. 'Haven't seen her since I finished her picture. What about the other girl you were telling me about – the one with the flowery name? Has there been any bloodshed?'

'You mean Dittany? Not that I know of. I suspect Penelope will have her hands full if she does marry him, though. He doesn't strike me as being exactly the one-woman type and he's an out-and-out charmer.' Melissa smiled at the recollection of Mitch massaging her hand, but her smile faded as she remembered the look on his face at his first sight of Dittany. Instinctively, she had scented trouble. It was true that Chloe, whom she met every Thursday at the college where they were both part-time lecturers, had made no reference to any tension during subsequent rehearsals. Penelope, however, was nobody's fool. With her immediate sights fixed on a substantial investment in her business, she would be very careful not to antagonise her potential backer.

Iris appeared to misinterpret Melissa's changing expression. 'Haven't fallen for this character yourself, have you?' She studied her friend with a beady eye. 'Know how susceptible you are.'

'Of course I haven't – what a cheek!' Melissa forebore to mention occasions when Iris herself had loved unwisely. 'By the way, what about those set designs you promised?'

'Nearly finished. Could bring them along to the next rehearsal, if you like.'

Melissa put down her empty mug and stood up to leave. 'Nothing to do with me, I'm afraid. I'll tell Chloe they're ready but she did say something about getting some of the students in the art department to paint the flats.' Seeing a look of disappointment flit across Iris's face, she added with a twinkle, 'If it's an excuse to meet Rich Mitch you want, I'm sure I can wangle it for you, but if the Hon. Pen has her engagement ring by then, she's the one you'll have to get past if you want a commission.'

Iris cocked her head on one side like a blackbird listening for worms in a lawn. 'Think so?' she said. 'Sounds to me like a man who makes his own decisions.'

It was almost a week later that Melissa sought out Chloe to hand over the portfolio containing Iris's set designs for *Innocent Blood Avenged*. She found her alone in the staff common room, staring out of the window, while her cup of coffee sat untouched on the table in front of her.

'You look like a woman with a problem,' said Melissa, sitting down beside her. 'Having a rough day?'

'No worse than usual. My first-year lot seem to think that the main reason for enrolling in a computer studies course is to play games, but otherwise . . .' With a shrug, Chloe took a sip from her cup, pulled a face and put it down. 'This stuff's foul even when it's hot.'

'Never mind, perhaps these'll cheer you up.'

'Oh, super!' Chloe's morose expression changed to one of

delight as she examined the sketches. 'Just the sort of thing I wanted . . . brilliant!'

'She's kept them very simple, but says if you want any help with executing them . . .'

'Oh, I'm sure the art students can manage. They'll be thrilled at the chance of working on something designed by Iris Ash. Please give her my heartfelt thanks, won't you?'

'If you want to do her a favour in return . . .' Melissa explained Iris's interest in meeting Mitch.

'Of course, she'd be more than welcome,' said Chloe warmly. 'We're rehearsing this evening, if she's free.'

'I'll tell her. How's it going, by the way?'

'So-so.'

'You don't sound very sure. Is there friction between Dittany and the gorgeous Penelope?'

'On the contrary, they're getting on quite well, after a shaky start. Penelope seems a good sort under that high-hat exterior. I can't say the same for her partner, though.'

'You don't mean Mitch? I thought . . .'

'No, not Mitch. Her partner in Dizzy Heights Boutiques, Lady Charlotte Heighton. A real gorgon. I get the impression she's the dominant one – Penelope's lamp burns less brightly when she's around.'

'She comes to the rehearsals?'

'Just the once.' Chloe fiddled with the tapes on Iris's portfolio. 'Melissa, if you're free I'd be glad if you'd come along this evening. There's something funny going on and I thought you might be able to help me figure out what it is.'

'What do you mean, something funny?'

'It's hard to say. Nothing I can put a finger on . . . just a hunch.'

'But there must be something.'

'Well, for a start, there's Will Foley. He still hasn't got a clue – he's absolutely hopeless.'

'I know the problem.' Melissa gave a sympathetic chuckle.

'I've got a student who hasn't a clue how to write but she keeps on coming to classes.'

'But she probably enjoys it, even if she's not much good.'

'Oh yes, she adores scribbling – turns out reams of stuff. She could paper the walls with her rejection slips, but she never gives up.'

'There you are then. This is different – Will simply hates acting. I heard him confiding to Dittany that he gets stage fright even at rehearsals, so why' – Chloe spread her hands and cast a despairing glance at the ceiling – 'does he carry on with it?'

'Have you asked him?'

'I never get the chance to speak to him on his own. When he's not on stage, he's in the bar chatting to the staff.'

'Try having a word with Mitch.'

'I have. I told him as tactfully as I could that I had several people who could play the part better, but all I got was, "Don't worry about Will, he'll be okay on the night."'

'Hmm. It almost sounds as if it's Mitch's idea for Will to play the policeman and Will's got to go along with it whether he likes it or not?'

'Exactly!' Chloe finished her coffee and replaced her cup on the saucer with a clatter. 'It's Mitch's party, of course, so he can do as he likes – and he does.' Chloe's mind raced off on another tack. 'I don't know what you'll say to his interpretation of your script, Mel. He's constantly ad-libbing – sends the rest of the cast rolling around laughing.' She gave a dramatic sigh. 'What with trying to get Will to loosen up and at the same time keep Mitch under control, I've got my hands full.'

Melissa grinned. 'So that's what's really bugging you – professional pride!'

Chloe shook her head. 'No, it's not only that. After all, the whole thing's a send-up anyway. What puzzles me is why a man like Will should allow himself to be pushed into doing something he hates. He doesn't strike me as the wimpish sort.'

Melissa shrugged. 'It's odd, I admit, but it doesn't sound particularly sinister. Is that the only strange thing you've noticed?'

'There's nothing really concrete – just odd remarks between the three men that sound almost like a code . . . or a sub-text spoken aloud . . . and once Will said something out of the side of his mouth to that chap Chris and they went out together.'

'To the bar, perhaps?'

'Chris doesn't drink.'

'Well, it doesn't seem much to go on.'

'I know it sounds feeble when I tell you but . . .' Chloe spread her hands in a gesture of frustration. 'Maybe it's my imagination, but I keep feeling that the whole thing is a charade and that Mitch's birthday isn't the real reason for putting on this show.'

'Chloe, what are you suggesting?' Remembering Joe's dark warnings about a possible scam, Melissa felt herself coming out in goose-pimples. 'Have any of the others noticed anything?'

'They don't seem to have done. They all like Will and give him lots of encouragement. As for Mitch, they think he's the bee's knees and they're having a ball . . . all except poor old Eric, that is.'

'Still yearning after Dittany?'

'The way he glares at Mitch and fingers his "prop" dagger when no one's looking, I get the impression he'd like to stick a real knife into him. Not that it'd get him anywhere – she'll never have him, poor lad.' Chloe gathered up her possessions and stood up. 'You will come along and let me know what you think, won't you? And bring Iris by all means, if she wants to come.'

'We'll be there.'

Melissa parked her dark green Golf in the forecourt of the Heyshill Manor Hotel, switched off the engine and opened the driver's door. A gust of wind almost wrenched it from her hand; as she locked the car she glanced up and saw a blanket of cloud unrolling from the west, rapidly obscuring the remnants of the sunset. Showers of dead leaves whirled in the air and skittered across the gravel.

'I think there's a squall blowing up,' she remarked.

Iris got out of the car, turned up the collar of her loose woollen coat and shivered. 'Think you're right.' She hugged her shoulders as she studied the scene with a professional eye. 'Dramatic, isn't it? I'd like to paint it in these conditions.'

Against the background of heavy cloud, the floodlit building stood out like a stage set. The trees where the lights were concealed rocked and creaked in the rising wind; shadows thrown by their flailing branches flitted to and fro like giant bats across the stone façade.

'Very dramatic,' repeated Iris thoughtfully, 'and somehow, menacing.'

It was Melissa's turn to shiver. 'Let's go in,' she said. 'Oh look, there's our nervous "policeman".' She pointed to where Will Foley, straddle-legged, hands thrust into the pockets of his waxed cotton jacket, was studying a large black American car parked against the hotel wall. A plaque fixed to the stonework stated that the space was reserved for the manager.

'Fancy one like that, Will?' called Melissa as she and Iris approached.

Will grinned. 'Beauty, isn't she?' He squatted on his haunches for a closer look.

'Ostentatious gas-guzzler,' sniffed Iris. 'Shows complete disregard for the environment.'

Will straightened up and looked at her enquiringly; Melissa introduced them.

'I'd have said it was more a sign of a healthy bank balance,' he commented as they shook hands. 'It must cost a fortune to run.'

Iris was unimpressed. 'More money than sense. I'd rather own a haunted manor.' She turned to Melissa with a glint of mischief in her eye. 'Seen the spook yet, Mel?'

Will was peering through the window of the driver's door at the console with its battery of instruments, twisting his head this way and that, one hand raised to blot out the reflection of light on the glass. He turned round on hearing Iris's question and before Melissa had time to reply, said with a grin, 'Not scared of ghosts, are you?'

'Of course not.' She pulled a face at Iris. 'Just at the moment, I'm interested in all things spooky. Writing this burlesque thing for Mitch has given me an idea for a creepy murder plot.'

'They've got a good spook here – several, in fact. This place has quite a gruesome history. You want to have a chat with Janice in the bar. Make your flesh creep, she will!'

'There you are, Mel,' said Iris triumphantly. 'Told you so!'

Reluctantly, it seemed, Will abandoned his inspection of the car. He stepped back and glanced at his watch. 'Time for a quick one before I'm on.' He gave a somewhat watery smile. 'Can't say I'll be sorry when this malarkey's over. Not really my cup of tea.'

He held the door open for the two women as they entered the hotel. Kim Bellamy, elegant as ever in a crimson velvet jacket over a low-cut black dress, was at the reception desk, speaking on the telephone. She raised a hand in greeting and the light from a chandelier drew points of fire from the diamonds on her fingers.

'See you later,' said Will and headed for the bar.

'Nice man,' commented Iris as she and Melissa made their way along the passage leading to the Priory Suite. 'Does seem a bit jumpy, though.'

Chloe and most of her cast had already foregathered. They had evidently been instructed to bring their costumes for approval. Eric Pollard and his friend Peter Little, who were playing the two villains, had turned up in waistcoats over collarless shirts with coloured handkerchiefs knotted round their necks and peaked caps pulled low over their foreheads. Sheila and Felicity, decked out in mob-caps and aprons over long skirts for their roles as servants, were parading for Chloe's inspection. Mitch, clad surprisingly in a baggy jacket and trousers with a black roll-neck sweater, was in earnest consultation with his minder in a far corner and paying no attention to the proceedings.

'Where's the Hon. Pen?' hissed Iris in Melissa's ear.

'Over there.'

Penelope and Dittany, the former wearing a sapphire-blue tailored suit and looking as if she had just stepped off the cat-walk in a Paris salon, the latter like a character from a Jane Austen novel in a dress of sprigged cotton, were examining the contents of a box which lay between them on a window-seat. They appeared totally relaxed, exchanging comments and friendly smiles.

'Never think they were after the same man,' whispered Iris.

'Chloe says Penelope's being very civilised. Come on, I'll introduce you.'

'The lady who designed our back-drops? I'm so pleased to meet you,' said Dittany warmly as she shook hands with Iris. 'I think they're simply lovely!'

'Masterly!' agreed Penelope.

'Thanks.' Iris peered into the box. 'What've you got there?'

'These are the props – Penelope's got hold of some super things.' Dittany rummaged and brought out a sack with 'Swag' stencilled on it in large letters. 'That's for Peter and Eric to put their ill-gotten gains in, and this,' she picked up what looked like an ordinary kitchen knife and waved it around, 'is what Eric murders me with.'

'I've never seen one of those before,' said Melissa. 'How does it work?'

'The point retracts into the handle, like this. When the killer strikes, it looks as if the blade has gone into the body.' Dittany demonstrated by stabbing a cushion; even at close quarters, the effect was surprisingly realistic. 'Of course, I have to grab the handle and hold it during my death throes, otherwise it'd fall over when Eric lets go.'

'Where's the blood?' Iris wanted to know.

'Here.' Penelope dipped into her box and produced a small bottle. 'It's the real, professional stuff, Kensington Gore! Oh, do be careful,' she warned, as Iris unscrewed the top and peered at the contents. 'It's terribly expensive. We don't use it in rehearsal, of course.'

'How does it work?' asked Melissa, thinking this might be useful information, if ever she set one of her murders in a theatre.

'I have a . . . well, the blood is in a . . . a sort of rubber bulb thing . . . I have to squeeze it to make it burst.' Dittany turned pink and Penelope looked amused.

'It's a condom, actually,' said a matter-of-fact voice. Chloe had appeared among them. She clapped her hands for attention. 'Prologue and beginners on stage, please.'

'Oh, that's me. See you later.' Dittany took the knife and hurried to the platform. Mitch, already in position with his remaining props, went to meet her. As he led her to her place, they exchanged a quick word and a smile.

Eric was glowering in a corner. Melissa glanced from him to Penelope, half expecting to catch some sign of jealousy or anger there as well, but there was none. She had closed the lid of her box and was sitting calmly, hands folded in her lap and a serene expression on her face, as if she were posing for a photograph.

Iris read Melissa's thoughts. 'Seen it all before, no doubt,' she whispered as they went in search of an inconspicuous corner to watch the proceedings. 'She'll reel him in if things get out of hand.'

'I expect you're right. Dittany's not in the same league, is she? I wouldn't like her to get hurt, though – she seems such a sweet kid.'

'Ready, Mitch?' called Chloe from her seat in the middle of the room. 'Haven't you learned your lines yet?' she went on a shade testily, on catching sight of the script in Mitch's hand. 'Oh no!' She slapped her forehead and turned her eyes to the ceiling. 'Don't tell me you've done another rewrite.'

'Funny you should say that,' said Mitch with one of his most disarming grins. 'I thought a bit of rap might be fun. How does this sound?'

With hunched shoulders and rotating hips, frenziedly thrashing the air with one arm and using the rolled-up script as an imaginary microphone, he pranced round the stage, chanting in a husky, rhythmic monotone:

> Now listen, man, there was these two broads
> And they both had hots for the guy next door.
> Well he loved one and not the other
> And that led to big trouble, brother.
> These broads, they worked for a classy dame.
> Miz Ann Bull, that was her name . . .

At this point his voice wobbled and he folded up, unable to continue for laughing. Everyone, even Penelope, joined in the mirth; from the back of the stage Dittany clapped her hands in delight.

'Whadya think, Chlo?' asked Mitch when he could speak again. 'Course, I'd need a backing, and some of the lines don't scan too well . . .'

'Whatever do you know about scansion, Mitch darling?' drawled Penelope, while Chloe struggled to recover her powers of speech. 'I'm surprised you've even heard of it.'

'Oh, I'm really into this poetry lark,' Mitch assured her, his eyes twinkling.

'Poetry!' exclaimed Penelope. 'Is that what you call it?'

'This stuff?' Mitch guffawed. 'No, course not. This is just for laughs. I mean the real thing. You ever read John Donne, Pen? Beeyootiful stuff he wrote – real sexy too, some of it.' He rubbed his hands together and winked.

Penelope's eyebrows lifted and her mouth became a cherry-pink 'O' of surprise. 'Where in the world did you hear about John Donne?'

'Oh, Dittany's been educating me, haven't you, doll?'

'Oh, yes,' Dittany confirmed eagerly. 'He's been to the library several times to borrow anthologies.'

'You amaze me.' The words were spoken lightly, with a faintly patronising smile, but it seemed to Melissa, who had been following the exchanges with close attention, that Penelope was more disconcerted than she cared to admit by the revelations. Mitch and Dittany had exchanged a glance that hinted at a growing intimacy.

'Could we please get back to the rehearsal?' demanded Chloe impatiently. 'Mitch, you aren't seriously . . .'

'No, sorry Chlo, just did it for laughs. I'll be good from now on – and I have learned me lines, honest!' As if to prove the point, he tossed his script away.

The air of mock contrition, the irrepressible good humour, the dynamism and the sheer charm of the man, transformed Chloe's frown of severity into an amiable smile.

'All right,' she said. 'But please, no more tinkering with the script. You'll upset our author.' She nodded in Melissa's direction.

'Oh, feel free,' said Melissa, who had laughed as loudly as anyone.

'Right. Are you ready this time?'

'Yes, ma'am.' Mitch proceeded to deliver his opening lines with a flourish and from then on Scene One continued with only minor interruptions from the producer.

While the stage was being set for Scene Two, Chloe said, 'Could someone pop along to the bar and remind Will that we'll be needing him soon?'

'I'll go,' volunteered Melissa. 'I want to have a chat with Janice.'

Chapter Four

The bar, low-ceilinged and wooden-beamed with inglenooks on either side of a glowing log fire, was almost empty – probably, Melissa thought, because most of the guests were in the dining-room, although a handful were sitting at low tables, drinking, smoking and chatting. A lad in a bottle-green waistcoat, sporting three gold rings in one ear and a haircut like an inverted boot-brush, was clearing used glasses from the tables, emptying ashtrays and exchanging pleasantries with the customers. Will Foley was not among them.

It was a room which might have been found in any one of a hundred country inns and hotels, with its velvet curtains, flower-patterned carpet and tub chairs of green leather trimmed with metal studs. The whitewashed walls were hung with a variety of iron and wooden artefacts; some, such as horseshoes, were easily recognisable, others suggested arcane but presumably rustic uses. These were interspersed with reproductions of early nineteenth-century advertisements for cattle-markets and horse-fairs. A local farmer was selling a grey mare and another a quantity of hay; there was even a chilling announcement of the public hanging of one Walter Heartfield for sheep-stealing.

Melissa strolled across to the oak counter which occupied the far end of the room. Will was not there either, but perched on a stool, with a glass in one hand and an expensive-looking cigar in the other, was Vic Bellamy, looking entirely at his ease as he lounged against a massive oak pillar. He had evidently been joking with the barmaid, for the two of them were laughing uproariously. The woman was middle-aged, with unnaturally black hair, pendulous cheeks and a generous bosom to which the hotel manager appeared to be paying close attention as it rose and fell while she loaded wine-glasses into a rack above her head. Melissa had entered quietly and it was several seconds before the two noticed her.

'Can I get you something?' asked the woman at length, while Vic gave a friendly nod and took a pull on his cigar.

'Actually, I was looking for Will Foley – I thought I might find him here.'

'He went out about ten minutes ago,' she said.

'I must have missed him then.' Melissa climbed on to a stool. 'I'll have a half of lager, please.'

'How's the show going, then?' asked Vic.

It was the first time he had addressed her directly. On her previous visit, she had been merely one of the group who left with Mitch's party and she was surprised that he was able to place her.

'Very well, I think,' she replied. 'Everyone seems to be having a great time.'

Vic gave a wheezy chuckle. 'They would, with Mitch around!' He emptied his glass and pushed it across the counter, which bore the patina of generations of elbows. 'Ta, Janice. See you later.' He slid from his stool and ambled out, ducking his head to avoid the low lintel over the door.

'I wouldn't say Will's been having a great time,' said Janice as she served Melissa with her lager. She rang up the money and handed over change. 'Seems to have quite a complex over this acting lark. Can't think why he let himself be talked into it.'

'Hasn't he said?'

'A favour for his old mate, Mitch, he says. Some mate, I told him, pushing him into something that gets to him like that.'

'Maybe he's shy of meeting people and Mitch thinks acting might be a way to overcome it,' suggested Melissa, reflecting as she spoke that it didn't sound a very convincing explanation, not at all in line with her own impressions of the man.

40

'Scared of Battling Bess, more like,' volunteered the lad in the green waistcoat, arriving at that moment with a trayful of glasses. He dumped it on the counter, ducked under the flap and began unloading the contents noisily into a sink.

'Careful, Kevin,' admonished Janice. 'We don't want any breakages.'

'Who's Battling Bess?' asked Melissa.

'The Heyshill Manor ghost,' replied Janice with some pride. 'One of them, that is.'

'Really? Do tell me about them.'

'Well . . .' Janice broke off to exchange a few words with a small group of Americans who announced that they were off in search of dinner. 'It's quite a story,' she said as the door closed behind them.

'I'd love to hear it, if you can spare the time.' Melissa glanced round the now unoccupied room. 'Why don't you have a drink with me, while things are quiet?'

A broad smile compressed Janice's double chin. 'I don't mind if I do. I'll have a port, thanks.'

'Kevin?'

'He's not allowed to drink on duty,' said Janice, before the lad could answer. She poured herself a generous port, rang up the money that Melissa handed over and took an appreciative sip. 'Mm, that's nice.' Kevin rinsed glasses under a tap, his face sullen.

'About the ghosts,' said Melissa. 'Do they ever appear?'

'I wouldn't say they *appear* exactly . . . you don't ever *see* anything, or at least, I don't know anyone who has.' The barmaid's tone was almost wistful. 'It's more of a creepy feeling you get when they're around. Of course, you hear them occasionally, when you're down in the cellar. Real spooky it is, down there – it's part of the crypt of the old priory, you know.'

'You mean the ghosts speak?'

'Not *speak* exactly . . . sort of murmurings . . . as if you were listening to a radio through a thick wall.' Janice, making short

41

work of the port, was warming to her subject. 'And there are other noises.'

'What sort of noises?'

'Oh . . .' Janice picked up one of the glasses that Kevin had just dried and held it up to the light. She handed it back to him. 'There's a smear on that one – give it another rub. The noises now – it's a bit hard to describe them, really. Sort of scuffling and slithering. And sometimes,' she lowered her voice and glanced round, as if fearful of being overheard by the spirits of the departed, 'you get this cold feeling, and smell a musty sort of smell – as if a grave had been opened up.'

'Isn't it always cold in a cellar?' Melissa had the impression that Janice was drawing rather freely on her imagination.

'Yes, it is, but this is different.'

'Have you heard these noises yourself?'

'Of course. Heard something earlier this evening, as a matter of fact.'

'Janice!' Kevin looked up in alarm. 'You never said.'

'Didn't want to scare you.' She patted his shoulder and winked at Melissa. 'Hates going down there after dark, don't you, Kev?'

Kevin fiddled nervously with his battery of earrings. 'You're not kidding. The girls won't go at all, not even in the daytime, not if they can help it. Real scared, they are.'

'But whose ghosts are they, and why do they call one of them Battling Bess?' asked Melissa.

'It seems that in olden times, poor widows who couldn't pay their taxes would hide in the monasteries with their children,' Janice explained. 'The monks used to look after them and give them food. Then old Henry the Eighth had the monasteries burned down. The story goes that a group of women turned up here for shelter, found the place ruined and deserted, and went into the crypt to hide. The sheriff's men tracked them down and tried to arrest them, but their leader, who was called Bess, persuaded them to make a fight of it. She got them to barricade themselves in and throw stones at the men

42

to drive them off. They succeeded at first, but the men came back later, closed the entrance to the crypt with rocks and went away.'

Melissa stared at her in horror. 'You mean, they left them in there to starve to death? What a fiendish thing to do.'

'Wasn't it?' said Janice, with something like relish. She emptied her glass and held it out for Kevin to wash. 'Real rotten times, they were.'

'Ain't much better nowadays for some people,' observed Kevin sourly. He glanced round as the door opened. 'Here comes a customer.'

Chris Bright entered, spotted Melissa and came across to her. 'Where's Will?' he asked.

'I thought he must be with you – he'd already left when I got here.'

'He hasn't shown up. Chloe's fuming.'

'Maybe he went for a turn outside,' suggested Janice. 'He told me he enjoys a stroll round the gardens.'

'He wouldn't see much in the dark, and anyway it's pissing with rain.' Muttering to himself, Chris went out. A couple entered; the woman went to a chair by the fire while the man came to the counter to order a gin and tonic and a pint of bitter.

'Lousy weather,' remarked Janice as she took down a tankard, held it under the tap and pulled the handle. There was a spluttering noise and a gush of froth. Her smile became a frown. 'Damn, this bitter's fobbing. Go down and put on another cask, Kevin.'

Kevin blanched. 'What, down the cellar?' he faltered. It was no act; the lad was genuinely scared.

'Where else, thickhead? And get a move on.'

Behind her back, Kevin scowled. Reluctantly, he reached up towards a heavy nail driven into the wall at the side of the counter. His expression changed from nervous apprehension to surprise. 'The key's not there.' He sounded almost pleased, as if its absence would relieve him of an unpleasant task.

'What d'you mean, not there?' Janice paused in the act of transferring ice cubes into a tumbler and went to look for herself. 'Funny,' she muttered. 'I could have sworn . . . maybe Vic took it.' She made an impatient gesture with her tongs. 'Well don't stand there gawping, go and see if he's down there. You can ask him to change the cask if you're too chicken to do it yourself.'

With a shrug, Kevin vanished. Moments later, he was back, his eyes starting from his head and his face as pale as if Battling Bess was at his heels. 'Someone come, quickly!' he gasped. 'There's been an accident.'

Melissa was nearest; she raced after him to where, at the far end of the passage, a heavy oak door marked 'Private' stood ajar. Kevin flattened himself against the opposite wall as if he was trying to disappear through it. With a shaking hand, he pointed. 'Down there,' he whispered. 'Mind you don't go head first like he must have.'

Melissa, her heart thumping, dragged the door fully open. A gust of chill air and a smell of beer rose to meet her. At her feet, a flight of worn stone steps plunged steeply downwards. Never at ease with heights, she experienced a surge of vertigo.

Under the cold fluorescent light, the vaults of whitewashed brick threw sharp black shadows that marched away into the distance like multiple reflections in a mirror. A tangle of pipes led down through the ceiling to a row of casks, flanked by tall cylinders standing shoulder to shoulder like faceless, armoured figures. At the foot of the steps lay Will Foley, face downwards in a pool of blood.

'Get an ambulance!' shouted Melissa. As fast as she dared, clinging grimly to the metal handrail, she descended the worn steps.

'What's going on?' It was a man's voice and it sounded impatient, almost angry. Vic Bellamy was at the head of the steps. 'What the hell was he doing down here?'

To her surprise, Melissa found herself suddenly disliking the man. As if explanations were important at a time like this.

'Never mind that now – we must get him to hospital,' she retorted, not caring if she sounded rude. 'And get some clean towels. I'll try and stop the bleeding.'

Over his shoulder, Vic shouted after Kevin, already on his way to call the ambulance, and then started down the steps. 'Is he badly hurt?' he asked.

Melissa did not answer; she was desperately trying to clear Will's mouth and nostrils with a paper tissue, alarmed at the quantity of blood he had already lost.

'I'd like to know what the hell he thought he was playing at, nosing around down here,' Vic muttered.

'You can ask him when he comes round.'

If he was aware of the sarcasm in her voice, he took no notice. It was plain what was uppermost in his mind. 'He must have pinched the key when Janice wasn't looking.' He seemed to be thinking aloud.

'For God's sake, where are those towels?' Melissa almost screamed in fear and frustration.

There was the sound of running feet, and Kevin, still pale and scared-looking, reappeared with a pile of paper towels, which he passed down with averted eyes. 'Will these do? I pinched 'em from the gents. The ambulance is on the way,' he said shakily.

'I suppose you know what you're doing?' said Vic as he handed her a wad of towels.

Ignoring the question, she applied pressure in an effort to staunch the blood still welling from a two-inch gash on Will's forehead, keeping the fingers of her free hand on the pulse in his throat. It was weak and fluttery, but it was there. She bent her ear towards his half-open mouth. 'I can't tell if he's breathing or not,' she muttered anxiously. 'He needs professional help quickly – how much longer's the ambulance going to be?'

'Should be here any minute – the station's not far.'

The seconds ticked away. Will showed no sign of returning consciousness. Melissa threw aside one saturated makeshift dressing and grabbed another. She was in agony from cramp and her hands were sticky with blood; the smoke from Vic's cigar crawled into her nostrils, mingled with the sickly smell of beer. She strained her ears, listening for the sound of a siren, but all she could hear was the whirr of an electric pump and the intermittent sound of muffled voices. She recalled Janice's highly coloured claims to have heard the Heyshill Manor ghosts, no doubt invented to tease the likes of the impressionable Kevin. She looked at her watch; the face was obscured with blood. Where the hell was the ambulance?

There was a commotion at the head of the steps. Glancing up, she saw Mitch's face appear over Vic's shoulder. 'Let me get to him!' Half frantic with anxiety, he tried to push past, but Vic restrained him.

'We'd better keep out of the way, Mr Mitchell.' He put a hand on Mitch's arm, urging him back up the steps. 'The lady's doing what she can till the ambulance gets here.'

Mitch, his face red and angry, threw off the restraining hand; for a moment it seemed there would be a confrontation. Then they heard the wail of the siren.

She had seen it all before, but only on film or during television coverage of some major disaster. This was reality: the wound swiftly covered; the deathly white face under the mask and the bag pumping air into feeble lungs; the intravenous drip set up with calm dexterity by a burly young man with 'Paramedic' on his shirt. Then came the competent manipulation of the stretcher, its burden firmly strapped into place. There was a moment of near-panic as Mitch, in an over-eager response to a request for a hand with the lifting, almost pitched down the steps himself.

Then they were gone and Melissa, leaning against the wall where she had retreated to be out of the way, was left alone with the barrels, the pipes, the stacks of crates, the blood-soaked paper towels kicked into a mangled heap by the ambulance crew. The ancient vaults stretched into limitless darkness. The whirr of the ventilation system filled her head, her stomach churned, her lungs pleaded for fresh air. Blindly, she groped for the handrail.

Vic came clattering down the steps with a mop and a bucket. She stood aside to let him pass.

'You'd better get cleaned up,' he said, eyeing her dishevelled appearance. He began stowing the debris in a plastic bag.

'Do you need any help?'

'I can manage.' He jerked his head towards the top of the steps, as if anxious for her to leave. 'My wife'll show you where to go.' She followed his upward glance and saw Kim standing in the doorway.

It was an effort to drag herself up the steps, clinging to the handrail. She paused halfway and glanced back. She was just in time to see Vic bend down and pick up something which, in her shock and agitation, she had failed to spot, which must have fallen from Will's hand as he fell. He dropped it into the bag – a pocket flashlight with a shattered glass.

Chapter Five

'My, you are in a state.' Eyeing Melissa's slacks and sweat-shirt with distaste, Kim hurriedly led her up a back staircase leading to the manager's flat. 'That lot won't come out without a good soak – you'd better borrow one of my track suits to go home in.'

'That's very kind of you.'

'The bathroom's in there.' Kim indicated a door on which was mounted a small reproduction of an impressionist paint-ing of a woman bathing. 'I daresay you'd like a shower.'

'That would be wonderful,' Melissa said gratefully.

'You'll find clean towels on the rail and I'll leave the trackie outside the door. Would you like some coffee when you've finished?'

'If it's no bother – but shouldn't you be down in reception?'

'It's okay – one of the restaurant staff is holding the fort.'

When she saw her reflection in the bathroom mirror, Melissa realised why Vic had been so anxious to get her out of the way; there had been enough disturbance in the hotel for one evening, without treating the unwary guests to a sight of this distraught-looking apparition with bloodstained hands, face and clothes. Such an encounter might not be too good for business, especially if the person in question had ever spent time in the bar soaking up Janice's highly coloured version of the saga of Battling Bess along with the after-dinner brandy.

Thankfully, Melissa peeled off her soiled clothes and turned on the water. As she waited for it to run hot, she glanced round the bathroom. It was almost as large as her sitting-room in Hawthorn Cottage and far more sumptuously appointed: thickly carpeted floor, a sunken bath complete with whirlpool

48

and gold-plated taps, an armoury of expensive beauty creams and lotions ranged on tiled shelves and several exotic flowering plants in porcelain *cache-pots*, supported on the outspread wings of delicately moulded swans. How the other half lives, she thought. There's a lot of money here somewhere. I wonder what their background is.

As she washed and dried herself, her writer's mind was busy, mentally recording impressions of the couple who managed this exclusive and highly successful hotel. Vic, she decided, if not actually top-drawer, was no further than second drawer down. His voice and bearing suggested a public school background. Kim, on the other hand, although poised, elegant and beautifully turned out, had a certain quality of over-refinement in her voice that suggested humbler origins. Perhaps she had been a model before she married Vic. She certainly had the looks and the figure – tall, slim and well-proportioned.

Liberally splashed – at Kim's express invitation – with Chanel *eau de toilette*, Melissa eventually emerged from the bathroom clad in a dark blue track suit embroidered with the logo of a top Italian designer. On a half-open door on the opposite side of the hallway, another reproduction – this time a still-life of a tall pitcher surrounded by apples – suggested that this might be the kitchen, a notion confirmed by the sight of Kim pouring coffee. Melissa knocked and entered, sniffing in appreciation.

'Oh boy, that smells good,' she exclaimed.

'Come and sit down.' Kim was already perched on a stool at a tiled breakfast bar where toaster, juice extractor and coffee machine were lined up beside packets of cereals and a fruit bowl piled high with oranges. 'Are you feeling better?'

'Yes, thanks. It's kind of you to lend me this.' She indicated the track suit. 'I feel very up-market – I'm afraid I get my casual things at a chain store.'

Kim smiled and stirred her coffee. She was older than Melissa had at first supposed – about her own age, in fact.

In other words, nearer fifty than forty, the careful make-up softening but not entirely concealing the age lines round her eyes and mouth, the throat already showing a tendency to sag. From the contents of the bathroom shelves it was plain that she was putting up a fight; Melissa could not help feeling a twinge of self-congratulation at the knowledge that, being blessed with an exceptionally good skin that needed little make-up, she managed to achieve a better result for a far more modest outlay. It was some compensation for having to be content most of the time with chain store clothes and costume jewellery.

'I wonder how he is,' said Kim, after a pause.

Melissa felt a stab of guilt. For the moment, she had totally forgotten the unfortunate Will Foley.

'I can't imagine what he was doing in the cellar in the first place,' Kim continued. 'Vic's very put out.'

'Yes, I noticed.' Melissa recalled the sight of him in the doorway, his head almost brushing the lintel, his face registering more anger than concern.

'I mean, if one of Mr Mitchell's friends wanted to look round, he only had to ask and Vic would have shown him. Not that there's anything to see down there except beer casks and our stock of bottles and canned drinks and so on.' A faint, nasal whine crept into her voice. 'I mean, why would anyone want to go poking around? You don't think he was planning to steal something, do you?'

Melissa shook her head. 'It seems unlikely. Maybe he's interested in ancient buildings – isn't the cellar the crypt of some old priory?'

'Oh yes, just a part of it. The rest was filled in and blocked off years ago.' Kim's dismissive shrug indicated a total lack of interest in the historic nature of the building. 'Anyway, like I said, he'd have been welcome to look, if he'd asked.'

'Well, let's hope he's not too badly hurt. He did lose an awful lot of blood, though. Did anyone go to the hospital with him?'

'Mr Mitchell went, and Mr Bright. The others were in the bar when I came up, waiting for him to ring through if there was any news.'

'The others – good Lord, I'd forgotten all about them! I'd better go down and join them, they'll be wondering where I am.' Melissa put down her empty cup and picked up her handbag. 'Thanks so much – I'll return your track suit tomorrow. Could you let me have something to wrap my own things in?'

'Sure.' Kim left the room and returned with a carrier made of heavy quality dark blue plastic with the legend 'Dizzy Heights' zigzagging diagonally across it in striking gold letters. Melissa studied it with interest.

'I see you patronise the Hon. Pen's boutique,' she remarked.

'Huh?'

'Penelope de Lavier – Mitch's, er, business partner.' She had been about to say 'girlfriend' but was unsure if that was strictly accurate. 'She's part owner of this outfit, isn't she?'

Kim shrugged. 'Is she? I dunno.' The telephone rang and she went to answer it; during her short absence, Melissa amused herself by examining more reproductions which, she guessed, identified the bedroom, sitting-room and dining-room. When Kim returned, she was on the point of asking for confirmation, but the question died in her throat at the sight of the other woman's expression.

'Vic's just had a call from Mr Mitchell,' said Kim, her voice unsteady with shock. 'Mr Foley died on the way to hospital.'

The rehearsal of *Innocent Blood Avenged* had come to an abrupt end when the company learned of Will Foley's accident. One or two people had left immediately, others repaired to the bar to steady their nerves while awaiting news. Eventually they, too, had begun to trickle out, expressing shock, anxiety and hopes for an early recovery. Everyone, it seemed, had a warm regard for Will.

It was nearly ten o'clock when Melissa entered the bar, an

hour when drinkers would normally be at their most relaxed and talkative, but apart from a group of young people standing at the counter with glasses in their hands, chatting to Janice, everyone seemed quiet and subdued. She guessed that news of the tragedy had filtered through.

Vic was helping Janice serve the customers. He caught Melissa's eye as she entered and jerked his head towards a corner where Penelope, Dittany and Iris sat half hidden by a wooden pillar. They looked up as she joined them, their faces sorrowful. Even Penelope seemed genuinely moved.

'Isn't it dreadful!' Dittany's expressive eyes were moist. 'Mitch will be devastated – he thought the world of Will.'

'However did it happen?' asked Penelope.

Melissa sank into a vacant chair and spread her hands in a helpless gesture. She felt utterly drained; the news of Will's death had been a blow whose effects were only just filtering through. 'We think he must have missed his footing and pitched down the steps from top to bottom, cutting his head open as he landed. He lost a hell of a lot of blood in a comparatively short time – and of course, there may have been other injuries as well.' She ran her fingers through her hair, still damp from the shower, and then pressed a hand to her eyes. 'I still can't believe it,' she muttered.

'What was he doing in the cellar anyway?' asked Iris.

'That's another mystery.'

'Here's Chris.' Penelope craned round the pillar and beckoned. 'Maybe he can tell us something.'

Chris could tell them very little. He leaned on the table, declined offers of a drink and announced that he had come to drive Penelope home, to say that Mitch would keep the business appointment arranged for the two of them for the following morning, and to make sure – here his normally taciturn manner softened slightly, as if he was making a subconscious effort to convey the spirit as well as the words of the message – that Dittany was feeling well enough to drive. She assured him that she was; by unspoken consent they all stood up and made for the door. Vic's smile as he called 'Good-night!' did little to conceal his relief at their departure.

It had stopped raining and the wind was slackening. As they made for their respective cars, Chris bent and said something in Dittany's ear. A quick lift of the head and a shy smile told the watchers that, despite the sadness of the occasion, the message had been received with pleasure.

'They certainly get some well-heeled customers here,' commented Iris as she and Melissa crossed the car park. 'Look at that gas-guzzler. Brand-new, diplomatic plates and all. Place must be a gold-mine.'

'I doubt if Mitch would have bought it otherwise.'

They drove home in almost total silence. It was still comparatively early and there was plenty of traffic about, many of the drivers impatient to the point of insanity. 'Accidents looking for somewhere to happen,' Iris observed caustically as a scarlet BMW hurtled past them on a blind bend. It was a relief to turn into the quiet lane leading to Upper Benbury; a few minutes later the Golf was bumping along the narrow dirt track that led to the pair of adjoining stone cottages where the two of them lived in neighbourly rural solitude.

The last of the storm clouds had cleared. A full moon, more brilliant than any floodlight, threw a wash of silver on darkened windows, cast inky shadows across the gardens and bleached every vestige of colour from the surrounding fields. All was silence except for faint rustlings from the tangle of brambles and long grass on the steep bank behind the cottages, beyond which the valley stretched away in a pattern of black and misty greys, like an artist's exercise in perspective.

'Bit different from Heyshill Manor,' Iris remarked, as she and Melissa contemplated the scene. 'But beautiful in this light. Think I'll do it in charcoal one of these days.' Receiving no response, she gave her friend a sharp glance. 'You feeling all right? Come in for a cuppa?'

'Yes, I think I will.'

'Suppose Mitch will abandon his plans for a party now,'

speculated Iris as she filled the kettle and rummaged in tins for an assortment of her home-made cookies.

'Probably. Unless . . .' Chloe's words came back to Melissa: *There's something going on . . . I keep thinking the whole thing is a charade*. Chloe was a clever, practical woman, highly numerate as well as artistic, something of a polymath, in fact. She was not the sort to let her imagination run away with her.

Iris pushed a steaming cup across the kitchen table and waved a hand at a plate of cookies. 'Help yourself. Unless what?'

Melissa told her of Chloe's misgivings. 'You were there this evening. Did you notice anything unusual while I was gone?'

'Not a thing. Seems to be going swimmingly. Not my idea of a birthday party but everyone to his own taste.' Iris looked thoughtful. 'Any ideas?'

'Several things are bugging me but I can't fit them together for the moment. I think we can take it that Will has been there for some reason other than his part in the show. Whatever it is, I suspect Chris is in the know as well because Chloe's seen them conferring. Will wanted to look round the cellar without Vic's knowledge – but why? After all, the place belongs to Mitch; he could have inspected the place from cellar to attic if he'd wanted to.'

'Most likely has already.'

'How do you mean?'

'With a surveyor. When he bought the place.'

'Of course.'

'Maybe' – Iris cupped her pointed chin in one hand and dunked her herbal teabag in a cup of hot water with the other – 'Will was looking for something that wouldn't be there if he viewed the place by appointment.'

'Such as?'

'Dunno. Maybe Vic's been working some fiddle over beer deliveries – charging for more than he receives and pocketing the proceeds.'

Melissa shook her head. 'You could hardly tell that from a

casual look round – you'd need to check invoices, delivery notes and things. And compared to the income from the hotel and the restaurant, it would only amount to peanuts.'

'Small beer, eh?' said Iris, with a cackle at her own joke.

Melissa managed a watery smile. 'Exactly – and hardly worth the risk of losing a well-paid job, to say nothing of a luxury apartment. Iris, you should see it.' She sketched a rapid word-picture.

Iris looked smug. 'Said they were ostentatious.'

'She is. I'm not so sure about him.'

'He's the one with the flashy car.'

'Yes, but she may have talked him into buying it. You know,' Melissa's brain was beginning to peck away at several ideas at once, like a bird at a patch of crumbs, 'they seem a well-matched pair on the surface but in some ways they're . . . not ill-assorted exactly, but . . . different.'

'How?'

'Vic's a good-looking, well-spoken man, rather distinguished in a florid sort of way. You could almost take him for one of the local landed gentry. I have the feeling that Kim's not in quite the same class. Oh, I know that's a snob word,' she went on hastily, seeing Iris's eyebrows shoot up. 'I don't know how else to express it.' Somewhat lamely, she tried to put her misgivings into words.

Iris frowned. 'You saying Vic married beneath him? "Wealthy hotel manager weds barmaid" – that sort of thing? So what if he did?'

'Nothing really, except that it might account for all the kitsch, using a reproduction Degas to indicate the door to the loo and so on.'

'Mm, that is a bit over the top.' Iris lifted out the sodden teabag and replaced it with a slice of lemon. 'Tell me about the other pictures.'

'I didn't recognise any for certain, except I'm sure the nude on the bathroom door was a Degas. From the brushwork, the still-life might have been a Van Gogh but I've never seen it before. Then there was one of some people sitting round a table and a maid carrying a teapot – I guessed that was the dining-room.'

Iris was beginning to look interested. 'Can you remember any more about that one?'

Melissa thought for a moment. 'I think there was an old man drinking from a cup, and a woman holding a plate.'

'Was the table round, and was there a tall cake-stand on it?'

'Now you mention it, I believe there was.'

'Just a tick.' Iris went out of the room and returned with a catalogue from an art exhibition. She flipped through the pages and laid it open on the table. 'Is that it?' She pointed with a lean brown finger to a picture entitled simply *Le Goûter*.

'Yes, that's it. May I see?' Forgetting for the moment the evening's tragedy and the possibility of illicit activity at Hey-shill Manor, Melissa turned the pages to admire the reproductions, some in colour, others in black and white. Many were of internationally famous paintings, others less well known. After a minute or two she recognised a second picture, which showed a couple in an armchair. 'She had that one too – I guessed that to be the sitting-room. Let's see if I can find the others. Yes, here's the Degas nude . . .'

'Renoir, actually,' interrupted Iris with a grin.

'Er, so it is.' Melissa grinned back. As usual, Iris's company, along with the herbal tea, had restored her to something like her normal frame of mind.

'And this is the still-life,' she went on. 'At least I was right about that being a Van Gogh so I'm not a complete ignoramus. And they had this one of a maid making a bed . . . I suppose Vic and Kim went to the exhibition too and bought some reproductions.'

'So maybe Kim isn't quite so uncultured as you thought?' said Iris slyly.

'Iris, don't exaggerate. I never said she was uncultured,' protested Melissa, who was beginning to wish she had never

voiced her impressions. 'But I ask you, if you had reproductions of old masters, would you use them as door-signs?'

'I wouldn't, but like I said, everyone to their own taste.'
Iris closed the catalogue and put it aside, looking thoughtful.

Melissa yawned and stood up. 'I'm off home to bed. Many
thanks for the tea.'

'Huh?'

'I said, thanks for the tea, and I'm going home.'

'Oh, right.'

Chapter Six

When Melissa came into her kitchen the following morning, the first thing she saw was the Dizzy Heights carrier containing her soiled clothes. She kept her head averted as she tipped the garments into the sink, turned on the cold tap and left them to soak. She doubted if she could ever bring herself to wear them again; the blood might wash away but the horror would be indelible.

Thanks to Iris's herbal tea she had slept reasonably well, but she had no appetite for breakfast. She brewed coffee, took it up to her study and made an effort to work. As usual, she began by reading the chapter she had finished the previous day. At the time, she had been pleased with it, but this morning it seemed flat and lifeless. The emotions experienced by her fictitious sleuth, Nathan Latimer, on finding a dismembered corpse, disgusted her with their facile shallowness. She closed her eyes and tried to relive her own thoughts and feelings as she knelt beside the dying Will Foley, but to exploit them for the sake of giving her readers a vicarious thrill seemed almost indecent, no better than the relentless pursuit of the recently bereaved by sensation-hungry journalists. She switched off the word processor and went downstairs.

There was a ring at the bell; Iris was at the door, asking how she felt, how she had slept. Chloe telephoned a few minutes later with a similar enquiry. 'Don't worry about me, I'm all right,' she heard herself saying repeatedly. Will's family were the ones who needed support and comfort, wherever they were. Mitch had said something about a daughter. And Mitch himself . . . he and Will had been old friends. She wondered if she would ever learn the true reason for his presence at Heyshill Manor. The thought was enough to kick her natural curiosity, never more than half asleep, into action.

Dittany might know. She had obviously been seeing quite a bit of Mitch lately; perhaps she had picked up something. It was worth a try. Melissa reached for the telephone directory to check the number of Stowbridge Public Library.

When Melissa reached the library she found Dittany busy stamping books for a small queue of borrowers. She was paler than usual and there were smudges under her eyes, her movements inclined to be jerky as she opened each volume and ran the electronic sensor along the bar code.

Last in the line was an elderly woman in a shapeless tweed coat and a felt hat like a pudding-basin, who scrutinised her with beady eyes as she dumped a stack of romantic novels on the counter. 'You're looking peaky this morning, my dear,' she said, in the conspiratorial manner of one hungry for confidences. 'Is anything wrong?' Dittany shook her head and said she was fine, thank you, but the woman was not to be discouraged. 'Having trouble with the boyfriend, perhaps?' she asked hopefully.

A faint glow lit up Dittany's grave face, as if a dying fire had suddenly shown signs of life. 'Oh no, nothing like that,' she replied. 'I just . . . had a bit of a shock last night, that's all.'

'Oh dear! Nothing too serious, I hope,' said the woman, in a tone that belied the words. She kept her eyes on the girl's face as she took her time about stowing the books in her shopping bag, plainly eager to hear more, but Dittany had caught sight of Melissa. After a brief word to a colleague, she escaped from behind the counter with both hands outstretched.

'I'm so glad to see you,' she said fervently. 'I hardly slept a wink last night.'

The inquisitive woman was still hovering; over Dittany's shoulder, Melissa could almost see her ears stretching. 'Why don't we go and have something to eat during your lunch break?' she suggested. 'I couldn't face breakfast this morning and I'm beginning to feel empty.'

'Me too.' Dittany glanced at her watch. 'I'm free now, actually.'

They found a corner table in a nearby café, which was quiet enough to make conversation possible but sufficiently busy to prevent their being overheard. During the short drive from Upper Benbury to Stowbridge, Melissa had been considering possible ways of raising the question that had been in her mind for most of the morning, but in the event she had no need of any of them. Dittany, too, had been giving the matter much thought.

'Mitch is so upset about Will . . . he keeps saying it's all his fault he's dead . . . have you any idea what he could mean?'

'None at all. I thought you might know . . . That is, I thought you might know what Will was doing at Heyshill Manor in the first place. As well as taking part in the show, which we all know he hated doing anyway.'

Dittany stopped her pretence of eating a mushroom omelette and began fiddling with her paper napkin. 'That's been puzzling me ever since we began rehearsals,' she said. 'The others thought it was a bit of a joke – poor Will, he was quite hopeless at acting – but it really wasn't funny. He went through agonies of nerves. He confided in me once, when I went to fetch him from the bar to play one of his scenes, that the thought of going on the stage – "making a prat of himself in front of everyone" he called it – quite turned his stomach.'

'So why was he doing it?'

'I asked him that, and all I could get out of him was "I owe Mitch one."'

'Have you asked Mitch?'

Dittany coloured slightly, and made another effort to eat the congealing omelette. 'I mentioned it once, and he just turned it aside. I . . . don't feel I know him well enough yet to ask too many questions.'

'But you've been seeing him – apart from rehearsals, I mean?' As she spoke, it occurred to Melissa that her own acquaintance with Dittany was even more slight than Dittany's with Mitch, but the question was received without resentment.

'We've been spending some time together, yes – when he can get away from his business commitments. I've never met anybody quite like him.' Dittany's oval face, with its delicate bones and large eyes, took on a dreamy expression. 'He's got so many sides to his character.' She smiled down at the tablecloth, as if remembering something that pleased her. Melissa ate her cheese salad and waited.

'Under that jokey Cockney exterior there's a very tough, quick-witted businessman,' Dittany continued after a pause.

'Well, there has to be, hasn't there?' remarked Melissa, as Dittany still appeared absorbed in her reflections. 'He'd never have built up that huge business empire without a hard nose and a lot of financial nous.'

'Of course, but he's got a soft centre – he's a devoted son to his old Mum and Dad.'

Melissa smothered a grin. 'So were the Kray twins, I believe.' Dittany bit her lip and Melissa touched her gently on the hand. 'Sorry – just my warped sense of humour. Please go on.'

'He really is a very sensitive, caring person . . . he supports a lot of good causes . . . and he's concerned about the environment . . . and he's keen on the arts, but he never learned much about them at school. I've been sort of helping him . . . We've had some lovely talks about books and things and he's really got a very fine mind, but . . .' Dittany broke off and stared down at her plate; the hand that held her fork was unsteady.

'Well?' prompted Melissa, after a further pause, during which her companion seemed to be making up her mind whether to continue or not.

'Last night, he said something rather strange and it made me a little . . . afraid. He phoned me after I got home. It was quite late, after midnight, and he was so apologetic at disturbing me but he said he just had to talk to me.' Another rush of colour to the face betrayed emotions that Dittany was plainly trying to hide. 'He was so upset . . . I was crying too . . . and he kept repeating that it was his fault Will was dead, and then he calmed down and said, very quietly, "I'll get the bastards, if it's the last thing I do." And you should have heard, Melissa, the . . . the rasp, the *hate* in his voice. It was quite horrible.'

'Let me get this straight,' said Melissa. 'Are you saying that Mitch believes someone else played a part in Will's death?'

'That's what it sounded like. He said there's to be an inquest . . .'

'That's normal in a case of sudden death.'

'And a post-mortem. Doesn't that mean the doctors suspect something?'

'Not necessarily – it just means they haven't been able to determine the cause of death by external examination. If it wasn't the head injury that killed him, they'll be looking for something like a stroke or a heart attack that could account for the fall.' A thought struck Melissa. 'I know this isn't a nice thing to suggest, but you don't suppose he'd had too much to drink, do you?'

Dittany shook her head. 'Oh, no,' she declared. 'He never had more than one or two drinks.'

'Those steps are very steep, and quite smooth and worn in places.' Melissa closed her eyes and shuddered at the memory.

Dittany pushed the mangled remains of the omelette to one side and took her capsule bottle from her handbag. 'I think I'll take one of these, I'm a bit on edge,' she said apologetically. She up-ended the bottle and shook it; it was empty. 'Damn, I meant to get some more . . . oh Lord,' she whispered, with a catch in her voice. 'Will was in such a tizzy the

62

evening he died, I gave my last two to him. I'm not sure he ever took them, though. He had a real fixation about any form of drugs.'

'But those aren't drugs?'

'Of course not – they're herbal extracts and completely non-addictive. I doubt if I convinced Will, though.' Dittany gave a sad shake of the head as she put the bottle away.

'Let's get back to Mitch,' said Melissa. 'You say he spoke about "getting" someone. Any idea who he was talking about?'

'None at all. I did ask him but he told me he'd been talking nonsense and I was to forget what he'd said . . . He sounded really furious for a moment and then he spoke gently again and said he'd call me this evening. You won't let him know I've told you all this, will you, Melissa? I don't think he'd like it, somehow.'

'No, of course I won't. But if you get the chance, I'd warn him against settling any private grudges. It could land him in serious trouble. Bad for his business image and all that,' she added, with an attempt at lightening the atmosphere.

A smile flickered over Dittany's wan face as she checked her watch. 'I'll have to be getting back to the library. It's been such a relief, talking to you.'

'I'm glad.' But I haven't learned much, thought Melissa as she made her way back to the car park. Except that Chloe was almost certainly right: the show was nothing more than an elaborate subterfuge. Something at Heyshill Manor Hotel was not what it seemed, and Will was there at Mitch's behest because he 'owed him one'. But what, exactly, had he been looking for? Why should Mitch adopt such a subterfuge when, as the owner of the hotel, he was in a position to ask any questions or carry out openly any investigation he wanted? And who else, apart from himself, was he trying to blame for Will's death?

It's none of your business, Melissa Craig, she told herself on the way home. It was pure chance that you happened to

63

be there when Will had his fall . . . if you hadn't taken that first-aid course you'd never have been involved. Keep out of it and get back to work or you'll have Joe Martin breathing down your neck and muttering about deadlines.

As for telling Mitch about the conversation with Dittany, it was unlikely that the occasion would arise. *Innocent Blood Avenged* was almost certainly a dead duck and there would be no more rehearsals for her to attend. She felt a twinge of disappointment; she had been pleasantly surprised at how slick and funny it was turning out under Chloe's direction.

When she reached home, she found Iris sitting in front of her cottage, working at her easel. After putting the car away, she strolled across for a chat.

'Mind if I look?'

'Help yourself. Tell me what you think.' Iris put her brush in a jar of water and sat back.

It was a simple study of their peaceful Cotswold valley, the foreground a random pattern of trees and pasture divided by low stone walls that curved and undulated along the uneven terrain, the background a checker-board of corn stubble and freshly turned earth. There was a glint of water from the brook, chestnut-brown cattle grazing on the hillside, a cloud of gulls wheeling round a tractor. It was a familiar scene, one they watched through the changing seasons with never-failing pleasure. By sheer skill with the use of colour, Iris had managed to convey the effect of the late September sun, which set the sky aglow and lay over fields and woodland like a haze of golden dust.

'Iris, that is lovely,' said Melissa warmly.

'You like it?' Iris gave her a keen look. 'Not just saying?'

'You know me better than that. The sunlight . . . it's got that special autumn quality – terrific.'

'Glad you like it. Been working on it for this "Patterns of Light and Shade" thing, y'know.'

'You mean the course you're giving in France next month? I'd forgotten about that – it's going ahead, then?'

'Always was. One or two students from last time signed on straight away.'

'Is Jack Hammond one of them?' asked Melissa slyly. Jack had taken a shine to Iris during the art course she had tutored the previous July; by coincidence he lived in nearby Somerset. Although Iris was being pretty cagey, Melissa had a shrewd suspicion that they had been seeing one another fairly often, and was glad. A stable relationship was exactly what Iris needed, after a couple of near-disasters.

Iris's mouth, which in repose had a certain uncompromising set, widened in a smile that softened her sharp features and brought a sparkle to her eyes. 'He's driving me down,' she said, in a vain effort to sound casual.

'That's great. How many have enrolled?'

'Eight so far, and several more enquiries.'

'Well, I'm sure they'll all want to know how they can achieve that effect.' Melissa gestured towards the easel. 'It almost makes me want to have a go myself.'

Iris grinned and took up her brush again. 'Must get on before the light changes. Care to come for supper?'

'Love to.'

As Melissa entered Hawthorn Cottage, the telephone rang.

'That you, Mel?' There was no mistaking the staccato London voice that made an unfinished 'w' from the final 'l' of her name.

'Mitch! How did you get my number?'

'Chris got it, no problem.'

So much for going ex-directory, thought Melissa resignedly.

'Mel, I need to talk to you.'

'What about?'

'Not on the phone. Have you got time this evening?'

'I'm having supper with a friend . . .' she began, but Mitch was quick to interrupt.

'This is urgent – can't you put him off?' There was a note of authority in his voice, the tone of a man accustomed to giving orders and getting his own way.

It seemed a good moment to make it clear that she was not prepared to be hustled. 'Not without a good reason,' she replied calmly.

There was a pause before he repeated, 'I don't want to discuss it on the phone.'

'I'm not asking for details . . . just some idea . . .'

'Okay then, if you insist. It's about Will Foley.' She waited, determined not to help him. 'I'm not satisfied his death was an accident.'

'Good Lord!' She hoped her exclamation conveyed genuine surprise. 'What are you suggesting?'

'I'm not sure what I'm suggesting . . . I'm just not satisfied.'

'Why tell me? If you've got suspicions, you should tell the police.'

'I haven't anything concrete to go on but there's a few things that don't add up. I thought you might help me figure them out . . . you being a crime writer and all that.'

So that was what he had in mind – picking her brains. Really, of all the . . .

'Look, are you going to come or not?' He sounded on edge; under the peremptory, almost hectoring manner was a man desperate for help.

'I'll think about it and call you back,' she said. He gave her the number with evident reluctance; she half expected a request not to divulge it to anyone else.

'Shouldn't do it if I were you,' said Iris when she reported Mitch's call. 'But knowing you, you will. Don't worry, we'll sup another time.'

'I haven't decided yet.'

Iris's only response was a sardonic cackle.

Melissa had still not made up her mind when the phone rang again. This time it was Joe. After the usual enquiries about progress on the novel and her state of health – in that order – he remarked casually, 'I see Rich Mitch has found something nasty in his cellar.'

'How did you know about that?'

'It was on the local radio. William Foley comes from London – he retired to a cottage not far from where I live when he left the force.'

'He was a real policeman?' Melissa could not control her surprise, and Joe was quick to react.

'What do you mean, a *real* policeman?'

'He was acting the part of a copper in my pantocrime,' Melissa explained. 'I didn't realise he'd actually been one. I wonder if that's why . . .'

'What?'

'Oh, nothing.'

'Come on, Mel, spill it. You've heard something.' There was a note of unease in Joe's voice. While he was never averse – after the event – to the publicity brought about by her occasional contact with actual crime, he was inclined to become agitated at the possibility of her being exposed to any risk. He always protested that he was concerned for her safety; Melissa, knowing that he would need little encouragement to show more than concern, made a point of keeping him at arm's length by maintaining that he was simply afraid of losing a lucrative client.

'I was there when the accident happened,' she said, and because her mind was still half on her conversation with Mitch, she added carelessly, 'Mitch thinks there's something fishy about it.'

'Fishy?' The familiar note of rising alarm in Joe's voice made her wince. Damn, she thought, I shouldn't have said that. Now he'll start fussing.

'Look here, Mel, I warned you not to get mixed up with that lot. All that rubbish about wanting a sketch for a birthday party – anyone could see through that. At least this gives you an excuse to keep out of it.'

'How d'you figure that out?'

'The show won't go ahead now, surely?'

'I don't see why not.' Melissa knew she was being perverse;

she had come to the same conclusion herself, but Joe had this effect on her.

'Well, whether it does or not, you keep out of it,' Joe reiterated. 'You'll let me have the new script by the end of next month, then?'

The opportunity to tease him was too good to miss. 'If I'm not too busy solving the Heyshill Manor Mystery,' she said, and put the phone down before he could reply.

Why, she asked herself as she dialled the number Mitch had given her, do men have to be so *bossy*?

Chapter Seven

Mitch brushed aside Melissa's assertion that she was perfectly capable of driving herself to his house.

'It's a sod to find – Chris'll fetch you in the Jag,' he said. Sensing that she was unlikely to get the better of the argument, she gave him directions to Hawthorn Cottage and went upstairs to get ready. It took her some time to decide what to wear; it was hardly a dinner date – although she hoped Mitch would remember that she had cancelled an invitation to eat with Iris – but perhaps to dress too casually would not be quite the thing either. She settled for a paisley skirt and shawl, a cream silk blouse and the opal pendant and earrings Guy had given her shortly before he was killed. 'Opals bring bad luck,' a friend had remarked on seeing them, but she had laughed away such nonsense. They suited her colouring and she wore them with joy and love. After the motor accident that smashed her world to pieces, she had continued to wear them in Guy's memory, in defiance of superstition. And as things turned out, despite the tragedy and the trauma of finding herself pregnant and rejected by her parents, life had been pretty good to her and her son. She reflected while she put on her clothes that Simon, grown-up now and helping to keep the oil wells of Texas in production, would be thinking it was time he had a letter from his mother. She'd write tomorrow – there was plenty to tell him.

She was giving her hair a final brush when through her bedroom window came a flash of headlights. She popped her head out and saw the Jaguar emerging from the gathering dusk.

'Chris'll have a job turning in that narrow space,' she

chuckled to herself with a certain malicious glee. She closed the window and drew the curtains.

The bell sounded almost immediately; to her surprise, Mitch was on the doorstep.

'Ready?' he asked.

'Almost. If you'd like to come in and wait while I do my hair . . .'

'What's wrong with it?'

Nonplussed, she put up a hand and brushed a loose strand away from her face. 'I usually tie it back or up in a knot for evenings.'

'Leave it like that, it looks great.' It was as if she had asked for his opinion which, once given, settled the matter once and for all. 'Come on, get your coat while Chris turns the car round.'

'I'm afraid he'll find the space a bit tight. Mine's only a small car and I find it tricky.'

'No problem. Chris can turn a ten-ton truck on a sixpence,' boasted Mitch. As he spoke, the car slid to a halt in front of them, its sleek bonnet pointing back towards the road. 'See what I mean?'

Round one had definitely gone to Mitch. Picking up her handbag and shawl, Melissa switched off the light and closed the front door. He handed her into the back of the car and climbed in beside her. It was almost like being kidnapped.

'Thought I'd come along too, so's I can give you a bit of background on the way,' Mitch explained.

'Yes, it would be nice to be put in the picture,' she said, thinking that a touch of sarcasm might have an effect where the direct approach had failed. He brushed aside the tiny barb with a chuckle and the kind of pat on the knee a rich uncle might give a favourite niece on taking her out for an afternoon treat.

'Yeah, well, I've always been a bit of a hustler. Wouldn't be where I am otherwise – right, Chris?'

'Right,' said Chris, without taking his eyes from the road.

'I got no secrets from Chris. Anything you find out, if you can't contact me, you can tell him.'

'Anything I . . . now, wait a minute. You wouldn't be suggesting I carry out some sort of private enquiry, would you? There are professionals who do that sort of thing. I invent scams, I don't investigate real ones.'

'I'm hoping I can make you change your mind.'

'Well, you won't. If that's what you're after, you're wasting your time. Please ask Chris to turn round and take me home.'

'No, wait a minute, you haven't heard what I've got to say.'

'I don't want to know.'

Stop kidding yourself, said a small voice in the back of her brain. *You're dying to know, so shut up and let the man talk.*

'Just hear me out, why don't you?' There was a subtle change, a hint of cajolery, in Mitch's tone. 'You broke your date – you want to go hungry?'

'I've got food in my freezer.'

'So who wants to dine on iced hamburgers? Listen, Mel, my housekeeper cooks like an angel, she's getting a meal for three and she won't half be wild if there's only the two of us to eat it.' His mouth wore the hesitant half-grin of a schoolboy trying to wheedle extra pocket money, but his eyes were steady and serious.

Melissa gave a resigned sigh. 'Oh, very well. But I'm not promising anything, remember.'

'Okay. Now, listen, here's how it all began . . .'

In the time that it took to arrive at Mitch's home, a converted farmhouse some twenty miles away, Melissa learned that he had acquired Heyshill Manor Hotel when it came unexpectedly on to the market after the sudden death of the previous owner in a riding accident. As it happened, he knew the place well, having regularly stayed there when visiting Gloucestershire from London to see how the work on his own house was progressing. He had for some time been on the look-out for

71

an opportunity of breaking into the leisure industry; here, it seemed, one was being served to him on a plate.

'Course, it was sad about the poor old geezer falling off his nag, but it did me one big favour, didn't it? He was a widower with no kids and no other relatives except an elderly sister living in Bournemouth. All she wanted was the ready – she couldn't sell quick enough.'

'How very convenient for you,' said Melissa, and promptly regretted it. 'I'm sorry, that must have sounded rude.'

He reached for her hand and gave it a squeeze. 'Nah, I know what you're thinking, but it was all kosher. I got what I wanted, but I paid a fair price. The place was in good nick; old Sir Whatsit had it done over two or three years before he kicked the bucket, but I had the conference wing built on. Kept the staff on as well – all except the chef, that is. Bloody Frog, stuffed everything full of garlic and gave it a fancy foreign name. When I told him I wanted roast beef and York-shire pud for Sunday lunch and the menus printed in plain English, he did his nut and walked out. What I say is, there's nothing wrong with good British grub.'

Gleefully, he rubbed his hands together as he recounted this gastronomic battle of Waterloo. It was plain that he was riding a favourite hobby-horse and Melissa could not contain a burst of laughter, in which he joined. 'Course, Pen thinks I'm uncouth, but they don't print menus in English in French restaurants, so what the hell?'

'Quite,' agreed Melissa, egging him on. 'And if people want French cooking, they can go to France, can't they?'

'Right. I can see you 'n' me'll get along just fine. Let's have some music.' Settling back in his seat with the air of one confident that a deal is all but in the bag, he pressed a button in his arm-rest and the slow movement of a Mozart piano concerto played softly from concealed loudspeakers. 'This is one of me favourites. They used it in some film or other, didn't they?'

'*Elvira Madigan.*'

'That's right. You know it?'

'Very well. I love all Mozart's music.'

'I don't know much, but I'm learning.'

From Dittany, perhaps? Melissa wondered. She, too, felt herself relaxing. The atmosphere was warm, the scent of leather overlaid with the fragrance of some expensive masculine toiletry, the upholstery soft and yielding. The big car purred along, the beams from its powerful headlamps sweeping the road ahead like searching fingers and kindling tiny flares in the eyes of nocturnal animals lurking by the roadside.

'Not far now,' said Mitch as they turned into an unmarked lane. During the drive, Melissa had been trying to keep an eye on the route they were taking. They had passed through Chipping Campden and headed towards Banbury, but after that they had turned on to minor roads and it was some time since she had seen a familiar name signposted. A vague feeling of disquiet made her shiver and pull her shawl more closely round her shoulders.

It was absurd, of course; Mitch was respectable, well-known and highly thought of in the world of business, not at all the sort of shady character who lures women into out-of-the-way places with felonious or murderous intent. He had brought her here quite openly; at the end of the evening he would arrange for her to be driven safely home. As for wanting to involve her in some as yet unexplained bit of private sleuthing – well, she could always refuse, couldn't she? Just the same, he was being unnecessarily evasive; perhaps it was time to pin him down.

'Look, Mitch,' she said, trying to sound brisk and business-like. 'You've told me how you came to buy a hotel and got rid of the French chef, and it's all very interesting and entertaining, but . . .'

'Nearly there,' said Mitch blandly. 'Lovely spot, this. Pity it's nearly dark – you'll have to come and see it in daylight some time.'

As he spoke, Chris swung the car into a concealed entrance

and along a narrow track, lit at intervals by mushroom lamps on either side. It snaked downhill through a series of tight bends, ending at a pair of wrought-iron gates set in a high stone wall. Chris had evidently actuated some remote-control mechanism, for there was a buzz, a click, and the gates swung inward. As the car crept forward, they closed behind it. Simultaneously, two dark shapes came padding out of the shadows and ran beside the car until it pulled up at the front door of the house.

Unusually for the Cotswolds, it was built of mellow red brick, with mullioned windows and carriage lamps on either side of the studded oak front door. The walls were partially covered in brilliant red Virginia creeper and scarlet geraniums spilled from tubs and hanging baskets. As the car stopped, the door was opened by a grey-haired, middle-aged woman. Her appearance and her smile of welcome were reassuring.

'Here we are, Mrs Wingfield,' called Mitch as he got out of the car. 'You wait there a tick while I introduce you to the boys,' he said to Melissa.

The instruction was unnecesssary. Faced with two pairs of baleful eyes and two gaping mouths full of spiky teeth, she had every intention of staying where she was. 'Okay, boys, she's a friend. *Friend*,' he repeated, opening Melissa's door and beckoning. Warily, she stepped out; to her relief, the dogs greeted her with wagging tails and amiably exploring muzzles. 'They know you now and they'll never attack you,' Mitch promised. 'Just let 'em have a sniff so's they recognise your scent. The brindle's Attila and the black one's Genghis Khan – Khan for short – and if anyone they haven't been introduced to tries to get in, they'll chew his balls off.'

'Charming,' murmured Melissa as she patted the rough coats.

The two German Shepherds followed them indoors, keeping close to their master's heels. Mitch led the way into a low-beamed sitting-room where a log fire burned cheerfully on a stone hearth.

'Have a seat. Drink?'

'Thanks – a gin and tonic, please.'

While he poured the drinks, she glanced round the room. Someone with taste and unlimited money had been given a free hand and the result would have graced the glossiest of magazines. Everything, from the heavy curtains in a random pattern of brown and cream like the fleece of a Jacob sheep to the huge copper warming-pan that reflected the glow of the log fire, had been carefully chosen and meticulously placed. Much of the furniture was antique and the pictures and ornaments looked valuable, with the exception of a couple of photographs in plain wooden frames, standing alone on a small table. Seeing her eye on them, Mitch picked one up and handed it to her along with her drink. It was of a beaming, rotund couple whose clothes were covered in white buttons; the man wore a cap, similarly adorned, and the woman a hat with a huge feather.

'Me Grannie and Grandad,' he said proudly. 'They was Pearly King and Queen of Bermondsey that year. That was taken on a costermongers' outing, just before the war.'

'Your grandfather was a costermonger?'

'And me Dad. They call 'em barrow-boys nowadays.' Mitch sat down beside her, took back the photo and studied it with an affectionate smile. Then he replaced it and picked up the second one. 'That's me Mum and Dad with their fruit barrow.' He pronounced it 'barrer'; his Cockney accent had grown markedly stronger as he handled the mementoes of his family.

'I know what you're thinking,' he said as he replaced the photographs, setting them in place with care. 'I'm out of me class, living in a place like this, owning Heyshill Manor, mixing with the nobs . . .'

'I'm not thinking anything of the kind,' protested Melissa, with total sincerity. 'You must have worked damned hard to get where you are.'

'That's what I tell Pen when she tells me off for not holding me fork right,' he said, with a lop-sided grin. 'And talking of forks, supper's ready.' Chris had appeared at the door and summoned them with a jerk of the head.

On the pretext that he didn't want to spoil anyone's appetite, Mitch steadfastly refused to discuss the real business of the evening until they had finished their meal of smoked salmon, roast beef and treacle tart. Instead, he encouraged Melissa to talk about her writing; several of her books had been set in other countries and he seemed to know them all well. 'Have to get about quite a bit, y'know,' he explained. 'Don't get much time for sightseeing, though. Lots of things I don't get enough time for,' he added, and his face softened as he spoke, as if a secret, pleasant thought had come to mind. Again, Melissa wondered if it had anything to do with Dittany.

'Well, now,' he said, as they returned to the sitting-room, where Chris was already pouring coffee for the three of them and brandy for Mitch and Melissa. 'Let's get down to the nitty-gritty.'

'Yes, it's about time,' said Melissa, stroking Khan's head. The great dog had sat beside her throughout dinner and now settled against her legs, yawning contentedly at the fire; after a moment he lay down with his head on her foot.

'He's taken a shine to you,' said Mitch, with obvious pleasure. 'You're one of the family now.'

A warning bell sounded in Melissa's head. *Watch it, girl. They're in it together, dogs and all, working to soften you up. Keep your head and don't let them flannel you into doing anything you don't want to do.*

Aloud, she said, 'I think it's time you told me exactly why you invited me here.'

Chapter Eight

'I dunno where to begin,' said Mitch in a dull voice. The cheerful front that he had kept up so far had fallen away and he sat staring moodily into the fire.

'Okay, let me do a spot of guesswork,' said Melissa. 'You suspect someone at Heyshill Manor of being up to no good – maybe trying to rip you off. You ask Will to do a bit of ferreting around. Next thing, Will dies as the result of a fall down the cellar steps, and you feel it's too much of a coincidence. Am I right?'

Mitch nodded, still gazing into the fire. 'Got it in one.'

'That much wasn't hard to figure out. Did the doctors find anything suspicious?'

'Not that I know of.'

'But you suspect Vic Bellamy of having had something to do with it?'

'Yeah.'

'That's a pretty serious allegation.'

Mitch ran his fingers through his neatly trimmed brown hair. 'I know, and I got no proof, just this gut feeling that he's either running some racket of his own or he's getting a hefty rake-off for keeping his mouth shut about somebody else's.'

'You must have some reason for believing this.'

Mitch stood up, returned his empty coffee-cup to the tray and began pacing up and down. On the instant, the dogs raised their heads. When they realised their master was not going out they settled down again, but their eyes followed his every movement.

'Heyshill Manor's a luxury hotel in a popular part of the

country,' he began. 'It's aimed at the nobs – jet-setters, property dealers, wealthy foreign tourists, people who don't have to worry about where the mortgage payments are coming from. So you'd expect to see plenty of Mercs and Jags in the car park, and the odd Roller and Bentley. But I got to wondering when I noticed the number of characters turning up in big Yankee cars, some of 'em with CD plates.'

'Maybe they'd heard about the change of chef and come in search of good British grub?' suggested Melissa, but there was no answering smile.

'They were coming before that. And twice, when I happened to be in Reception when one of them turned up, I noticed that Kim made a point of calling Vic and introducing him. There was something about the way they greeted each other, like the first polite exchanges when you're negotiating a deal. Nothing significant in itself, just the usual guff from Vic – "Hope you'll enjoy your stay, the staff are at your service", that sort of thing. He'd even take 'em up to their rooms himself.'

'Well, if they were VIPs of some sort . . .'

For a second time, Mitch ran his fingers through his hair, twisting his head this way and that as if trying to shake out the words he needed. 'There was more to it than that. I can't explain any clearer. When you've done as many deals as I have, you get to know the drill – it's almost like a ritual dance – shake hands, exchange small talk, size one another up, watch the body language. Those guys weren't just there for a holiday, I'll stake my life on it.'

His look challenged Melissa to make some reply, but she could only shake her head and he gave a grunt of exasperation.

'Then there's Vic's own life style,' he went on. 'Flashy car, villa in Spain, membership of a snooty golf club, goes hunting with the local gentry – and have you noticed all that ice Kim wears?' Each point was accompanied by a stabbing gesture with the right forefinger and Melissa found it easy to picture him in the chair at a business meeting, haranguing his directors, brushing aside objections. 'I pay 'em well and so did the previous owner, but not enough to run to that lot.' He lifted his hands and thrust his chin forward as if winding up a case against which there was no argument.

'Could he be siphoning off some of the profits – the bar takings, for example?'

Mitch brushed aside the suggestion with a sweep of his arm. 'Not big enough. Besides, our accountant's been through the books with a toothcomb, checking against stock. No, it's gotta be something on the side.'

'But not necessarily illegal,' Melissa pointed out.

'Do me a favour! If it's on the level, why all the secrecy?' Mitch turned to look her straight in the face. The lines round his wide, mobile mouth had become hard and his blue eyes cold, laying bare the vein of ruthlessness that had driven him onwards and upwards from a street market in south-east London to the chairmanship of a multi-million pound corporation. 'I'm not having one of my managers involved in shady deals,' he snapped. 'Mitchell Enterprises is a tightly run ship, it's a clean ship, and that's how it's staying. Okay, so I can't be behind everyone all of the time, but I keep as close a check as I can. I've built up a reputation for straight dealing and if I catch anyone on the fiddle, he's out!' He thrust his hands into his pockets and stood with his back to the fire, glowering down at Melissa as if challenging her to an argument on business ethics.

Deliberately, determined to show that she was not to be browbeaten, she put down her coffee-cup, leaned forward and caressed Khan's head. He responded by sitting up and laying his black muzzle in her lap.

'Has it occurred to you that Vic may have a private income?' she said. 'He's quite a distinguished-looking chap; maybe he comes from a well-to-do family.'

'Nah!' Mitch dismissed the idea as if it were a fly not worth the effort of swatting. 'If you've got that sort of bread, you don't work as a hotel manager. In any case, don't let the posh accent fool you. He comes from a working-class family, same as I do.'

'How do you know that?'

With a suddenness that took her by surprise, his manner changed. His sense of humour came bubbling through the anger, bringing the familiar twinkle back to his eye. 'Made a few enquiries, didn't I? His Dad was a milkman and he grew up along the road from me in Walworth. The difference between us is, he put on a bit of la-di-da and the old school tie on his way up the ladder. I got further up, though.' His smile radiated self-satisfaction.

Melissa smiled with him, but her brain was busy. 'I suppose,' she said thoughtfully, '*Innocent Blood Avenged* was simply a device for allowing Will to carry out a discreet investigation – find out whatever he could without arousing suspicion or frightening the horses.'

Mitch grinned. 'In a manner of speaking, but it didn't start like that. In the bar one night me and Chris saw this notice about the Stowbridge Players putting on some kinda revue. I said, "Why don't I get them to do something to entertain the mob at my birthday knees-up?" and Chris said, "What a good idea." That's right, innit, Chris?' He shot a glance towards the corner where his minder sat, silently nursing his coffee-cup and saucer.

'Right,' Chris agreed.

'So Chris got in touch with Chloe, and Chloe got in touch with you, and that's how it all started, right, Chris?'

'Right.'

'I'm beginning to understand,' said Melissa. 'When you saw my script and realised there was a detective in the cast, you hit on the idea of inviting a friend who was a retired policeman to play the part.'

Mitch's expression of astonishment was comical. His mouth fell open and his eyebrows leapt towards his hairline. 'How d'you know Will was an ex-copper?'

'It crossed my mind when I first met him that he might have been in the force at some time.'

'No kidding? What gave you that idea?'

'A friend of mine is in the local CID and he has the same way of looking you straight in the eye that Will had.' It was perfectly true so far as it went and she saw no particular point in adding that she had confirmation from another source.

Mitch nodded and gave a wistful half-smile. 'Yeah, I know, like he could see the inside of your skull. When I was a kid and he caught me getting up to no good, he always knew if I was fibbing.'

'You've known him a long time?'

'All me life. Him and me Dad were best mates from their schooldays.'

'So the scheme was that during rehearsals, when he wasn't actually needed on stage, he could go off and chat up the staff, or maybe turn up early and wander round the grounds before it got dark, keeping his eyes and ears open to see what he could pick up.'

'You got the idea.'

'And you still made him go through with it, even when you realised he found acting such an ordeal?'

'I never *made* him, honest.' Mitch sat down opposite her and leaned forward, hands tightly clasped, his eyes fixed on hers, imploring her to believe him. 'I wanted to drop the idea when I saw how it was churning him up. I told him, forget it and we'll think of something else, but he wouldn't hear of it. He never was one to give up, once he'd got his teeth into something. His manor took in parts of dockland and things can get pretty rough round there. He said no one was going to call Will Foley a wally for being scared of a bit of play-acting.'

'He'd been in the force a long time, I take it?'

'Ten years on the beat, then moved over to the CID. He wasn't flavour of the month with the local villains, I can tell you. A gang of 'em followed him one night when he was off

81

duty and started to work him over. Me and me Dad saw it and pitched in to help him. He never forgot it.'

So that was what Will had meant when he told Dittany that he owed Mitch one. He had died while trying to repay the debt; Mitch had persuaded himself that he was partly to blame and was trying to expiate his guilt.

There was a short silence, during which she tried to think of some way of persuading him that, without even one piece of hard evidence to justify voicing his suspicions to the police, he should either hire a professional private investigator or let the matter drop. She wanted no part of it, could not in any case accept his reasons for suspecting Vic Bellamy. In running an hotel, as in any other business, it was the job of a manager to keep the customers happy. So far as she could see, the man was doing a good job.

Mitch had leaned back in his armchair, looking emotionally drained. Their eyes met; his said, as plainly as if he had spoken aloud, *I'm out of my depth, I don't know where to go from here – please help me.* It would have taken a harder heart than hers to ignore the appeal.

'Tell me,' she said gently, 'did Will find out anything at all?'

'I think he might have been on to something, from what he said to Chris, but he wouldn't be drawn. Wouldn't stick his neck out unless he was sure.'

'What did he say, Chris?' she asked.

Chris glanced at Mitch as if seeking permission to answer, and received a nod in return. He cleared his throat.

'He took me out one evening to have a look at Vic's car, asked me if I noticed anything about it. I couldn't spot anything out of the ordinary till he pointed out it had twin exhausts and one looked cleaner than the other. He wanted to know if that was usual.'

'And is it?'

'No.'

'Did Will give you any idea of why he was asking?'

'No.' From his wooden expression and vague shrug of the shoulders, Melissa deduced that Chris was more accustomed to answering questions than analysing what lay behind them.

'You said it wasn't usual, but it could happen? If one silencer developed a fault or got damaged if the car hit a rock or something and had to be replaced, the new exhaust would look cleaner than the other, wouldn't it?'

Both men looked at her in surprise. Plainly, they had not expected a mere female to know about such things.

'Oh, sure,' agreed Chris.

'Did you tell Will that?'

'Yes.'

'What did he say?'

'Nothing. He just stood there sort of whistling through his teeth, and then we came back indoors.'

'I remember now,' said Melissa, 'he was looking at Vic's car yesterday evening, when Iris and I arrived to watch the rehearsal. He was peering through the driver's window.'

'Now, why would he do that, I wonder?' said Mitch.

'Checking the mileage?' suggested Chris.

'Maybe he wanted to know if it had been on any long trips since he last looked at it,' said Melissa. A thought struck her. 'You mentioned Vic and Kim had a villa in Spain. Do they use it often?'

Mitch considered. 'Dunno exactly. Several times a year – I'd have to ask the Joyriders. The department at head office that keeps an eye on the outposts of me empire,' he explained, in response to Melissa's questioning look. 'I call 'em that 'cos it gives 'em any God's amount of excuses to swan round doing on-the-spot check-ups. I send Chris out now and then to check on the checkers,' he added. He seemed anxious to impress her with the efficiency of his control system, but she was only half listening.

'Does he go by car?'

'Can't say as I've ever asked him.'

'Who runs the hotel while he's away?'

'A relief manager and his wife. It's a long-standing arrange-ment with the previous owner.'

'Have the Joyriders vetted him too?'

Mitch chuckled. 'Chris has. He's clean. Retired from full-time work a few years ago on health grounds, but does the odd stint here and there to top up his disability pension.' He gave her a keen look. 'You got something in mind?'

'Nothing specific at the moment. I'm trying to figure out why Will should be so interested in the exhaust. It's a pity he played everything so close to his chest.'

Mitch sighed. 'That was Will for you.'

'Chris, haven't you any idea?'

Chris did not appear to consider it part of his remit to have ideas. 'Haven't a clue,' he said, his face a blank.

'But you are something of an expert on cars.'

'Course he is,' said Mitch proudly, as Chris gave another shrug. 'What he doesn't know about 'em isn't worth knowing. Mind you,' he grinned at Melissa, 'imagination's not his strong point. You have the ideas, he'll tell you if they'll work. I reckon you two'd make a great team.' His eyes swivelled from one to the other. 'I was right to rope her in, wasn't I, Chris?'

'Right,' Chris agreed, predictably.

'But I haven't done anything,' protested Melissa. 'And I'm not sure I . . .'

'Not yet, but you will. I've got this gut feeling.'

Melissa caught the faintest movement in Chris's left eye and bit her lip to kill the smile that might betray an inclination to weaken. 'You seem to be strong on gut feelings,' was the only comment she could think of.

'Sure I am. Half me business decisions are made on that basis. And talking of business, that's another reason why I want this done nice and discreetly. No adverse publicity that might scare off the customers. We find out what Vic's up to and confront him with it, he goes quietly, problem solved.'

'*We* find out?' Melissa raised a cynical eyebrow.

Mitch treated her to a full frontal smile – the complete works, as she later recounted to Iris: white teeth, dimples, blue eyes alight with whimsical humour.

Once again, she found herself exchanging glances with Chris. Until now, she had sensed that his attitude towards her, while by no means hostile, was at best one of resigned acceptance. Mitch wanted her there, Mitch was the boss, and that was that. By that flicker of an eyelid, Chris had shown that he too welcomed her presence.

They're in it together, dogs and all. As if to reinforce the recurring thought, Khan, who had once more settled down to sleep at her feet, stood up, yawned, stretched himself, and then shoved his nose under her hand, his tail gently wagging.

'Tell you what, I've just had this great idea.' Mitch was on his feet again but this time there was no restless pacing to and fro. He was like an athlete before the start of a race, tense and ready for the gun. 'You told us over dinner your next book's set in an old house with a spook, right?'

'Right,' Melissa agreed, wondering where the question was leading.

'You wanna get the atmosphere spot on, don't you?'

'Ye . . . s.'

'So you oughta spend a few days in a spooky old house, to get the feel of it.'

'What are you getting at?'

Like a salesman brandishing a sample of his most seductive product, Mitch held out both hands and treated her to yet another blinding smile. 'Be my guest at Heyshill Manor for a few days – do some field research. Give you the perfect excuse to snoop around.'

There was a pause, during which Melissa's sense of adventure did battle with sound and sober judgement.

Mitch made an impatient gesture. 'Well, what do you say?'

'You're serious?'

'Course I am. Will you do it?'

A long-case clock in the far corner of the room struck eleven.

She heard it with relief and seized the opportunity of playing for time. Gently pushing Khan's head aside, she stood up. 'I had no idea it was so late, I must be going,' she said.

'You haven't given me an answer.'

'I'll have to think about it. It's very generous of you, but I'm not sure I want to commit myself to . . . what you're asking of me.'

But she was already committed, even if she was not prepared to admit it just yet. The whiff of mystery was like a heady perfume in her nostrils, exciting, irresistible. All the same, she was not going to let Mitch think she was a pushover. 'I'll let you know in a day or two,' she promised.

As if recognising that to press her further could be counter-productive, Mitch nodded to Chris, who picked up the keys of the Jaguar and left the room without a word. By the time Mitch and Melissa reached the front door, having said their good-nights, he had already started the engine and was standing by the front passenger door, holding it open for her. She thanked him as she climbed in and received a brief nod in return.

For the first two or three miles he drove in silence, giving her an opportunity to observe him out of the corner of her eye: a rounded forehead beneath cropped hair, a jutting lower lip that put her in mind of the young Winston Churchill. She wondered how he had come to be associated with Mitch and was trying to devise a tactful line of enquiry when, without warning, he spoke.

'You gonna do it, then?'

With some vague notion of giving herself time to prepare a noncommittal reply, she was on the point of lamely responding 'Do what?', but for a fraction of a second he took his eyes from the road ahead and looked directly at her. Even in the semi-darkness, she could read their message: 'No bull-shit – just tell me straight.'

There had been no opportunity to confer with Mitch; he was doing this off his own bat. It wasn't idle curiosity, he wasn't that sort of man. He wanted to know because of his one hundred per cent loyalty to his employer. He deserved a frank reply, and she gave it to him.

'I'm not really convinced that there's any mystery about Will's death,' she said. 'So, if I accepted Mitch's invitation to stay at Heyshill Manor as his guest, it'd be a great benefit to me as a writer, but I'm afraid he mightn't get value for his money.'

'But you'd do as he asks – keep your eyes peeled, maybe ferret around a bit?'

'Oh sure, I'd do that all right.'

'Then what's the problem?'

'Let *me* ask *you* a question. Do you agree with Mitch that Vic's up to some sort of scam?'

'Mitch doesn't make many bum judgements about people.'

'But have *you* noticed anything?'

Chris shrugged. 'Wouldn't know what to look for, would I?' He slowed, changed gear and turned into the lane leading to Melissa's cottage, but instead of driving on he pulled off by the entrance to a field. Still looking straight in front of him, he said, 'I tell you this. Will Foley was no fool either, and he thought he was on to something.'

Without thinking, Melissa remarked, 'Mitch seems to inspire great loyalty among his friends.'

'Too right. You know why?'

'Tell me.'

'Because he's never done a dirty deal and because he sticks by his mates. Look at me . . . I came out of the army to find my wife had been screwing with some rich bookie. Did six months for breaking the bastard's jaw. Couldn't get work when I come out of the slammer, hit the bottle, was on the point of ending it in the river. Met up with Mitch by chance when he was visiting his Mum and Dad. He got it all out of me, gave me the bollocking of a lifetime and then offered me a job.'

'You knew one another as kids?'

'At school. Mitch was always the bright boy – everyone knew he'd go a long way.'

For a short while they sat in silence in the warm darkness of the car, surrounded by their own thoughts. Then Chris said, 'Maybe I've said too much. I just wanted you to know, that guy's pure gold. If you take it on, and you need back-up, you can count on me.'

'Thanks. As I said, I'll have to think it over.'

'Oh, sure.' He said nothing more for the rest of the way, and only a brief 'Good-night' as she got out of the car at her door.

Chapter Nine

'Stay out of it,' was Iris's predictable reaction.

Melissa put down her knife and fork and began fiddling with the stem of her wine-glass. 'I'm very tempted,' she said. 'It'd be a great opportunity to get the atmosphere just right for my book . . .'

Iris tilted her head and looked down her nose. 'Stop kidding yourself,' she said bluntly. 'Plenty of other pubs in the county with a tame spook – try one of those for atmosphere. Folks love helping writers with research, or so you keep telling me.'

'Yes, but chatting to someone over a bar isn't the same as actually staying in a place.'

'Treat yourself to a weekend in one of them. No strings, no funny business.'

'It wouldn't be the same. Mitch has promised to let me see round the oldest parts of Heyshill Manor and show me some of the old documents and things he got when he bought the place. And Janice is full of stories . . .'

'Nothing you couldn't get in the library. Talk to Dittany if you want to research local history.'

'That's not a bad idea. More quiche?'

'No, thanks. What's for pud?'

'Blackberry and apple crumble.'

'Super.'

It was Saturday evening and the two friends were eating supper together, as they often did when neither had an engagement, taking it in turns to cook the vegetarian dishes upon which Iris insisted. It had been a fine, sunny day, perfect for gardening, but as the afternoon wore on and the sun began to sink, a chilly breeze brought a reminder that summer was past.

'I suppose it won't be long before you're off to France,' Melissa remarked as she served the crumble. Iris owned a small house in Provence, where each year she took refuge from the Cotswold winters.

'Couple of weeks.'

'So soon? You don't usually go till November.'

'"Patterns of Light and Shade" starts at Les Châtaigniers, on the twentieth. Not much point in coming home for a few days – might as well go straight on.'

'I suppose that makes sense.'

Iris's annual departure marked the advent of short days and long nights, when gales roistered through the valley bearing rain that turned fields and gardens into quagmires. There were times when frost made rope ladders out of spiders' webs, when the drive to the cottages became a skating rink and snow was liable to block the lanes for days at a time.

Normally, Melissa found plenty of compensation in the beauty of the winter landscape, exhilarating walks in the cold, clean air, seasonal events at Upper Benbury village hall and invitations to the homes of nearby friends. Although she missed Iris's company, the absence of daytime distractions and the enforced solitude did wonders for her creativity.

Today, however, her friend's announcement brought to mind thoughts of grey days when the sun cowered beneath spongy clouds; of homecomings in the dark to an empty cottage with no friendly light behind the next-door curtains; of black shadows and creaking branches and the moan of the wind through the ruins of a long-abandoned shepherd's hut. She was not a nervous woman, but she felt a pang of dismay and desolation. She had once, for a short period, been a dog-owner; now, recalling the warmth of Khan's powerful body leaning protectively against her, she thought what a comfort it would be to have him as a companion.

Then she pictured Iris's reaction to such a possibility and her mood lightened.

Iris saw her smile. 'What's so funny?' she demanded.

Melissa explained. As she expected, Iris's first thought was for her beloved half-Persian cat. 'Can't do that. You know how Binkie hates dogs!'

'Would Binkie rather I was mugged by an intruder?'

'No muggers round here.'

'You never know.'

Iris glowered and Melissa laughed. 'Don't worry, it was just a thought. I'm not serious.'

'Should hope not. Unreliable creatures, dogs. Know where you are with a cat.'

Melissa decided against an argument. Iris could be set in her ideas at times, and in any case there were more important things to think about. She was relieved when her friend got up to go home.

At the door, Iris remarked, 'Suppose you'll do it?'

'I haven't made up my mind yet.'

'Heard that one before!'

As she went about the nightly routine of locking doors and checking window fastenings, Melissa found her thoughts returning yet again to the previous evening. It was all as clear in her mind as if she were watching the scene on film: the comfortable room with the glowing remains of the fire; Mitch holding her shawl and wrapping it round her shoulders; the short walk across the hall to the front door with the dogs padding at their heels. It had seemed perfectly natural, after shaking hands with Mitch and promising to be in touch soon, to give Khan a farewell pat. 'He's your mate for life,' his master said, and there had been quiet satisfaction in the smile that puckered his mouth, the smile of a man used to getting what he wanted and confident of doing so.

But it was the drive home, with Chris so unexpectedly communicative, that she relived again and again. A man of few words, almost a total stranger, he had revealed a painful episode in his life out of simple loyalty. It must have cost him a great deal; to refuse to help the man to whom he owed that loyalty would be to undervalue it. If she had had doubts, that realisation was enough to tip the balance.

She glanced at the clock. It was gone eleven, too late to telephone Mitch this evening. And tomorrow was Sunday. Well, it wouldn't do him any harm to wait another day or so. In any case, there was something she wanted to do first.

It was some time since her last contact with Detective Chief Inspector Kenneth Harris. He sounded both surprised and pleased to receive her call.

'How nice to hear from you, Mel,' he said. 'Committed any good murders lately?'

'Not exactly, but I'm working on it. May I pick your brains for a few minutes?'

'With pleasure. Why don't we meet for a noggin – or a spot of lunch, maybe?'

She was taken aback. They had had the odd drink together in the past, but never before by prior arrangement.

'That'd be nice,' she said.

'Twelve thirty at the Grey Goose in Stowbridge?'

'You're on.'

He was there before her, standing at the bar with a tankard of ale, head turned towards the door as if watching for her. For a moment she hardly recognised him.

'You've lost weight. Has Isobel put you on a diet?'

'In a manner of speaking. What'll you have to drink?'

'A St Clements, please.'

'That's orange juice with lemon, isn't it? Sure you wouldn't prefer a gin and tonic?'

'And have you book me on a drink-driving charge?'

He chuckled, bought her drink, tucked a menu under his arm and led the way to an empty table by the window. In the diffused light filtering through the frosted glass, she studied his face.

'There's something different about you and it's not just the weight loss.'

'Don't you think it suits me to be lean and fit?' His grin compressed his cheeks into cushions of pink flesh.

'I wouldn't describe you as actually *lean*,' she teased him. 'You've lost a chin or two, and the chair didn't groan when you sat on it, but . . .'

'But what?'

His eyes, on the small side but shrewd and candid as ever, met hers over the rim of his tankard. They held an expression she had not seen before and found difficult to fathom. Hitherto, their relationship had been that of professionals whose jobs now and again impinged – once or twice when they had become involved in a case of murder, but more often by no more than a telephone call when she needed to check some point of police procedure. She was curious to learn what lay behind the invitation.

'I know,' she said, affecting a flash of inspiration. 'You've been punching iron at that new health studio in Stowbridge. Whose idea was it – yours or Isobel's?'

The smile faded. He put down his half-drained beer tankard and handed her the menu. 'Isobel left me six months ago for the pro from her golf club,' he said, and his voice, which she had once in conversation with Iris likened to oily sandpaper, was grittier than usual. 'What d'you fancy to eat? The lasagna's pretty good – they use fresh pasta.'

'Ken, I'm so sorry.'

'Forget it. We'd been drifting for a long time – and you were right about the diet. She's a superb cook and loves rich food.' He gave a short laugh. 'The irony is, *she* never put on an ounce. I'm the one who got fat.' Another laugh, this time with a harsher edge. 'Maybe that's why she went off me. Well, have you chosen yet?'

'The lasagna will be fine.'

She gave him back the menu; he snapped it shut, drained his glass and stood up. 'Want a refill?'

'No, thanks. Maybe later.'

She studied his back as he went to the bar to give their order. His hair, greyer than she remembered, was neatly trimmed. His suit fitted his slimmer shape so well that it had to be new. He had certainly not been crushed by the breakdown of his marriage, but she wondered how badly he had been hurt.

'So what skulduggery are you working on at present?' he asked when he came back with a fresh pint.

'I have this idea for smuggling stuff in a car fitted with a false silencer.'

'What sort of stuff – drugs?'

'Not drugs – I've done that before and anyway it's old hat. I thought perhaps stolen jewellery, or art treasures – small stuff, of course, miniatures or statuettes, or maybe counterfeit money.'

'Why ask me? An art dealer or museum director would know more about it.'

'I'm talking about the actual modification to the car. Do you know anyone who could tell me if it's feasible?'

Harris thought for a moment. 'You might try Stumpy Dart.'

'Who?'

'Real name, J. Edgar Hoover Dart.' He gave a chuckle. 'The men in his mother's family were all in the force and she was a great admirer of American police methods. It nearly broke her heart when her son never grew tall enough to follow the family tradition.'

'And he knows a lot about cars?'

'You could say he's a lifelong enthusiast. He trained as a mechanic; a few years ago he bought an old Morris Cowley and rebuilt it. When he'd finished, someone offered to buy it for a ridiculous sum and he went out looking for another. If he'd branched out, taken on a partner maybe, he could have made a fortune, but he was always a bit of a loner.'

'He sounds just the man I need.. Where will I find him?'

'He's got a small workshop out on the Evesham Road. If you want to get on the right side of him, don't let on you know what the initials stand for. Ah, here's our food.'

They ate in silence for a few minutes. Then Melissa remarked, as casually as she could, 'That was a nasty business at Heyshill Manor the other night.'

Harris's eyes met hers over the rim of his tankard. 'I wondered when you'd get round to that.'

'I heard there was to be a post-mortem.'

'That's right.'

'And?'

'It wasn't a stroke or heart attack.'

'So what was the cause of death?'

'They don't know yet.'

'They must have some idea, surely.'

'They're running more tests, that's all I can tell you. How's your lasagna?'

'Good, thanks.' She hesitated for a moment before asking, 'Ken, do they suspect drugs?'

'They have open minds at present – they're just following standard procedure.'

She shook her head in bewilderment. 'I can't believe it of Will – he was an ex-copper, a very steady sort of chap.'

'How come you know him?'

Without revealing her particular interest, she explained. Harris gave an ironic laugh. 'Everyone to their own amusements, I suppose. I'd rather spend my birthday with just one special person.'

'I dare say Mitch would as well,' she replied, thinking of Dittany. 'I imagine this shindig is mainly for his business cronies.'

'You reckon it's still going ahead, then?'

'So I understand.' She finished her meal and laid down her fork. When she looked up from her plate, she caught Harris looking at her with a hint of uneasiness.

'This fellow Mitchell, you aren't . . . involved with him, are you? Not that I've any right to ask, I know, but . . .'

'But what?'

He shifted in his chair and toyed with a pepper pot. 'People with his sort of money . . . who move in that sort of milieu . . . are liable to have some funny friends.'

'Oh, Ken, you sound just like my agent,' said Melissa reproachfully, but she spoke with a smile to let him know there was no offence taken.

He glanced up at the clock on the wall and said, 'I'll have to leave you, I'm afraid. I hope I've been some use.' As he helped her on with her coat, he said, 'Maybe we could do this again some time. One evening, perhaps?'

'I'd like that.'

'I'll call you.'

'Do that. And thanks for the lunch.'

When she reached home, she rang Mitch to let him know her decision. All he said was, 'I told Vic to keep a room for you from tomorrow.'

'But you didn't know I'd be coming.' She pictured his smug grin as she added, 'A gut feeling, I suppose.'

'Got it. Feel free to order whatever you fancy. I'll pick up the tab.'

'Wouldn't it be better if I settled the bill myself and you paid me later? Vic might think it's an odd arrangement.'

'Not a bit. I've told him it's by way of compensation for the shock you had, finding Will – and a "thank you" for writing the script of *Innocent Blood Avenged*. You're working on your latest blockbuster and you're in search of local colour. Poke around as much as you like.'

'All right. I'll keep in touch.'

'Better not call from the hotel.'

In case the enemy overhears, I suppose, she thought as she put the phone down. Really, the whole enterprise might be an adventure story for schoolkids, something straight out of a comic paper ... except for the disturbing fact of Will's unexplained death.

October was in a mellow mood. When Melissa opened the window of her room at Heyshill Manor Hotel, the air had a softness that was almost springlike. The outlook, however, was wholly autumnal. In the distance were brown fields on which the first shoots of winter crops made narrow bands of tender green, and patches of woodland arranged in abstract patterns of yellow and bronze. In the foreground, beds of chrysanthemums and dahlias, untouched as yet by frost, bordered a well-tended lawn.

Close to the house, an elderly gardener was plodding to and fro behind a machine that noisily sucked up the day's scattering of fallen leaves. He was working on a section that Melissa guessed was the Bellamys' private corner of the garden, since it was separated from the rest by a low box hedge that ran without a break to a stone boundary wall. In an angle of the building, almost immediately below her window, was a small patio. Pots of winter-flowering pansies made a bright splash of colour at the feet of a stone shepherdess who gazed, shading her eyes like Bo-peep, into the distance.

Melissa turned to take another look at the room. It was evidently part of the original building and had all the period features so beloved by tourists: beamed ceiling, bulging whitewashed walls and a fine old oak door, complete with iron latch and hinges and secured with a massive key. The furniture was mostly reproduction but of good quality and carefully chosen. The polished wooden floor, liberally scattered with rugs, looked original but probably wasn't, and she was relieved to find on inspection that the bathroom facilities were modern.

Kim Bellamy had personally shown her up, falling over herself to be obliging. 'I think it's ever so exciting, having a famous writer staying with us,' she had gushed. 'Mr Mitchell has told us to help you in any way we can.'

While Melissa was unpacking, the telephone rang. It was Mitch.

'Settled in okay? Got everything you need?'

'Everything's fine, thank you.'

'Listen, Mrs Wingfield's cooking a special dinner for Dittany and me this evening. How about joining us?'

'That's very nice of you, but I wouldn't want to intrude.'

'You won't be. Chris'll pick you up at seven.'

'Well, if you're sure . . . thank you, I'll look forward to it.'

She put the phone down and reached for the Yellow Pages. 'Might as well do something to justify all this VIP treatment,' she said to herself as she flipped through the directory until she came to the entry, 'J. E. H. Dart. Cars Rebuilt and Repaired'.

The first thing she heard when the call was answered was the sound of pop music, playing very loudly. Above it, a man's voice shouted 'Hello!'

'Is that Mr Dart?'

'Speaking.'

'My name's Melissa Craig, I'm a writer,' she began.

It was her standard opening when approaching a stranger and the usual response was a guarded, 'Oh, yes?' In this case, all she got was, 'Eh? What? Can't hear you.'

'I'm a writer,' she repeated, raising her voice. 'I wonder if you . . .'

'Hang on a minute.' After a couple of seconds the row was turned down. 'Say all that again.'

Melissa told the same story she had given to Ken Harris. Stumpy Dart's reaction caused her pulse to notch up an extra beat.

'Funny you should ask that,' he said. 'I did a job like that not long ago. Gentleman who takes his car to foreign parts where things are liable to get pinched – wanted a safe place to hide his valuables. Tell you what,' he went on

98

before she could get in another word, 'if you'd like to come round to the workshop, I'll show you a drawing of what I did.'

'That's very kind of you.'

'No trouble. Tomorrow afternoon be all right? Got an urgent job to finish in the morning.'

'That'll be fine.'

She put the telephone down and checked the time. It was only three o'clock, a little early for afternoon tea. She decided to take a stroll round the gardens.

Vic Bellamy was at the reception desk as she made her way to the door. He glanced up and nodded, but did not smile. As she stepped outside, she had an uncomfortable feeling that he was staring after her, his gaze far from friendly. She had a vague sense of being threatened, then told herself not to be stupid. He was a busy man; he probably saw her as a tiresome female scribbler who would waste his time with a load of silly questions.

She made her way round the side of the building and almost immediately bumped into an elderly woman in a tweed coat and skirt, carrying a small dog under one arm and apparently in a state of great excitement. 'The Heyshill Martyrs!' she exclaimed, clutching at Melissa with her free hand. 'They're here!' She released her grip and made a sweeping gesture that seemed to encompass the entire extent of the grounds. 'Isn't it wonderful?'

Completely taken aback, Melissa stared in all directions and said, 'I don't see anything.'

The woman looked scornful. 'Of course not. I didn't *see* anything either. Didn't you know – they don't *show* themselves. But just now,' she dropped her voice, as if about to speak of something holy, 'I sensed their presence all around me!'

'In the garden? I thought they were supposed to live in the cellar,' said Melissa, and received a look of disapproval from piercing blue eyes.

'It's plain you know nothing about the history of Heyshill,' the woman retorted.

'I know about the legend of Battling Bess – Janice told me,' said Melissa defensively.

'Janice!' The woman's upper lip curled in scorn. 'What does an insensitive creature like *Janice* know about the spirit world? You have to be *psychic* to make contact with them – or an animal, of course. Dandie knew they were there, didn't you, my precious!' She bent her head; from the bundle of fur nestling in the crook of her arm, a small pink tongue emerged and licked her face. 'You should have seen his little hackles rise – he was aware of them before I was.'

She gave Melissa a triumphant smile, as if the behaviour of Dandie's hackles put the matter beyond doubt, and deposited the dog on the ground. He wandered on to the grass and began sniffing at the base of a tree. 'Not too far, my precious,' cooed the woman, 'or the nasty man will get cross again. Really, that gardener!' She jerked her head towards the rear of the house. 'He got so angry, just because Dandie had strayed on to a bit of garden marked "Private". You've never heard such a fuss. Then when I went to pick him up – I'm afraid he was a bit naughty, he didn't come the minute Mummy called him – the fellow positively shouted at me. Of all the impertinence – I've a good mind to complain to the manager!'

The afternoon was wearing on and the air was becoming cooler by the minute. Melissa, anxious to continue her walk, began to edge away. 'Well, I'll be on the look-out for them, the ghosts, I mean,' she said. 'If I should see anything' – she caught the woman's eye and hastily corrected herself – 'if I should *experience* anything, I'll let you know. I take it you're staying in the hotel?'

'Room 32. Millicent Clifford.' A gloved hand was graciously extended. 'Of course, it's highly unlikely that dear Bess and her friends will reveal themselves to *you*. No offence, of course' – a superior smile exposed an expanse of pink

100

gum above well-kept teeth – 'but I doubt if you have the necessary *aura* to make contact with the other side. Enjoy your walk.'

Chapter Ten

'Found anything yet?'

Mitch's question was addressed to Melissa, but his gaze was fixed on Dittany, who responded, as she accepted the drink he handed her, with a shy but intimate smile of thanks. As he sat down beside her on the couch, and before Melissa had time to reply, she turned to him and shook her head in reproach. 'She's hardly had time to unpack yet. You shouldn't be so impatient.'

Dittany was, Melissa thought, looking quite lovely in a dress of pleated cream silk, her hair piled like a swirl of rich brown honey on top of her head. It was plain that Mitch thought so too; from the look on his face, it was evident that the reason for his question was momentarily forgotten. Melissa, seated opposite them with Khan stretched out at her feet, glanced across to where Chris sat sipping orange juice. His left eye flickered for a moment and she guessed that he shared her thoughts.

'As a matter of fact,' she began, and at the words, Mitch's head jerked towards her as if a string was attached to his ear.

'You're on to something!' he said.

'Just a bit of spade work,' she replied, and told him about her conversation with Stumpy Dart.

Mitch's eyes grew bright. 'That's amazing! It could have been Vic's car he doctored.'

'It could. And the reason for wanting the mods done could be perfectly genuine. We know he visits Spain regularly, and the papers are full of reports about cars being broken into out there. Maybe he's had property stolen in the past.'

'But just think, he could hide all sorts of stuff in a secret

102

compartment like that.' Mitch was carried away by the idea, excited as a schoolboy. 'Drugs, maybe . . . forged currency, dud passports, anything.'

'I'm sure Melissa's thought of that.' Dittany's quiet voice reminded him that he was stating the obvious. 'Would it be worth having a chat to Kim about it?' she suggested. 'You said she was quite friendly, Melissa – she might let something drop.'

'Forget that.' Abruptly, Mitch released the hand he had been gently caressing, got to his feet and went over to the drinks trolley. 'She might mention it to Vic, and he'd be sure to smell a rat.'

Seeing the girl's downcast expression at having her idea so summarily rejected, Melissa interposed, 'I'm sure Dittany only meant, ask her if they'd had any bad experiences. I might learn something . . .'

'Nah!' Mitch waved his glass at her in a gesture that was unmistakably a command. 'If he is up to something, we don't want to give the slightest hint we're on to him. Besides, Mel, you're only supposed to be interested in spooky old buildings, remember.'

'Talking of spooks . . .' Melissa described her encounter with Mrs Clifford. 'Actually,' she went on, when they had finished laughing, 'she might be quite useful. She implied that she knew a lot about the history of the place.'

'Yeah, well, remember what you're really there for.' Mitch was still smiling and his tone was bland, but the look in his eyes reminded her that he expected value for his money. He drained his glass. 'Refill, anyone?'

There was a general shaking of heads; Mitch returned to the couch and put his free arm round Dittany's shoulders. Once again, the two exchanged a quick, loving glance. There seemed to be no doubt which way things were heading; the Honourable Penelope, Melissa reflected, would have to accept honourable defeat.

'That's all you've got to report, then?' There was a brisk,

almost peremptory note in Mitch's voice that he might have used when speaking to an underling. Melissa pictured him behind a desk, a battery of telephones at his elbow and a secretary or two hovering, notebooks at the ready.

'That's all for the moment,' she replied.

Mrs Wingfield appeared and announced dinner. As they settled at the table, Mitch remarked, 'Got those drawings for you to look at presently. And Dittany's been doing a spot of research in the archives, haven't you, love?' He winked. 'You'll never believe what some of those old monks got up to.'

Over the meal, Dittany gave a surprisingly racy account of the fall from grace of the members of the Heyshill monastic community. Over a period of years, tales had filtered out of over-indulgence in secular pleasures and a neglect of spiritual duties. In the opinion of one historian, the sheltering of destitute women in the crypt had begun long before the Reformation and was not prompted solely by considerations of charity.

'Things got so bad that the Bishop intervened, had most of the crypt bricked up to put a stop to the naughty goings-on and eventually disbanded the community altogether,' Dittany explained. 'In any case, the quarry was worked out so they had no source of regular income.'

'What quarry?' asked Melissa.

'There's a disused quarry, adjacent to the edge of the manor grounds. Last century, archaeologists investigating the site came to the conclusion that the builders of the abbey discovered it when they were digging the foundations, and continued to work it for several years.'

'I noticed this afternoon how the land falls away on the other side of the boundary wall,' said Melissa. 'Are there any plans that show the layout of the original buildings?'

'Dunno,' said Mitch. 'I've only seen the drawings old Sir Whatsit had done when he refurbished the place. They're in my office – if you've all finished eating, we can go and look.'

He stood up. Melissa and Dittany followed him from the

room, but Chris remained behind and began clearing the table. As usual, he had said very little throughout the evening, although he had joined in the laughter at some of Dittany's tales and Mitch's mildly ribald comments, even occasionally adding one of his own.

Mitch's office was at the back of the house. It was equipped almost as luxuriously as the other rooms, with a deep carpet, velvet curtains, desks and bookshelves of polished wood and padded leather chairs. The filing cabinets were wooden-fronted to match the rest of the furniture and the walls were hung with reproduction old masters; the only items of undisguisedly modern appearance were telephones and a fax machine, a word processor and a computer.

'This is how I keep in touch with me empire,' said Mitch. 'Course, me head office is in London, but I do as much from home as possible. The drawings are over here.' He led them to a table at the back of the room and switched on a reading lamp.

After a good dinner they were all in a relaxed and mellow mood. As they began their examination, Mitch regaled them with anecdotes about his negotiations with the executor of old Sir Whatsit's estate, whom he described as 'a toffee-nosed git'. When they came to a plan showing the position and layout of the cellar, however, their laughter died away and they fell silent. Dittany shivered and moved nearer to Mitch, who put an arm round her and held her close, his head bent over hers. Melissa shut her eyes, reliving the horror of the previous Thursday, the interminable wait for help to come as she tried to staunch the wound in Will's forehead. She recalled the pain in her cramped legs and the chill air of the cellar with its sickening overtones of beer and blood and cigar smoke, heard the murmuring voices from the bar, saw Mitch's anguished face over Vic Bellamy's shoulder as he tried to reach his friend.

A thought struck her. She opened her eyes, reached out for the ground floor plan and studied it for a second time, comparing the two. 'That's odd,' she said, half to herself.

'What's up?' asked Mitch. 'Spotted something?'

'The cellar – I thought it was directly under the bar.'

'Nah. It runs in the opposite direction. What of it?'

'Oh, nothing. I just . . . no, it's nothing.' She pushed the plans away and thought, *This isn't real, I'm being fanciful. Too much wine, I expect – that and listening to Janice and old Mrs Clifford with their ghost stories.* But it surely hadn't been her fancy that while she was crouched beside Will there had been faint, muffled voices not far away. She had assumed, without thinking, that they came from overhead, from the bar . . . but now it was plain that was impossible. And in any case, the sounds had died away, almost as she became aware of them.

Sort of murmurings . . . as if you were listening to a radio through a thick wall, was how Janice had described the ghostly manifestations. *And a musty sort of smell, as if a grave had been opened up*. The hairs rose on the back of Melissa's neck; despite the warmth of the room, she felt cold. She pushed the plans away. 'I've seen all I want to,' she said, trying to keep her voice even. 'I don't think these help very much.'

'Feel free to look at them again, any time,' said Mitch. He rolled up the drawings and slid them into a cardboard tube, which he stowed away in a drawer. 'Have to keep the place tidy or I get an earful from Medusa. Me secretary,' he explained, nodding towards one of the desks. 'Her name's Joan, but she's a right battle-axe, gets her knickers in a twist if there's a paper-clip out of place.'

Evidently, he had noticed nothing untoward in Melissa's manner, but as they left the room, Dittany whispered in her ear, 'Are you all right?'

'I'm fine.' Melissa managed a smile. 'But I am a bit tired. Mitch, if you don't mind, I'd like to be getting back to the hotel.'

'Sure.' He raised his voice. 'Chris, bring the Jag round!'

'Feeling better?' asked Chris, after driving a mile or two in silence.

Melissa glanced at him. In the dim light reflected from the headlamps, his face was expressionless, his eyes fixed on the road. 'I don't know what you mean,' she said.

'Yes, you do.' He halted at a junction; as he waited for a car to pass, he looked her full in the face and said, 'Something happened while you were in Mitch's office. You came out looking as white as a sheet. Didn't the others notice?'

'Dittany asked me if I was all right and I told her I was tired, that's all. I don't think Mitch was looking at me.'

Chris gave a hoarse chuckle. 'He doesn't look at anyone else when she's around.'

'Do you think he's serious about her?'

'Never known him so serious about anyone in his life.' After a pause, he said, 'You haven't answered my question. What made you look as if you'd seen a ghost?'

Melissa's first impulse was to stall but she knew it would be a waste of time. In his way, Chris was as shrewd as Mitch.

'I didn't *see* a ghost,' she said, 'but I think I may have heard one. Several, in fact. Not just now, but last Thursday, down in the cellar.' She explained, thinking how improbable and absurd it sounded. 'You must think I'm hyperimaginative, and you're probably right. I was overwrought . . . my ears must have been playing tricks.'

'I guess that's it.' It was clear that Chris wanted no truck with the supernatural. 'Here we are.' He brought the car to a standstill at the front door of the hotel and she got out. 'Be seeing you,' he said, and drove away. She watched the car disappear and went inside.

A night porter at the reception desk smiled and nodded as she went through; there was no sign of the Bellamys. The door to the lounge stood open, revealing a glimpse of Mrs Clifford seated in an armchair by the fire with Dandie on her lap. She was addressing an elderly man who wore a hearing aid; her voice was raised and as Melissa hurried past, she was repeating her claim to have made contact with Battling Bess and the Heyshill Martyrs. 'They're all around us,' she was saying, her voice pursuing Melissa along the corridor and up the stairs. 'If you're psychic, like me, you can feel their presence everywhere!'

'Damn the woman!' Melissa exclaimed aloud as she unlocked the door to her room. She felt thoroughly edgy and ill-at-ease; a pleasant evening had ended on a disturbing note. She wished she was back at home in Hawthorn Cottage, where she could have called Iris and shared a cup of herbal tea with her. Dear, down-to-earth Iris, with her clipped speech and her common sense, would soon have dispelled these idiotic fancies. Ghosts, indeed! She could almost hear the contemptuous sniff that would have greeted her story.

A quiet read in bed would calm her nerves. Thank goodness the hotel provided an electric kettle and tea-bags. Parts of the building might be old and spooky but there was nothing antiquarian about the service. In fact, the central heating was almost too efficient; the room was uncomfortably warm. She turned down the radiator and opened the window a fraction. An hour later, relaxed and drowsy, she put out her light.

Almost immediately her mind, no doubt prompted by memories stirred earlier in the evening, turned to *Innocent Blood Avenged* and the final scene in which the spirit of the murdered heroine returned to accuse her killer. It was to be the high spot of the piece, intended to give the audience a deliciously scarey finale to their Hallowe'en entertainment. Penelope had gone to town on effects; Dittany was to appear in a long white gown, heavily stained with Kensington Gore and treated with some luminous substance to give a spectral appearance. As Melissa drifted off to sleep, the darkened stage seemed to materialise before her eyes and Dittany entered, hands clasped to her breast, her costume with its scarlet stain shedding a faint, unearthly glow. But there was something wrong; the pain and terror in the girl's eyes were real and no make-up could have produced such a deathly pallor on living flesh. The front of her gown lay open to reveal a frightful wound, spurting blood that poured through her fingers, spread along her wrists and arms and dripped on to the stage. People in the audience were screaming, and Melissa awoke, gasping and trembling.

She sat up, trying to get her bearings in the unfamiliar room. There was a rustling sound, and a pattering; for a terrifying moment she thought the dream had caught hold of her again and she tried to fight it off, then realised that these were natural sounds of rain falling on glass and curtains rustling in the wind. Muttering to herself and still heavy with sleep, she got out of bed, stumbled over to the window and closed it.

There was no moon, and no light in any of the windows. All the outside lighting had been switched off, but the reflection from the illuminated sign at the front of the hotel gave a faint glow which intensified as her eyes became accustomed to the gloom. Gradually, she made out the roof-line of the building and the black shapes of the trees. Below her window, a vague, grey figure slowly emerged from the background. She strained her eyes, peering through the rain-spattered glass; it was the stone shepherdess, of course, but there seemed to be a strange, will-o'-the-wisp glow at its feet. It gave the illusion of movement, as if the statue were floating, first this way, then that, yet all the time remaining exactly where it was.

A sudden squall threw a flurry of rain against the window. When it had passed, the one remaining light had been extinguished and the stone shepherdess was nothing but a motionless blur. Shivering, Melissa groped her way back to bed.

Chapter Eleven

By morning, the rain had stopped and the sky was blue and cloudless. There was still enough heat in the early autumn sun to coax a gentle exhalation of steam from the soaked earth; it rose in soft swirls and drifted over the fields like a thin layer of fog. In the garden below Melissa's window, a blackbird wallowing in a stone bath sent arcs of sparkling water flying in all directions; a robin, perched on the arm of the stone shepherdess, proclaimed for all the world to hear that this territory was his.

Reflecting that there could hardly be a more peaceful, more reassuringly normal scene, determinedly dismissing from her mind the oneiric fancies of the night, Melissa made a cup of tea and drank it while waiting for her bath to fill.

A short while later, as she passed through Reception on her way to breakfast, she was greeted, with unexpected cordiality, by Vic Bellamy. After enquiring if she had slept well, he said casually, 'Mr Mitchell mentioned you'd be interested in a proper look at the cellar. I'm expecting a delivery from the brewers at ten o'clock and I'd be happy to show you round – if you feel you can face it after what happened, of course.'

'That's really very kind of you,' said Melissa. She went in search of breakfast, reflecting that he was not such a bad sort after all.

She made for a corner table, hoping to be able to read her morning paper in peace, but was beckoned by Mrs Clifford, who, in between mouthfuls of scrambled egg, was loudly complaining at not being allowed to bring Dandie into the dining-room. 'He wouldn't be a mite of trouble,' she grumbled, glowering at a waitress who arrived at that moment with coffee and toast as if holding her personally responsible for Dandie's banishment. The girl backed away with a nervous smile and Mrs Clifford rounded on Melissa.

'The poor darling simply *hates* being left alone in a strange room,' she confided. 'Especially after last night.'

'What happened last night?'

'My dear, he was so excited when we got back from our late-night walkies, he was trembling all over.'

'Don't tell me you bumped into the ghosts again!' said Melissa in an exaggerated stage whisper, but Mrs Clifford was too carried away to notice the disrespectful levity of her tone.

'I wasn't aware of them myself, not then, although I'm sure they couldn't have been far away,' she said earnestly. 'But Dandie could sense them, I know he could.' She scythed the air with a slice of buttered toast to emphasise her point. 'I don't suppose you'd care to come for a stroll through the grounds with me later on this morning?' she continued. 'I've been to the reference library to study some reports of the local archaeological society about the history of the priory, and I've made simply *sheaves* of notes. I thought I'd see if I could trace the original site.'

'Are you an archaeologist, then?'

'Oh, bless you, no!' Mrs Clifford laughed horsily at the suggestion, causing several heads to turn in her direction. 'It's not the *buildings* I'm interested in so much as who *lived* there . . . and,' she lowered her voice and leaned towards Melissa with a conspiratorial air, 'the *ambience* they left behind!'

'Ah! Yes, of course . . . well, I'd love to come with you,' said Melissa politely. It might turn out to be a complete waste of time; on the other hand, she might pick up something to include in her report to Mitch. It would at least help to prove that she was taking her assignment seriously. 'I'll be busy for a while, though. Would eleven o'clock suit you?'

'Jolly good. Eleven o'clock's fine. See you later.'

Mrs Clifford departed and Melissa drank a second cup of coffee before repairing to the lounge, where she settled down to do *The Times* crossword while awaiting the arrival of the delivery lorry. Shortly before ten o'clock, she spied it turning into the hotel entrance. She slipped upstairs for a coat and then wandered outside to see what was going on.

The lorry was parked at the rear of the building. The tailboard was down and the driver and his mate were unloading barrels, crates and cartons, which they stacked beside an open trap-door. Near by stood Vic, clipboard in hand; as each item was taken from the lorry he ticked it off his list. When they had finished unloading, the two men disappeared down a wooden ramp and began rolling up the empty barrels. Vic caught sight of Melissa and waved.

'You've timed it just right,' he said. 'This way.' He led her back through Reception and along the passage to the cellar entrance. The door stood wide open, but a bar had been placed across the opening, evidently as a safety measure. Vic lifted it and signalled to Melissa to descend, which she did with some hesitation, clinging grimly to the rail and staring straight ahead with gritted teeth. Reaching the bottom, she stepped quickly past the spot where Will had been lying, averting her eyes and drawing a deep breath to quieten the spasm in her stomach.

It all looked so different from the other night, and so innocent, with no dark corners, no menacing shapes or mysterious shadows. As well as the fluorescent tube on the ceiling, there was sunlight streaming through the trap. The stainless steel pipework, the walls and arches of whitewashed brick, the rows of metal shelving laden with cartons of canned drinks and almost as many varieties of snacks as could be found in the average supermarket – all had an air of almost mundane normality.

The men had sent up the last of the empty barrels and were now disposing of crates of bottles which Kevin, clad in jeans, T-shirt and trainers, was lugging to the base of the ramp.

When the last load of empties had gone up, full ones were sent down, followed by case after case of cans; lastly came the barrels, bumping and rumbling their way down the wooden slope. Melissa noticed that Vic checked every item a second time. It was hard to see how any fiddling could be going on here.

'I'll be back in a tick,' he told her, when the last item had been accounted for. He scribbled a signature, tore the top sheet from the clipboard and ran nimbly up the ramp. Through the opening, Melissa saw him hand the paper to the driver; then, without warning, the daylight disappeared as the trap-door closed.

It was so unexpected that she experienced a moment of panic as the heavy slab of wood fell into place with a thud that echoed among the vaults. Without the sun, the temperature plunged and the place took on an eerie, almost hostile quality. Above the low hum of machinery was the sound of muffled voices; for one uneasy moment she fancied there were ghosts crowding around her, then realised that it was only Vic taking leave of the brewer's men on the other side of the trap-door. Kevin had climbed the ramp to bolt it from inside; on his way down he caught her eye. He must have read her thoughts, for he said, without a trace of a smile, 'It's all right, lady, they ghosts only chatter after dark.' He looked none too happy himself as he began stowing away the day's delivery, hurrying to and fro with crates and casks as if anxious not to remain in the cellar a moment longer than necessary.

Feeling slightly foolish at her momentary attack of nerves, Melissa began to look round. It would be as well to think of some questions to ask, to support her reasons for being here. She wandered over to the far wall. It too was built of brick, and whitewashed. The total area of the cellar was smaller than she had imagined; even so, there was a fair amount of unused space. Electric cables ran here and there, serving the light, the air-conditioning unit and a large refrigerator which stood in one corner. She moved up and down, examining the floor, walls and arches, hardly knowing what she was looking for and finding nothing remarkable.

The door at the top of the steps opened and Vic reappeared. 'Seen all you want to see?' he said.

'I'm not sure what I expected,' she told him. 'Is this really the original brickwork?'

'As far as I know. I can't say I've ever delved into the history of the place; all I can tell you for sure is that it's a listed building and can't be altered without permission.'

'But the original crypt was larger than this, wasn't it? I was told a large part had been bricked up.'

'That's right.' Hands in pockets, Vic glanced round, as if sizing up the place. Then he looked down at Melissa and grinned. 'That was before they had all the rules and regulations.'

'Where would the other part have been? I mean, in which direction?' With one hand on a brick pillar, Melissa turned slowly round, trying to orientate herself. She glanced upwards, thinking she might find some clue from the arrangement of the vaults and wishing she knew a little more about architecture, but all she saw was more electric cable.

'I've no idea.' Vic glanced at his watch. 'Look, I don't want to rush you, but . . .'

'Of course, you must have loads of things to do.'

At the top of the stairs, as she waited while he replaced the barrier and relocked the door, she asked, 'Have *you* ever heard the ghosts of Battling Bess and her friends?'

She had expected him to dismiss the whole matter of ghosts as superstitious nonsense, but his tone was serious as he replied, 'I can't deny there's a strange atmosphere down there sometimes, especially at night.'

'You've felt it too? Janice claims to have actually heard the ghosts talking.'

He gave a slightly contemptuous laugh. 'I wouldn't pay too much attention to Janice – she has a vivid imagination and she enjoys putting the wind up the youngsters.'

'The customers seem to enjoy her stories. Don't any of them ask to go down there and listen for themselves?'

'It has been known but we don't encourage it. Guided tours of the cellar aren't included in our tariff!' he added with a grin.

'Well, thanks very much for giving me one,' said Melissa cordially. 'By the way, I heard there was a disused quarry near where the old priory used to stand. Can you tell me anything about it?'

They were back in Reception, where Kim was dealing with a guest who was settling his account. She appeared to overhear the question and gave a sharp glance first at Melissa and then at her husband. It was only for a split second; almost immediately she turned back to the departing guest with one of her polite, professional smiles as she handed him his receipt and wished him a safe journey home, while Vic replied in a casual tone, 'Yes, the remains of the quarry adjoin the hotel grounds, but it's quite inaccessible. Anyway, it's in a dangerous state. I'd keep away from it if I were you.'

'Yes, I will. Thank you once again, Mr Bellamy, for sparing me so much of your time.'

'No trouble.'

It was a little after half past ten. There was just time for a cup of coffee before her appointment with Mrs Clifford.

The first half-hour of the walk was one of the most frustrating Melissa had spent in a long while. Mrs Clifford had obtained a photocopy of an old map of the area, on which the presumed site of Heyshill Priory, said to date from pre-Tudor times, was marked with a dotted line, but it was obvious that she had no sense of direction and much time was spent wandering in circles, with frequent pauses to allow Dandie to stop, sniff and lift his leg. Not until Melissa persuaded her to relinquish the map, thus revealing the beautifully executed compass rose that she had been covering with her thumb, did they manage

115

to establish the orientation of the site and relate it to the existing building.

It was at this point that Mrs Clifford became excited. Ignoring Dandie's desire for a prolonged inspection of a tree, she set off back towards the house, muttering, 'Of course, of course, that explains it!' under her breath. Totally bemused, Melissa followed her; when she reached the edge of the plot presided over by the stone shepherdess, she swung her arm to and fro like a policeman directing traffic. 'This,' she suddenly bent her head and lowered her voice to a reverent whisper, 'is hallowed ground!'

For one moment Melissa was convinced she was going to fall to her knees. She stood with clasped hands and a look of ecstasy on her large, pale features. Dandie, meanwhile, took advantage of his mistress's preoccupation to trot forward on his extending lead and hop over the miniature hedge, heading for the patio and some promising stone urns that stood there. Halfway across the lawn, he stopped short and began growling softly.

'I think Dandie's spotted a cat or something,' said Melissa.

If Mrs Clifford's behaviour so far had been eccentric, it now became positively bizarre. 'He feels them, he feels them!' she declared in tones of awe. 'And I can feel them too. Listen, oh, listen! Any minute now we may hear their spirit voices.' She closed her eyes and assumed a trance-like expression. 'Bess, Bess!' she cried. 'Speak to us! We are fellow women and we know how you have suffered!'

The woman's out of her tree, thought Melissa, *I must get away from her*. She was on the point of making her escape when Mrs Clifford opened her eyes, grabbed her by the hand and said in a hoarse whisper, 'Now you must *surely* feel them. Close your eyes and *experience* their vibrations!'

But Melissa had had enough; looking around for some diversion, she found one in Dandie. Whatever had caught his attention had evidently gone away; he was on the patio, doing the round of the pottery urns and cocking an optimistic leg at each. 'I think you'd better call your dog off before someone sees him,' she said. Without waiting to hear Mrs Clifford's response, she tugged her hand free and hurried indoors, hoping that her afternoon visit would be more profitable.

Twice, Melissa drove past the narrow track leading to Stumpy Dart's workshop as she looked in vain for the sign he had assured her was there. It was only when she left the car on the grass verge to investigate on foot that she saw the board, with the name amateurishly painted in green, propped against a hedge and almost invisible from the road. It was not a promising start.

The track was muddy and uneven, ending in a clearing littered with the rusting wrecks of half a dozen cars which, she suspected, had been picked up from scrapyards, cannibalised and then abandoned. The workshop, which had a second, more legible sign fixed to the wall, was a breeze-block structure under a galvanised metal roof, with several broken windows crudely mended with sticky tape and a heavy sliding door covered in peeling green paint. From outward appearances, Stumpy Dart was not making a fortune from his business.

The door was partially open and through it came a blare of rock music at maximum volume. Buried somewhere in the din was the strident jangle of a telephone. Picking her way across the uneven ground, Melissa reached the entrance just as the ringing ceased, and peered inside.

The place was lit by bare fluorescent tubes and smelled strongly of motor oil. The floor was of concrete and the walls, their greyness partially disguised with a roughly applied layer of white paint, were hung at roof level with cobwebs. Lower down, they were bedaubed with irregular patches of colour, obviously applied with a spray and no doubt for practical purposes, but accidentally giving a random, abstract touch of brightness to the dingy surroundings.

A workbench, littered with tools and spare parts, ran along

one side, there were old tyres piled up in one corner, a welding booth, and several other pieces of equipment which Melissa could not identify. There were two cars, one a fairly new hatchback which she guessed was Stumpy's own vehicle, the other an elderly Morris Traveller on which he had evidently been working when interrupted by the telephone. A transistor radio, still playing loudly, stood on the floor beside it.

A man's voice could just be heard from the far end of the building but its owner was invisible. It was several minutes before he appeared from the partitioned-off corner which presumably served him as an office.

It was easy to see how he had come by his nickname. At five feet five inches in her flat shoes, Melissa was a good half a head taller. He was stockily built, broad-shouldered and short-necked, with squat features topped by a straggle of unkempt brown hair. As he approached, he pulled a rag from the pocket of his grimy overalls and wiped his fingers, looking vaguely uncomfortable, as if afraid he might be expected to shake hands. He did not return Melissa's smile.

'Mr Dart? I'm Melissa Craig. We spoke on the phone yesterday morning. I asked you about fitting a dummy silencer.' She waited for him to respond, but he did not, nor did he meet her eyes.

'You promised to show me . . .' she continued, but before she could finish, he said brusquely, 'I've been thinking it over and it can't be done.'

'But you told me . . .'

'Not feasible. Can't be done,' he repeated, still avoiding eye contact. He threw down the rag and picked up a spanner. Plainly, he intended the conversation to end there, but Melissa was not prepared to be so easily put off.

'Look here,' she said, raising her voice above the inane babbling of a disc jockey. 'You said you'd already done it for someone, so how can you pretend . . .'

'You must have misunderstood. I only said it might be possible. I've thought it over, and it isn't.'

118

He began tinkering with the Morris, his back towards her and his face hidden.

'I don't believe you,' she said, suddenly angry. 'I remember distinctly . . .' A thought struck her. 'That job you told me about on the telephone, for the gentleman who travels abroad . . .' The spanner slipped from Dart's hand and he swore as he reached into the engine to retrieve it. 'That job,' she repeated, 'was it by any chance for a man called Bellamy?'

He straightened up and turned round, his hand clenched round the spanner and his expression grim. 'Don't you understand plain English?' he said harshly. 'I told you, I've never done a job like that.'

His attitude was threatening. The cacophony from the radio seemed to increase in intensity, bouncing off the bare walls and roof in harsh echoes that punished Melissa's eardrums and tore at her nerve-ends. She felt her knees begin to wobble, but she stood her ground.

'How much did he pay you to keep your mouth shut?' she asked. 'Or did he threaten you with something nasty?'

It was a shot in the dark, but she saw the muscles round his mouth tighten and knew she was on the right track.

'Just bugger off and leave me alone!' he shouted, taking a pace forward and brandishing the spanner. Melissa stepped back, lifting her hands in a gesture of capitulation.

'Okay, I'm going,' she said.

She walked back to her car with as much dignity as she could manage on unsteady legs. She was shaken by the encounter, but at the same time seething with excitement. The look in Stumpy Dart's eyes when she accused him of lying under duress had not been anger, but fear.

Chapter Twelve

The road back to Heyshill Manor was long, straight, and reputed to be of Roman origin. On either side, the rolling landscape was a palette of rich autumnal colour, but Melissa, absorbed in her own thoughts, barely noticed it. It was mid-afternoon and there was very little traffic to disturb her concentration, which was directed towards linking together and making sense of the jumble of fact and speculation presently whirling in her head like leaves tossed by the wind.

Go back to the beginning, she told herself, *take things in order, maybe then some kind of pattern will emerge.*

First there was Mitch, suspecting that the Bellamys were living beyond their legitimate means and using *Innocent Blood Avenged* as a device to plant Will Foley at Heyshill Manor for one evening a week to do some quiet probing.

Next, there was Will's exploration of the cellar. He had taken a flashlight, presumably because he wanted to search in corners and cupboards, or maybe behind pillars, where the electric light might not penetrate. Since neither Chris nor Mitch had referred to his motive for going down there, it was a reasonable assumption that he had not told them. He had gone to his death – the cause of which was still not known – without revealing that particular secret.

So what could he have been expecting to find? Surely not a cache of stolen goods or drugs? No one in their right mind would store such things, even for a few hours, in a place to which members of the hotel staff had free access – however reluctantly, in view of the sinister reputation of the cellar, they might go down there.

So, if Will had hoped to find something incriminating, it

would seem he had been barking up the wrong tree. By giving her the opportunity to visit the cellar, Vic had shown that he had nothing there to hide. In which case, Mitch's belief that the hotel manager was somehow involved in Will's death would seem to be groundless. Unless, of course, he was on to something else, something too hot for him to be allowed to live, of which he had said nothing. If only he hadn't been so tight-lipped.

Then there was the question of the alleged haunting. The previous evening in Mitch's house, as she examined the plans that had awakened such disturbing memories, Melissa would almost have been willing to swear on oath that she had witnessed something supernatural. Now, she was less sure. Having that morning seen the cellar under normal conditions and in daylight, she found it difficult to relive fears experienced under stress. But, if those voices were natural, where did they come from, and did they have any sinister meaning?

Most puzzling of all was the way Stumpy Dart had changed his story. It was possible that, out of a sense of responsibility to his customer, he had decided to clear her request before revealing details of the dummy silencer. So far from being given permission, he might have been ordered to deny all knowledge, or maybe bribed or coerced into doing so. In that case, although the customer could still be Vic Bellamy, it could as easily be someone else.

On the other hand, if by chance either of the Bellamys had overheard her telephone conversation with Stumpy – at this point she recalled Mitch's injunction not to call him from the hotel – the same thing could have happened, except that in that case the car could only have been Vic's. Either way, the indications were that the purpose of the dummy silencer was to conceal something more valuable than a few personal belongings.

By the time she had reached this point in her deliberations, Melissa was less than half a mile from Heyshill Manor. A short distance ahead was a lay-by with a telephone box. She

pulled over, switched off the engine and took from her handbag the notebook with Mitch's telephone number.

A secretary answered and she asked to speak to Chris.
There was an interval, during which she was regaled with an
electronic rendering of 'Knocked 'em in the Old Kent Road'
before he came on the line.

'I think I may be on to something, but I don't want to say
anything to Mitch till I'm certain,' she said. 'Can we meet?'

'Sure. Where are you?'

She told him, and they arranged to rendezvous in a village
midway between the hotel and Stumpy's workshop.

'Be with you in twenty minutes,' he said.

He was there in just over fifteen; she saw him park the
Jaguar a short distance away and flashed her lights to attract
his attention. He came and slipped into the passenger seat
beside her.

'So, what's new?' he asked. She told him, and he nodded,
lower lip jutting.

'You don't seem surprised.'

'Not entirely. That gas-guzzler of Vic's – remember I said
I didn't know much about Yankee cars?'

'Yes?'

'Well, I know a man who does. Imports them for certain
people with dough that needs laundering.'

'And?'

'That model that Vic drives doesn't have twin exhausts.'

'I wonder if Will knew that.'

'He could easily have found out.'

'I've just had a thought,' said Melissa after a pause. 'If you
were in Vic's shoes, and you knew someone was going to make
some unwelcome enquiries, what would you do?'

Chris shrugged. 'Do what we think he did – get the guy
who did the job to keep his trap shut. Bribe him, or threaten
to have his place turned over . . . or worse.'

'I think I'd go further than that.' He waited for her to go
on, not making any visible effort to keep up with her train of

thought. 'I'd get the car up to Stumpy's workshop pronto and have that dummy silencer whipped off and hidden until things had cooled down.'

'You could be right.' Chris sat for a moment in silence, digesting this new possibility. Then, uncharacteristically, he came up with an idea of his own. 'In which case,' he said, 'it's probably in that workshop now.'

'We can soon check if that's what happened. When I go back to the hotel, I'll have a look at the car. If the second exhaust pipe is missing . . .'

'Does Stumpy live on the premises?'

'I don't see how he can – it's just a shed.'

They turned to look at one another. Melissa felt a tingle of excitement as the idea took shape in her head like a Japanese paper flower growing in water. 'Are you thinking what I'm thinking?' she said.

'A silencer isn't something you can stuff in a drawer. Should be easy to find.'

They arranged to meet at nine o'clock, when it would be quite dark and there was unlikely to be much traffic.

'That's assuming the second exhaust has gone from Vic's car,' Melissa pointed out. 'If it hasn't, I'll call you straight away and we'll have to think again.'

She was dismayed to find, on returning to the hotel, that the car had been backed into position, making it impossible to see what she wanted by a cursory glance. It would be simple to walk up to the wall and examine the car from there, but it would look extremely odd. She had a shrewd idea that it had been done deliberately; there was also a chance that someone was keeping a look-out.

While she stood hesitating, help arrived in the shape of a small Yorkshire terrier. Dandie had managed to evade his mistress and came toddling in her direction. He went straight past her, making a beeline for one shining rear wheel, which he eagerly sniffed before cocking his leg.

'Oh Dandie, you are naughty!' exclaimed Melissa, leaping

forward and pouncing on him. He gave an indignant yelp as she scooped him up, just as Mrs Clifford arrived in a state of agitation and a great kerfuffle took place as she reclaimed her pet.

'I've been looking for him *everywhere*,' she panted. 'He disappeared while we were walking up by the old quarry. I was *terrified* he'd get into the road and be run over. Thank you so much for rescuing him.'

'It was nothing, really. He'd come home by himself,' Melissa assured her.

'And your nice jacket – it's all muddied. You must let me pay to have it cleaned, I absolutely *insist*.'

'Don't worry, it's an old one, and anyway I'm sure it will brush off.' At that particular moment, Melissa would not have cared if the jacket had been ruined. She had seen what she wanted to see.

Chris had said, 'Wear something dark'. Melissa had packed a navy blue track suit, but if she wore that down to dinner it might look odd, and she did not want to draw attention to herself by changing before going out. Instead, she put on a black, high-necked sweater and long black flared pants. As she entered the dining-room, Mrs Clifford caught her eye and beckoned.

'Do come and join me! Have an apéritif!' She reinforced the invitation by waving her own drink; the hint of a slur in her speech suggested that it was not her first. Melissa accepted a small dry sherry and as soon as she had given the order, Mrs Clifford went on, 'I can't thank you enough for rescuing Dandie. Did the mud brush orf?' Under the influence of two martinis, her accent had become exaggeratedly 'county'.

'Oh, yes,' said Melissa.

'*Awfully* glad to hear it.'

'Did you say you'd been walking in the old quarry?'

'Not in it. Can't do that – it's enclosed by a fence, to keep the animals from falling down, don't you know. There's a footpath that goes near it, into some woods. It's *such* a pretty walk – would you like me to show you tomorrow?'

'That would be lovely, if you can spare the time.'

'Time's one thing I've got plenty of, m'dear.' Mrs Clifford had, it emerged, a passion for walking. 'Can't go as far as I used to, of course, not with my gammy knees.' She turned out to be an even more compulsive talker; over their first course, and throughout the meal, she regaled Melissa with her life history. She was a widow of independent means; her home was a flat in London in which she spent as little time as possible. In summer she travelled abroad; in the autumn she stayed in hotels in various parts of the country.

'Shan't be using this one again,' she declared. 'Never told me I couldn't bring Dandie into the dining-room. Pity,' she went on, spooning redcurrant jelly on to her saddle of lamb. 'The food's tip-top. Sensible menu, too. I hate it when everything's something à la something, *haw haw haw*!'

Mrs Clifford's appetite, like her laugh, was hearty and unrestrained. She took twice as many vegetables as Melissa and finished in half the time.

If Melissa had any fears about having to detach herself without inviting awkward questions, they were soon dispelled. As soon as she had finished her dessert, which she did in record time, Mrs Clifford put down her spoon.

'I must go and see to Dandie,' she said. 'Do please excuse me. It's been *awfully* nice having your company.'

Twenty minutes later, Melissa left the hotel for her assignment with Chris, wrapped in a dark blue car coat. A relief receptionist was on duty. That was good; with any luck, neither Kim nor Vic would realise that she had gone out.

Chris was at the meeting-place before her. As soon as she parked her Golf, he came over. 'We'll use the Jag,' he said. 'It's got longer legs. Just in case we need to hurry,' he explained. A nerve twitched in the pit of her stomach. It had not occurred to her that they might have to make a dash for it.

Following her directions, Chris turned into the entrance to the track leading to Stumpy's workshop, then backed round and parked on the verge, close to the hedge. He switched off the lights; before locking the car, he opened one of the rear doors and a dark shape spilled out. It was Khan.

'Thought he might as well come along,' Chris remarked. 'Attila's looking after things at home.'

A gibbous moon was partially obscured by clouds, but there was a bright glow over Evesham and the occasional flash of headlights from a passing car. Their eyes gradually adjusted to the gloom as they crept along. Khan padded at their heels, barely visible but for a glimmer of white teeth. He had not greeted Melissa nor invited a caress; he seemed to understand that this outing was strictly business.

'Any idea how the front door's fastened?' whispered Chris as they reached the building.

'I think it's bolted from inside.'

'That means a window – unless there's another door at the back.'

There was another door. Cautiously exploring with the aid of a torch dimmed with a cloth, Chris located it in a matter of seconds. A few seconds more and he had it unlocked. They were in.

'We won't chance the electric light,' said Chris. He removed the cloth and sent a powerful beam on a circle of exploration. Everything was much as Melissa remembered it from her afternoon visit; tools scattered untidily on the bench, the Morris with the bonnet still open. And, behind the Morris, the new red hatchback.

'That's funny,' she said, not bothering to keep her voice down. 'I'm sure that's Stumpy's own car. I wonder why . . .'

She broke off on hearing a low growl from Khan, who had been stationed close to the door with the command 'Guard'. Chris grabbed her and pulled her behind the Morris. In the split second before he switched off the torch, she could see the outline of the dog against the wall, crouching, wolf-like, with shoulders hunched and hackles raised.

'Get down!' commanded Chris in a low voice.

They held their breath and waited. The darkness seemed absolute until, straining her eyes, Melissa could just make out the dim squares of the windows. For a few seconds, they heard nothing; then came the sound of footsteps, slow and cautious, first dragging through grass, then picking their way across the rough hardcore, past the main door and along the side of the building. They stopped; there came the sound of a handle turning and a rectangle of grey appeared, framing the dark silhouette of a man. Then the electric light clicked on. From their hiding-place they could see, reflected in a window at the far end of the building, a shirt-sleeved Stumpy Dart, shotgun at the ready.

'All right, whoever you are, come out with your hands up!' he shouted.

There was a pause, during which Melissa could feel her heart pounding in her chest. Stumpy was peering nervously this way and that, swinging the barrel of the gun in all directions.

With perfect timing, Chris gave a low whistle and Khan sprang out from behind the half-open door. The next minute, a bewildered, terrified Stumpy was spreadeagled face down, with one arm gripped in the dog's powerful jaws and the gun spinning away out of his reach. Chris stepped out and stood in front of him as he wriggled, gasping and groaning, struggling to raise his head to look at his attacker.

'If you want to stay joined to that arm, you'd better lie still,' said Chris, his tone almost conversational.

'Call him off,' whined Stumpy. 'He's hurting me.'

'He's not even trying.'

Chris picked up the gun, opened the breech, shook out the cartridges and examined them.

'Blanks,' he called, with a glance in Melissa's direction. 'We've got a real tough egg here.'

'It's only to scare people off.' Stumpy's face was contorted with pain and fear. 'Living out here with no one else around . . .'

'You live in this dump?'

'I've got a caravan at the back. Who are you, what do you want, for God's sake?'

'I want to talk about a silencer,' said Chris.

'What silencer?'

'The false one you took off Vic Bellamy's car.'

'I don't know what you're talking about.'

Almost casually, Chris strolled across and stood over Stumpy. Then he lifted one foot and brought it down hard on the man's head, driving his face against the concrete. There was a thud and a howl of anguish; Melissa, watching from behind the Morris, gasped and covered her eyes.

'The dummy silencer,' repeated Chris. 'Where d'you say it was?'

'All right, I'll tell you. For Chrissake, call off that fucking dog!'

'That's better.' Without undue haste, Chris removed his foot. 'Khan, leave!'

The animal released its grip, retreated a few paces and sat on its haunches, still alert, eyes fixed on the target. Whimpering, one hand clutching his bleeding nose, Stumpy got to his feet. Over his shoulder, Chris called to Melissa. 'Our friend here is going to tell us all about it.'

Slowly, Melissa walked out from behind the Morris. Stumpy's eye's stretched. 'You . . . you meddling cow, you put him up to this! Oh my God, what have I let myself in for?'

He was a pitiable figure, standing there shivering in a thin shirt, his shapeless trousers tucked into shabby cowboy boots. His hair was tousled, his damaged face covered with blood and dirt from the floor. Melissa felt a wave of revulsion at what Chris had done; she had not bargained for anything like this. Her voice shook as she said, 'Why don't we go to your

128

caravan to talk it over? If there's no one else there, that is?'

'Who d'you think I've got there – a bird?' said Stumpy dejectedly. 'Yeah, why not, if it's okay with your gentleman friend, that is.'

'Not till you tell us where you've hidden the silencer,' said Chris implacably.

Stumpy, utterly defeated, pointed upwards.

'Can you see anything, Melissa?' asked Chris, without shifting his gaze.

'Some planks lying across the beams supporting the roof. There's something up there covered with sacking but I can't see what it is.'

'Stumpy will get it down for us, won't you, mate?'

'You ain't going to take it away?' pleaded Stumpy, and now there was naked terror in his eyes. 'He said it was more than my life's worth if I breathed a word . . .'

'Who said? Vic Bellamy?'

'He never told me his name. Honest!' The man was not far from tears. 'Look, what is all this about?'

At this point, Melissa intervened. 'Can't we look at the thing later – it won't run away,' she said. 'I'm getting frozen. Let's go over to the caravan.'

'Okay,' said Chris. 'Maybe our host will make us some coffee.'

'Bloody cheek!' Stumpy muttered.

They locked the door, leaving Khan on guard. Stumpy led the way round behind the workshop to where the caravan stood against a hedge, its position invisible to anyone approaching in the normal way. Soft lighting glowed through curtained windows, giving it a cosy, welcoming appearance. Inside, it was comfortably warm.

Stumpy filled a kettle and lit a small gas stove. 'Not sure if I've got three decent mugs,' he grumbled. 'You'll have to take pot luck.'

'We'll manage. Make mine strong, not too much milk, no sugar.' Chris sat on a cushioned seat at the rear of the van and stretched out his legs. 'Well, isn't this cosy?' He whistled a few bars of 'Mack the Knife', then broke into song: *On the sidewalk, Sunday morning, lies a body, oozin' life*. Poor Stumpy, measuring out instant coffee, trembled so hard that the spoon rattled against the mugs.

Melissa was becoming more uncomfortable by the minute, as well as concerned about the abrasions on Stumpy's face.

'I think you should clean up,' she told him. 'The skin's broken – have you got any antiseptic?'

'Got some Dettol somewhere.' Leaving the kettle to boil, Stumpy vanished into a cubbyhole and they heard the sound of running water.

'Is the psychological warfare really necessary?' said Melissa unhappily. 'The poor chap's scared out of his wits.'

'Fine. Let's keep it that way.'

'You could have broken his nose or something.'

'Yeah, you're right. I could have done.' Chris seemed mildly amused at the thought.

There was a drumming sound on the roof; it had begun to rain.

'Poor Khan will get soaked,' said Melissa.

'He'll survive.'

They waited. She looked round the caravan. It was built and equipped on luxury lines with good quality fittings, but it had obviously seen better days. The cupboard doors were scratched and chipped, the carpet and upholstery worn, the curtains faded and grubby. Stumpy had probably picked it up at a bargain price when the previous owners had finished with it. From what Ken Harris had told her, he came from a respectable family and had had a good upbringing. She wondered what had brought him to this solitary existence, and how he had become involved with Vic Bellamy.

Stumpy reappeared. One side of his face was swollen and bruised, but he had washed off the blood and dirt, combed his hair and covered his soiled shirt with a sweater. He took the kettle from the stove and poured hot water into the mugs,

brought out a carton of milk from a small refrigerator and a
packet of sugar from a cupboard, and put the lot on a battered
tin tray which he set down on a table in front of his uninvited
guests.

'What, no biscuits?' taunted Chris.

Stumpy glowered. 'Wasn't expecting company, was I?
Look, just get on with it, will you – what's your game?'

'That,' said Chris, reaching for a mug, 'is what you're going
to tell us.'

Chapter Thirteen

'It started a couple of months ago,' said Stumpy. 'This bloke with a posh accent turned up in a bloody great Yankee car and spun me a tale about wanting a place to hide his valuables when he went abroad. It had to be somewhere your ordinary thief who broke in to pinch the stereo wouldn't think of looking.'

'Was the dummy silencer his idea, then?' asked Chris.

'No, it was mine.' Stumpy stopped fingering his bruises for a moment and straightened in his seat. 'I thought of it, I designed it and I made it.'

'And fitted it?'

'Of course.' Stumpy's tone held a hint of confident pride. For the moment, mastery of his craft had given him the edge over Chris.

'Didn't it ever enter your head,' Melissa asked, 'that what he wanted to carry might be something illegal? Drugs, for instance?'

Stumpy put down his mug and wiped his mouth with the back of his hand. 'Why should I care what he wanted it for? As far as I was concerned, it was a job – and he paid well, cash on the nail.'

'How much?' asked Chris.

Stumpy scowled. 'That's my business.'

Melissa saw Chris's expression darken. Fearing that things were about to get rough again, she frowned at him, shook her head and said quickly, 'It doesn't matter. How long did it take?'

'Can't remember exactly. A week, maybe a bit less. The biggest problem was finding a place to fit the thing. As it was,

I couldn't make it as big as he wanted it, but he said it would do.'

'How did he get the car to you?'

'Some bird in a blue Renault came with him to drive him back, and again when he came to pick the car up.'

'Kim, I suppose,' Melissa remarked to Chris. 'What did this woman look like?' she asked, turning back to Stumpy.

'Dunno. She never got out of the car.'

'And you say the man didn't give his name?'

'Never thought to ask him. He gave me some bread in advance, to cover the materials I needed. I never doubted I'd get the rest, and I did.' Stumpy dabbed gingerly at his face and rubbed his sore arm, wincing. 'Got more'n I bargained for, didn't I?' he grumbled.

'Right,' said Chris. 'That brings us up to date. Now finish the story. When did this bloke bring the car back to have the dummy silencer taken off?'

'Yesterday evening. He rang about four and said he had an urgent job for me. I told him I couldn't fit anything in before the end of the week, and he said "Stuff that, I want it done right away, it won't take long." He sounded pretty het up, so I said I'd do it after hours, but it'd cost him. He said, "Don't worry, it'll be worth your while," and hung up.'

'So what time did he show up?'

'Must have been well after eight.'

'Did he say why it was so urgent?'

Stumpy shook his head and looked down at his boots. When he raised his eyes, Melissa saw the fear she had noticed earlier creeping back into them. 'He never said a word till the job was done. Just stood there fidgeting and telling me to get on with it. When I'd finished, he said, "Hide it away somewhere safe till I need it. And if anyone comes here asking questions, you don't know nothing, understand?"'

'Is that all he said?'

Stumpy chewed his lower lip and his voice fell to a hoarse whisper. 'He said something like, "I've got friends who could make life uncomfortable for you if you go telling tales." He meant it too. He was smiling, but there was a sort of cold look in his eye that gave me the willies. Then he gave me a fistful of tenners and left. I hardly slept last night, wondering what I'd got into.' He looked from Melissa to Chris with a beseeching expression. 'You ain't going to let him know I've told you? He'd half kill me, I know he would.' His voice became a tremulous squeak.

'No, I can promise you that.' Chris stood up. 'Now let's have a look at this brilliant invention of yours.'

'You ain't planning on taking it away?' pleaded Stumpy. 'If I can't produce it when the bloke comes back . . .'

'Just show us, will you?'

The rain had almost stopped. Guided by Chris's torch, they went back to the workshop, picking their way round the puddles. Khan appeared from the shadows; Chris patted him, said 'Good boy' and gave him a tit-bit which he acknowledged by circling round them, tongue lolling and tail swinging, then spraying them with water as he shook himself dry.

'He's off duty for the moment,' said Chris with a grin. 'Unless, of course, we have any trouble from our little friend.'

At the word 'little', Stumpy shot a glance of pure hatred at Chris, but he said nothing. He fetched a ladder and brought down a heavy bundle, which he laid on the bench and unwrapped.

'That's a weird-looking thing,' Melissa remarked. In the workshop of the garage where she had recently taken the Golf to have new tyres fitted, she had noticed racks of exhaust systems of every shape and size, but none resembling this.

Stumpy said nothing, but his condescending expression indicated that it was only what could be expected from a woman. Chris was examining the object minutely, turning it in his hands.

'Look at this, Mel. See how that section hinges back?' He demonstrated, revealing an elliptical compartment some two feet long. 'You stuff your loot in there, snap it shut, and this piece,' he indicated the straight end of a loop of piping welded to the closure, 'lies snugly by the genuine exhaust, as natural as can be.'

The interior of the compartment was clean. Melissa ran a finger over the surface and then examined it. It told her nothing.

'Ingenious, innit?' said Chris. 'He's a bright lad, our Stumpy.'

Stumpy gave a flicker of a smile that faded as he said nervously, 'Look, mate, you've seen what you want. Now get the hell out of here, will you?'

'Okay,' said Chris, with a wink at Melissa. 'Do we need to take this with us?'

'For God's sake,' whispered Stumpy. 'D'you want to get me torn apart?'

'Of course we don't want to take it,' said Melissa firmly, with an angry glance at Chris. 'We're going now.'

At the door, Chris said, 'No need to tell your customer about our visit.'

'You've gotta be kidding!'

'And thanks for the coffee.'

'Oh, piss off, the pair of you!'

The road was still wet and glistening as they drove back to where Melissa had left her car. Water swished under their tyres, approaching traffic flung out fountains of spray that glistened in the headlights and fell in a fine mist on the windscreen. Throughout the short journey, Melissa sat staring ahead, saying nothing.

Chris parked the Jaguar and switched off the engine. As Melissa, still not speaking, reached for the door catch, he said, 'You didn't care much for that, did you?'

'No,' she said through her teeth. She would have found it difficult to express politely just how little she had cared for her first taste of real-life violence.

'Had to make him talk, didn't I?' Chris's tone was matter-of-fact, almost casual. She did not reply. 'You look as if you could use a drink,' he went on. 'There's a pub across the way.'

She got out of the car and crossed the road, still without speaking. The interior of the pub was warm and welcoming, not crowded but comfortably full of cheerful, chattering people. She felt alienated from them as she sat at a corner table, reliving in her mind the scene in Stumpy's workshop, hearing once more the sound of his face making contact with the floor and thinking, *I wish I'd never got into this. Joe was right. Iris was right. I wish I'd stayed at home.* It was an effort, when Chris returned with a glass of wine for her and an orange juice for himself, to smile and thank him.

After a moment's pause, he asked, 'Did you pick up anything from inside that thing?'

'No, nothing at all. It looked almost surgically clean.'

'Any ideas on what Vic's been carrying in it?'

'Not the slightest.'

'So what do we do now?'

'I suppose we'll have to tell Mitch what we've found out.'

'I'm not sure that's a good idea.'

'Why not? We'll have to say something – he already knows I was going to see Stumpy.'

'Yeah, that's right.' Chris frowned. 'Anyway, he's out tonight. Some business do with the Hon. Pen – he's staying in London till tomorrow.' He glanced at his watch. 'I'd better get back soon. He'll be checking in later on.'

'Is the Hon. Pen back in the picture, then?'

'She's hanging in, hoping he'll get tired of the other bird.'

'You mean Dittany? He's still keen on her?'

'Oh, yeah.' Chris swallowed a mouthful of orange juice. 'Look, this doesn't solve our problem. What're we gonna do about this phoney exhaust on Vic's car?'

'But it isn't on Vic's car,' Melissa pointed out. 'And unless we can get Stumpy to give evidence, which he's obviously much too scared to do, we can't prove it ever was. And even if we could, how can we be sure it's been used for anything crooked?'

136

'No one goes to all that trouble if he's on the level.'

'I agree, but that's hardly evidence.'

'Yeah, I know. That's why I'm in two minds whether to tell Mitch. He'll go up in the air like a Roman candle, thinking he's got Vic by the short and curlies. He won't like it when I point out how things really are.'

'Well, it's up to you now.'

He looked dismayed. 'You're pulling out?'

'There's nothing more I can do, is there? It's obvious Vic's going to lie low for a while, and I can't keep up this research charade much longer. If Mitch wants to know what he gets up to with that gadget on his car, he'll have to have him watched to find out when he has it put back, and then have him tailed. It's a job for a professional – I'm not taking it on.'

They had finished their drinks and by unspoken agreement they got up to leave. As they returned to their cars, he said, 'You're okay on your own?'

'Of course. And tell Mitch I'll be checking out of the hotel by lunchtime tomorrow.'

'He won't like it.'

'Too bad.'

'There's a rehearsal in the evening – won't you be coming to that?'

'So the show is going ahead, in spite of what happened?'

'Course it is – big PR exercise innit? Good for business, keep the customers in a good mood, all that crap.' From his tone, it was plain that Chris had jaundiced views on the subject of corporate entertaining.

'I don't see any reason for me to be there. Anyway, I've got things at home to catch up with.' She got into her car and wound down the window, conscious that her tone had been far from cordial and trying to make amends. The man had simply been doing his job in the only way he knew. He, Mitch and their associates lived in a different milieu, another world; it was time for her to creep back into hers and close the door like a caddis worm. 'Good-night,' she said, 'and thanks for the drink.'

'Sure.'

When she re-entered the hotel, she was disconcerted to find both Kim and Vic at the reception desk, apparently studying some paperwork. They raised their heads with polite smiles. Kim asked if she had had a good day.

Vic's gaze raked her briefly from head to foot. 'Been out ghost hunting?' he enquired. His tone was bantering but his eyes, as they finally made contact with hers, held an expression that called Stumpy's description to mind: 'a sort of cold look . . . it gave me the willies.' It was an effort to respond naturally and her knees shook a little as she went up to her room.

She kicked off her shoes, pulling a face as she noticed the splashes of yellowish mud from the dirt track leading to Stumpy's workshop. The bottoms of her trousers had similar stains and there were bits of grass clinging to the damp cloth. 'Bother!' she muttered crossly as she put them on a hanger. 'Something else for the dry cleaners.'

She lay awake for a long time that night. There was no further doubt in her mind that Mitch was right; Vic was up to his neck in some kind of racket. He was illegally carrying or preparing to carry, during his trips abroad, some goods or substances for which wealthy people were willing to pay handsomely. She recalled what Mitch had said about visitors to the hotel turning up in large, expensive cars and receiving the VIP treatment. It pointed to deals actually taking place on the premises, presumably in the Bellamys' private apartment. Deals in what? Her mind kept throwing up drugs as the obvious answer, yet she was not convinced. It might be something else. In any case, she kept reminding herself, she had played her part. If there was any more sleuthing to be done, others could do it.

Just the same, she felt uneasy. There had been something

disturbing about the way Vic had looked at her when she came in, as if he knew perfectly well that her presence in the hotel, and her professed interest in its history, were subterfuge. He could not, of course, be aware that she had paid Stumpy a second visit, but he had almost certainly known about the first. Even if he believed her story, he was not prepared to take any chances.

She had achieved something, but very little, and even that could turn out to be counter-productive. Forewarned that he might be under observation, Vic had caused the one tangible piece of evidence to be removed. He might put the whole operation – whatever it was – on ice, perhaps indefinitely. She had come to a dead end . . . unless she could find out something else. Something irrefutable. *No, forget it, Melissa. You're pulling out, remember?*

She got up, went to the window and drew back the curtains. The sky had cleared and the air was still. The garden lay bathed in moonlight; the stone shepherdess was poised serenely on her plinth, with no lurking phantoms in the shadows or imaginary will-o'-the-wisp lights at her feet. Nothing to worry about. None of her business anyway. Tomorrow night she would be looking out on the familiar scene from her own bedroom. She closed the curtains, went back to bed and fell almost immediately into a heavy sleep.

At breakfast next morning Mrs Clifford, brisk and cheerful as she despatched a hefty helping of eggs and bacon before wading into the toast and marmalade, reminded Melissa of their plans to go for a walk. They agreed to meet at ten o'clock.

Kim was on duty when Melissa went to announce that she would be leaving before lunch. 'I understand you'll be sending my bill to Mr Mitchell,' she said.

'Yes, that's right.' It might have been imagination, but it seemed to her that Kim's smile was a trifle forced. 'I hope you've enjoyed your stay,' she said. Her voice had a metallic edge as she uttered the polite formula, in marked contrast to the effusiveness of her welcome.

At ten o'clock, Melissa and Mrs Clifford set off on their walk. A short distance along the road past the hotel, a sign indicated a footpath. They climbed over a stile and began to cross a field of pasture that sloped gently upwards.

'That's good – no sheep today,' said Mrs Clifford. She let Dandie off his lead and he went scampering off, nose to the ground, propelled along by his short legs like a clockwork toy. His mistress sighed happily. 'He just *loves* it here,' she said. 'If it wasn't for that silly rule that keeps him out of the dining-room, this place would be *ideal* for us both.'

At the top of the field they paused to look back. 'Now you can see the old quarry,' said Mrs Clifford, pointing with her walking-stick. 'All overgrown, of course. Hasn't been touched for centuries, I should imagine. You can see how close it is to the hotel – must have been very convenient for the builders of the original priory.'

'They didn't use stone for the crypt, they used brick,' said Melissa. 'I wonder why.'

'Ah, that's easy.' As if preparing to deliver a lecture, Mrs Clifford leaned on her stick and planted her feet well apart. 'They only came across the stone deposits by accident, y'see, when they'd nearly finished excavating for their foundations. So they'd have used up their bricks for the crypt and then built above ground using stone. That's the theory, anyway.' She gave Melissa a sudden, sharp look. 'You've been down in the cellar, then?'

'Yes.'

'Lucky old you! You might have encountered Bess and her friends.' Excitement glowed in Mrs Clifford's pale eyes, then died away as she added dismissively, 'But of course, you wouldn't have been aware of them. You aren't psychic.'

Melissa was studying the position of the hotel building in relation to the quarry, trying to remember how it appeared on the ground plan that Mitch had shown her. 'I suppose,' she said, thinking aloud, 'the crypt originally extended in this direction. On the other hand, it might have run *away* from where we're standing, but it would definitely have been east–west, wouldn't it?'

'Of course.' Mrs Clifford shaded her eyes against the sun and considered, then suddenly let out a hoarse cry of excitement. 'That's it! What did I tell you?' She grabbed Melissa by the arm. 'It *did* run this way – below that part of the garden where the man shouted because Dandie ran on to the grass. I *knew* Bess wasn't far away, and I was right. There she was, beneath my feet – oh, how absolutely *marvellous!*' Wearing an expression of almost religious fervour, she clasped her hands round her stick and held it before her face as if it were a holy relic.

Uncertain how to respond, Melissa said nothing, but if she had spoken it was doubtful whether Mrs Clifford would have heard. She was in a state of euphoria with only one thing on her mind. 'Do forgive me, but I simply must get back to the hotel,' she said. 'I'm going to speak to the manager and ask permission to visit that part of the garden again. I'm *sure* Bess has a message for me.'

She was already on her way back across the field. She had an awkward, ungainly way of walking, due no doubt to the gammy knees of which she had earlier complained, but she set a pace that Melissa could only just match without breaking into a run. 'Where's Dandie got to?' she puffed, without slowing down. 'Ah, there he is. Come on, you little scamp!'

Dandie had just emerged from an exploration of the wood. He bounded across the grass towards them, then suddenly changed direction and tore off in pursuit of a rabbit. They saw the white scut vanish on the other side of the perimeter fence; the next minute there was a startled yelp and Dandie also disappeared.

'Oh, my goodness! He's gone down the rabbit-hole!' wailed Mrs Clifford. 'He'll get stuck – whatever shall we do?' She rushed towards the fence, repeatedly calling the dog's name. From somewhere not far away, they heard a pathetic whine.

'I think he's fallen into the quarry,' said Melissa.

141

'Oh, the poor darling!' Mrs Clifford gripped the top of the fence and shook it. 'How can we get to him? I can't climb over, not with my knees. Melissa, do you think you could possibly . . . would you . . . please?'

'I'll try.' The fence was too high to vault and too unstable to climb. Eventually, Melissa found a couple of large, flat stones which she placed one on top of the other to form a step. With the aid of Mrs Clifford's supporting arm and the loan of her stick, she managed to clamber over. Cautiously, she approached the edge of the quarry.

To her relief, the drop was not sheer and at this point the distance to the bottom was not much over ten feet. Dandie was sitting on a ledge about six feet from the top, whimpering and trembling. When he caught sight of her, he jumped up and scrabbled at the face of the rock with his front paws.

'I can see him. He can't get back by himself, but he doesn't seem to be hurt,' she called.

'Oh, thank God! Can you reach him?'

'I think so.'

An elder bush made a handhold as she scrambled down, carefully testing each projecting rock before putting her weight on it. Reaching Dandie, she picked him up and prepared for the return trip, then realised that the branch she had used to steady herself on the way down was now out of reach.

'I can't get back the same way,' she shouted. 'There's a track over there – it probably leads to the road. You go on and I'll meet you.'

'Righty-ho! You're sure Dandie's all right?'

'He's fine.'

She was only about four feet above the ground at this point and her main difficulty was not the descent but the tangle of brambles that lay at the bottom. They stretched across to the far wall of the quarry which, owing to the slope of the land, was considerably higher than the one she had just come down.

'Lucky for you, you didn't fall over there,' she informed the small bundle of brown fur tucked under her arm. Dandie wriggled, eagerly licking the air in the direction of her face.

Thankful that she was wearing thick shoes and slacks, she slithered the rest of the way down and began trampling a path through the undergrowth. A clump of hawthorn and elder lay between her and the track; she was seeking a way through them when she heard the sound of an approaching car.

She was not doing anything wrong. Although she was, technically, a trespasser, there was no reason to suppose that the owner of the land was going to berate her for straying on to his property to rescue a dog. So why, she asked herself as she crouched out of sight among the bushes, thankful that they had not yet shed all their leaves, was she hiding? All this spook- and crook-hunting must be making her paranoid.

The car seemed to be coming straight towards her; then it swung to the left and vanished behind an angle of rock. There was a pause; she heard the engine idling, speed up again as if it was being driven slowly forward, and then die. Moments later came the sound of a heavy door closing.

Melissa waited for a minute or two but no one appeared. She straightened up, squeezed through a gap in the bushes and went to investigate. At the far end of what was evidently a well-used track, a metal up-and-over door had been let into the quarry wall. Probably, someone had converted an old tool or dynamite store into a garage. There was nothing unusual or suspicious about that, she told herself as she hurried to rejoin Mrs Clifford. Nothing at all.

Except that, although she had been unable to identify the driver, she had caught a glimpse of the badge on the bonnet of the light blue car. It was a Renault.

Chapter Fourteen

On returning to the hotel, Melissa went upstairs to pack, leaving Mrs Clifford putting her case for permission to go ghost-hunting to a less than enthusiastic Kim Bellamy.

When she went downstairs again, the position was evidently not yet resolved. Mrs Clifford was sitting in a chair beside the fire with Dandie on her lap, drumming on the floor with her stick and glowering towards the desk, where Kim, paying no attention to her whatsoever, had spread a selection of brochures for the benefit of another guest.

'Is there a problem?' asked Melissa.

'It's like trying to get into Buckingham Palace,' snapped Mrs Clifford, making no attempt to lower her voice. 'She won't agree to it – says I have to speak to her husband. Did you ever hear anything so ridiculous? Ah, about time!' She rose to her feet as Vic Bellamy appeared, suave and self-possessed in a dark suit, white shirt and bow tie. 'Now, look here young man, this is a perfectly simple, reasonable request . . . !'

Melissa left them to it and headed for the car park with her suitcase, her mind on other things. All the time she was packing, she had been pondering on the significance of the blue Renault. Stumpy had mentioned that the woman who accompanied Vic to the workshop had such a car. She had immediately assumed that woman to be Kim – but Kim was on duty when she and Mrs Clifford went out and was still there when they returned; obviously, she had not been driving on this occasion. It might not have been the same car – after all, it was a fairly popular model and there was more than one shade of blue. The car she had just seen might belong to a total stranger who either owned or rented the garage, its similarity to Kim's car – if indeed it was hers – nothing but coincidence.

All the same, it was an odd place to have a garage, with no house near by; odd, too, that the driver had closed the doors and remained inside. Unless . . . Melissa's heart began thumping as a new possibility mushroomed in her brain. Supposing . . . no, it was too fantastic . . . but surely, worth looking into. She would need Chris's help, of course . . . Her resolve to have nothing more to do with the affair flew out of her head as she got into the Golf and started the engine.

As she was waiting to turn out of the hotel entrance, she spotted something that made her pulse give yet another blip of excitement. About a hundred yards along to her left, having apparently emerged from the track leading to the quarry garage, was the blue Renault. Because of its position, as the driver sat watching for a gap in the traffic, it was impossible to see who was at the wheel. When it pulled out, heading towards Evesham, Melissa followed without a second thought.

Had she at this point been asked what she was hoping to achieve, she would have been hard put to it to think of a sensible reply. For some reason, it seemed important to know the identity of the driver. If the theory burgeoning in her mind was correct, it *was* possible for Kim – or possibly Vic – to be at the wheel. If so, it would not by itself prove anything, but it would be another piece of evidence to support the case that was slowly building up against them. Still only circumstantial evidence, she reminded herself as she drove past the telephone kiosk from which she had intended to call Chris. She could talk to him later – this evening, perhaps. She might go to the rehearsal after all.

She chewed over various possibilities while keeping the Renault in sight but not getting too close. It took the Evesham by-pass, heading towards Stratford-upon-Avon. By the time they entered the town, they were separated by several other cars; at a set of traffic lights it was only by putting her foot down and shooting across on the amber that Melissa managed to keep the Renault in sight. A couple of minutes later she found herself fourth in a queue to enter a multi-storey car park.

The Renault had reached the entrance; it stopped briefly as a woman's hand took a ticket from the automatic dispenser and then swung away to the left towards the first ramp. Still Melissa could not get a glimpse of the driver's face, although it was possible to see that there was only one person in the car. At least, she had been able to read the registration number, which she repeated over and over while waiting her turn to enter.

The second driver in the queue managed to stall his engine; the next pulled up too far from the machine and Melissa sat fuming while an elderly man took what seemed an eternity to unhook his safety belt, get out to take his ticket and get back in again. By the time she had found a space to park her own car and located the blue Renault another two levels up, it was standing empty and there was no other person in sight.

Faced with the possibility of an unlimited wait, she felt her enthusiasm for the adventure oozing away. A multi-storey car park is not the most congenial of places to while away the passing hour, especially on a chilly autumn day. Still, having come thus far, she was loth to abandon the project altogether. She decided to bring the Golf up to the same level as the Renault, where there were several unoccupied spaces, in order to keep watch in comparative comfort.

She had just made this decision and was heading for the passenger lift when the door opened and a man came out. He hurried towards her, ignition key at the ready, parking ticket clutched in one hand. She glanced idly over her shoulder as he made for the far end of the line of cars, then continued towards the lift, reaching it just as the doors were closing in response to another call. As she stood waiting, one finger on the button, she heard the sound of an engine starting up. Looking back, she saw the blue Renault reverse out of its bay and drive at speed towards the exit. Helplessly, she watched it go, realising that by the time she reached her own car, the Renault would be out of the building and out of sight.

'That was a complete waste of time,' she heard herself informing the control panel of the lift as it creaked towards the street level. A second occupant, a tired-looking young mother with a chocolate-coated toddler, looked at her curiously.

'You what?'

'Oh, nothing. Just thinking aloud.'

Adjacent to the car park was a shopping precinct. Melissa wandered through it, thinking of possible explanations for what she had just seen. She reached the river, found an unoccupied bench and sat staring at the grey-green water, its slow-moving surface speckled with fallen leaves among which the population of ducks and swans glided and pecked and squabbled.

She calculated that the blue Renault had stood empty for something like ten minutes; an unidentified woman had left it there and a man she had never set eyes on before had driven it away. Perhaps he was borrowing it, or perhaps he was the owner and the woman had been returning it. Perhaps they were husband and wife; he was using the car for some errand while she remained in town shopping. But why, if the explanation was a simple, straightforward one, had they not arranged to hand over the car in the open? Street parking in the town centre was normally impossible but there were plenty of little side streets within easy walking distance where one could wait for limited periods. Apparently, these people did not wish their manoeuvre to be observed – which could mean the car was being used to hand over something in which the police might be interested. Something, perhaps, that had been stored in the mysterious quarry garage?

Aware that she was beginning to feel hungry, she headed back into town in search of lunch. On the way, she passed the Royal Shakespeare Theatre and called in for a programme. For some inconsequential reason, she thought of Ken Harris and wondered if he would follow up his suggestion of a date. Her thoughts strayed for a moment in a different direction until, as she strolled along the High Street, a new and elegant shop front attracted her attention. The framework was dark blue, with the name 'Dizzy Heights' inscribed in gold on the fascia-board.

The door stood open. Inside, workmen were busy installing fixtures and fittings, while at the rear of the shop, supervising the erection of a partition, were two women. One, whose outline was instantly familiar, had her back turned; the other, a petite figure with a bush of ash-blonde hair and round tinted spectacles, caught sight of Melissa and came to the door with a coloured brochure in her hand.

'I am afraid we shall not be open until Saturday,' she said, 'but please take this and peruse it at your leisure. You will, I am sure, find much to interest you.' Despite her small stature, she had a commanding air, and she handed over the brochure like a headmistress giving out homework.

This, thought Melissa, must be the Honourable Penelope's formidable partner. Her surmise was confirmed as Penelope herself, having finished instructing the fitters, came forward. Her smile had the brightness of sunshine on snow.

'Melissa, what a surprise! Charlie, this is Mel Craig, who wrote the show for Mitch's birthday party – Charlotte Heighton.'

'Delighted to meet you.' Lady Charlotte brushed Melissa's hand with her fingertips. 'I wonder if you would care to join us for cocktails at our preview tomorrow evening?' Her pronunciation had an almost mechanical perfection, as if each word had been individually cut and polished before being spoken.

'Oh, yes, do come!' urged Penelope. Melissa was conscious of two pairs of eyes appraising her plain tweed skirt and four-year-old car coat. 'We'll be showing some simply lovely clothes and I'm sure we can tempt you with something. By the way,' she turned to her partner, 'I spoke to Mitch this morning and he's promised to be with us if his business commitments will allow.'

148

'Of course, he will be with us.' Lady Charlotte's smooth delivery had acquired a jagged edge, faint but unmistakable. 'It will be our first joint promotion since the start of our association, and a very significant occasion in more ways than one.' Eyes like bluish-green marbles fixed Penelope with a gaze that was almost hypnotic. 'He knows how important this is to you.'

The two women exchanged confident, almost conspiratorial smiles which they then turned on Melissa, moving closer together as if to impress her with their combined strength. Like a pair of tigresses, she thought, taking control of their trainer in a bizarre reversal of rôles. It crossed her mind to wonder just what chance Dittany stood against these two. Penelope on her own was a rival to be reckoned with; backed up by Charlotte, who had all the makings of a scheming duenna, her advantage might prove overwhelming.

'You will come, won't you?' they urged, almost in unison.

'It's very kind of you, but I'm afraid I have another engagement,' said Melissa untruthfully and they responded with formal expressions of regret.

'And what brings you to Stratford, Mrs Craig?' asked Lady Charlotte. 'Are you going to a Shakespeare matinée? That reminds me' – she turned back to Penelope – 'I have reserved a block of seats for the evening performance on Saturday. *Twelfth Night* – I believe dear Mitch will find it most enjoyable.'

'I'm sure he'll love it,' purred Penelope.

'Well, I mustn't delay you any longer,' said Melissa, seizing the opportunity to escape without answering the question. 'I hope the new branch is successful.' Amid a flurry of polite exchanges, she went on her way.

Over a lunch of quiche and salad in a cafeteria, she returned to her speculations over the possible significance of the quarry garage and the blue Renault. It was still not definitely established that it was the same car that Stumpy had noticed. If he had happened to spot the registration number, or if he could describe the shade of blue more accurately . . . people who worked with cars often got into the habit of noting such details . . . his workshop lay on her route home . . . it was worth a try. She finished her meal and hurried back to the car park.

The first thing she noticed as she drew up outside the workshop was the silence. The raucous clamour of the transistor was missing. It might mean that Stumpy was out, but more probably he was in his caravan, eating a belated lunch. She walked behind the workshop to investigate, gave a horrified gasp and stopped dead in her tracks. The van was a burnt-out wreck.

Her first reaction was one of terror – terror that Stumpy might not have been able to escape the flames, that what remained of his body might be lying inside the blackened ruin. Her heart thumped in her chest as she moved closer, shaking her head in shock and bewilderment on realising the extent of the destruction. Hardly anything was left of the van itself but the chassis and the twisted metal frame. With the exception of the little stainless-steel sink unit and the jagged fragments of a metal gas container, almost the entire contents had been reduced to a charred, unrecognisable mass – insufficient, she realised with relief, to conceal a corpse.

She swung round on hearing a sound behind her. Stumpy had emerged from the workshop carrying a heavy spanner in one hand. His face, still discoloured and swollen from its encounter with the floor, wore an expression at first wary and apprehensive, swiftly changing to one of mingled anger and disbelief.

'You!' he exclaimed, his voice thick with fury. 'You've got a nerve, showing yer face here!' He took a step towards her, brandishing the spanner. 'Get out, if you know what's good for you.'

She backed away in alarm, fearing he was going to attack her; then she saw that he was trembling. He was not so much angry as scared. It was hardly surprising in the circumstances.

'Look, I'm sorry about last night. I didn't know things were going to get so rough,' she said. Stumpy's lip curled but he made no comment. 'I didn't expect you to be pleased to see me,' she went on, 'but there's something else I need to know. It seems I couldn't have come at a worse time.' She gestured at the wrecked caravan. 'How did it happen?'

Stumpy fingered the spanner, avoiding her eye. 'Gas cylinder blew up,' he muttered.

'How awful. Were you hurt?' He shook his head, but she saw his knuckles whiten as he increased his grip. 'What will you do? Are you insured?'

'Insured?' He gave a scornful laugh. 'Who'd insure that heap of junk? Besides,' he added, almost to himself, 'there'd be questions.'

'What do you mean? What sort of questions?'

'Nothing. Forget it. And for pity's sake, get out of here before . . .'

'Before what?' she asked, as the sentence remained unfinished.

'Just leave me alone. Haven't you caused me enough trouble?' His glance slid past her to what had once been his home; then he turned on his heel and walked back towards the workshop, dragging his feet, a man cowed and defeated. 'Go away, and don't come back,' he called over his shoulder.

'But I only wanted to ask you a simple question,' pleaded Melissa, hurrying after him. He quickened his step, reached the door first and slammed it in her face.

'I don't know nothing,' he shouted from inside.

'But I only want to . . .'

'I'm not saying another word.' His voice was breathless, vibrating with fear. 'I don't care if you and that sod come back with half a dozen Rottweilers, you'll get nothing out of me.'

There was no point in pressing him. Frustrated yet again, Melissa marched off without troubling to pick her way through the mud left by last night's rain. She glanced down at her shoes as she opened the car door and muttered an angry exclamation at seeing the state they were in. 'That's the second pair I've mucked up in two days,' she grumbled aloud as she wiped away the yellowish deposit with a rag.

The second pair! Her mind switched to the previous evening. Vic Bellamy had been at the reception desk when she got back; he had glanced at her feet and made some wisecrack about ghost-hunting. He would know that she could not have picked up that particular shade of mud anywhere near the hotel; he must have guessed where she had been. It was odds on he had been to see Stumpy and frightened him into admitting that he had disobeyed orders. Stumpy had given a defective gas bottle as the cause of the fire, but she had had her doubts at the time; now she was certain. The burnt-out caravan was to serve as both punishment and warning.

Melissa drove back to Hawthorn Cottage feeling cold, miserable and sick. The whole enterprise was a shambles; as a result of her meddling, a man who was trying to make an honest living and had acted in good faith, had been roughly handled and had his home destroyed. Even though she felt certain in her own mind that Vic Bellamy was behind Stumpy's misfortunes and – as Mitch had been maintaining all along – that he was involved in some very shady activities, she had nothing, not one shred of hard evidence, to show for her efforts.

Her mood of pessimism took a further knock when she got indoors and found a note on the hall table. It read, 'Gone to a private viewing in London, staying till Sunday,' and was signed with the initials I.A. entwined in an elegant monogram. Underneath was scribbled, 'PS Gloria swapped days, coming to you Friday.'

'Damn!' said Melissa. She had been looking forward to a comfortable chat with Iris. On second thoughts, it might not have been so comfortable. Iris had very firmly warned her against becoming involved with Mitch's scheme.

She cheered up on re-reading the postscript. Apart from her amazing capacity to get through housework in record time, Gloria Parkin's bouncy good humour, combined with an insatiable appetite for gossip, were guaranteed to lift the lowest of spirits. Already, as she went upstairs to unpack, Melissa felt more optimistic.

She brewed some tea while considering whether to call Chris, and if so, how much to tell him. She had no doubt that, if he knew the full story, he would be only too willing to try to break into the quarry garage. Excitement at the thought made her nerve-ends tingle; once more, common sense and the resolve to opt for a quiet life were in retreat, beaten back by relentless curiosity. She rinsed out her cup and picked up the phone.

Mr Bright, she learned from the secretary, was not there; he had driven to London to meet Mr Mitchell and they would not return until late. When Melissa enquired if that meant they would miss tonight's rehearsal, she was informed that it had been cancelled.

While she was trying to decide how to spend her evening, the telephone rang; Detective Chief Inspector Kenneth Harris was on the line.

'I've been trying to get you for a couple of days,' he said.

'I'm sorry, I've been away since Tuesday. Is it something important?'

'In a manner of speaking.' There was a momentary pause; then he said, 'About that date we spoke about . . .' and left the words hanging in the air in a way quite unlike his normal businesslike approach.

'Yes?' she said.

'I was wondering . . . are you free for dinner tomorrow?'

'That would be lovely.' She did not have to simulate the pleasure she could hear in her own voice, and she was aware of the tension leaving his as he said, 'There's a new French restaurant opened recently in Stowbridge. I'm told it's very good.'

'I don't mind where we go as long as it's not Heyshill Manor.'

Chapter Fifteen

The following morning, Melissa got up at her usual time. She ate her breakfast of cereal and toast standing by her kitchen window, admiring the view and thinking how good it was to be home. The sun was shining from a clear sky; a touch of overnight frost was rapidly disappearing, except for a few patches of rime lying like spilt sugar in the shade of the hedgerows. The valley bottom was a shallow sea of mist, out of which trees and bushes rose like the turrets and domes of a miniature city, tinted bronze and gold.

There was a yowl and a thump as Binkie landed on the window-sill and demanded admission. Melissa opened the back door and he rushed in, at first coiling himself round her legs in ecstatic loops and purring hysterically, then padding over to the refrigerator and back, fixing her with pleading yellow eyes.

'Don't try and kid me you're starving,' she admonished him. 'I know jolly well Iris has organised your food. Oh, all right, I'll give you some milk.' She put a saucer on the floor and the cat settled down to drink while she poured a second cup of coffee and began planning her day.

She really should get back to her novel. She was behind schedule; any time now, Joe would be on the line demanding a progress report. Resisting the temptation to go out for a walk, she went up to her study and began re-reading the early chapters, with Binkie snoozing on her lap.

An hour later, Gloria arrived, her moon face pink with the cold, her plump body encased in a quilted anorak patterned with flowers. 'My Stanley got it for me off a friend what runs a stall in Gloucester market,' she explained, in response to

Melissa's admiring comment. She took it off and handed it over for inspection, accompanied by a wave of unfamiliar fragrance.

'New perfume?' asked Melissa, sniffing.

Gloria nodded her blonde head, currently a mass of crimped curls. 'It's from the Green Shop,' she said. 'En-viron-mentally friendly.' She pronounced the unfamiliar word with care. 'The kids have been doing this project at school about saving the rain forests, see, and I thought I'd better show willing.'

'Quite right,' said Melissa. She had a feeling that Gloria was getting her causes muddled but to point out the distinction might lead to a time-consuming discussion. 'Well, I suppose we'd both better get down to work. I'll be in the study if you need anything.'

Gloria rolled up her sleeves. 'See you at coffee-time.'

On the stroke of eleven, she re-entered the kitchen, peeling off her rubber gloves. She washed her hands at the sink and perched on a stool to drink the coffee Melissa had just made.

'Miss Ash says you've bin staying at a fancy hotel,' she remarked. 'In London, were it?'

'No, Heyshill Manor, the other side of Cheltenham. It's a very historic house, like the one I'm writing about in my new book. I was doing some research.'

'Oooh, my! That were a nasty accident, when that gentleman fell down the cellar steps. Was you there?'

Melissa evaded the question, unwilling to supply the gory details Gloria would surely expect. 'How did you hear about that?'

'My Stanley's auntie works there.'

'Really?'

Gloria nodded, setting the curls bouncing. 'Auntie Muriel. Bit of a come-down for her, doing domestic work after being a lady's maid, but she don't complain. She does for Mrs Bellamy, the manager's wife, twice a week in her private flat.' A husky giggle erupted unexpectedly from Gloria's corsage and the twinkle in her toffee-brown eyes was like a nudge in the ribs. 'Mrs B.'ll do for her, if she finds out about the picture she broke yesterday.'

'Oh dear, how did that happen?'

'Fell on the floor while she were dusting it. Glass everywhere. If Mrs B. had been there, she'd have had a fit. You like to know what Auntie did?' Gloria wriggled on her stool, dying to tell. Melissa nodded, resigned to the fact that, like it or not, she was going to hear.

'She took another picture about the same size from the spare room and hung it in its place. Then she sneaked the one that got broke out in her shopping bag. She reckons she'll get away with it while it's being mended 'cos Mr and Mrs B. got no one staying just now and they only uses the dining-room when there's posh visitors – they mostly eats in the kitchen like us. Clever, weren't it?'

'Very clever,' agreed Melissa. Nine people out of ten would be found out in such an obvious piece of substitution but, knowing how close Gloria's husband sailed to the wind in running his second-hand car business and how rarely his peccadilloes came to light, she suspected that Auntie Muriel would get away with it. That sort of luck tended to run in families.

'Fancy you staying at Heyshill,' said Gloria. 'I'll bet you got all they stories about Battling Bess and her mates.'

'I did indeed. Has Auntie Muriel ever heard the ghosts talking?'

'Course not.' The curls quivered in scorn. 'Loada rubbish, innit?'

'A lot of people seem to believe in it. Janice says none of the staff'll go down in the cellar at night if they can help it.'

'Yeah, I know. Auntie Muriel says' – here Gloria paused to take a noisy swallow from her mug – 'she thinks Mr Bellamy maybe puts they stories around 'cos he keeps something hidden there. She reckons he might be a crook.'

'Whatever makes her think that?' Melissa found herself beginning to take an interest in Auntie Muriel.

Gloria selected a chocolate wafer and crunched it between her small white teeth. 'Dunno really, 'cept he's in with the local big-wigs and they're all on the fiddle, ain't they?'

'I don't think you should say things like that,' said Melissa primly, remembering that, should she be rash enough to agree with any of Gloria's wilder assertions, she was liable to be quoted. 'As a matter of fact, Mr Bellamy showed me round the cellar yesterday morning and there's nowhere he could hide anything.'

'Oh!' Gloria's moon face fell, then brightened as she remembered something else. 'Tell you what, though. He once came to my Stanley's showroom, looking for a big American car. Offered cash on the nail.'

'Really?' Melissa's flagging interest was once more aroused, but she kept her voice casual as she asked, 'How long ago was this?'

'Dunno.' Gloria brushed biscuit crumbs from her blouse. 'Couple of months maybe.'

'Did your Stanley sell him a car?'

''Fraid not, he didn't have nothing suitable.'

They finished their coffee. Gloria rinsed the mugs and returned to her cleaning duties. Melissa went back to her study and tried to continue work on *Dancing with Death*, but found her concentration had been disrupted by what she had just heard. It was significant that Mitch was not the only one to have doubts about Vic Bellamy. However, the fact that he was 'in with the local big-wigs' who, Gloria claimed – probably with some justification – were 'all on the fiddle', would hardly support an application for a warrant to search the premises. On the contrary, when dealing with individuals who had friends in high places, any police officer with an eye to promotion would need to watch his step with more than usual care.

A succession of telephone calls distracted her still further: first the anticipated lecture from Joe, once more reminding her of her deadline; then a request to give a talk to a local branch of the Women's Institute and an invitation to a charity coffee morning in the village. When the phone rang yet again, she swore aloud as she reached for the receiver.

'Hello!' she snapped.

'What's up with you, then?' asked Chris.

'Oh, it's you. Sorry, I didn't mean to bark, but you're the fourth person to ring in half an hour, and I do have this novel I'm trying to write.'

'I was just returning your call. We can make it some other time if you like.'

'No, I wanted to talk to you.' She gave him an account of the previous day's adventures.

His response was predictable. 'We've got to get inside that garage. What are you doing this evening?'

'Having dinner with a member of the local CID,' she said.

His voice betrayed no reaction as he said, 'Well, leave it till tomorrow. Saturday might be better; it's the busiest night of the week so the Bellamys should be well tied up for the evening.' There was a pause. 'I don't suppose your policeman friend . . . ?'

'No chance,' Melissa interrupted firmly. 'He'd only tell me what we already know – there's nothing to justify an investigation.'

'What about the damage to Stumpy's van?'

'Yes, and what about the damage to Stumpy's face?' she countered. 'Forget it, Chris. Stumpy will stick to his story of a defective gas cylinder come hell or high water. He's much more scared of Vic's mob than of the police. By the way, what about asking Mitch to replace the van? After all . . .'

'Don't worry, he will. I'd already thought of that.'

'That makes me feel a lot better.'

'So, what time do we meet tomorrow? Ten o'clock?'

Melissa hesitated. She thought of the ruthless treatment meted out to Stumpy and felt a fierce desire to help bring

159

those responsible to justice. On the other hand, if they were caught, and could show no evidence of wrong-doing . . . She quailed at the thought of Ken Harris's reaction.

It was as if Chris could read her thoughts, even over the telephone. 'Don't tell me you've got cold feet,' he taunted her.

'I'm just thinking of what DCI Harris would say. He'd go bananas if he knew what I'd been up to so far. Breaking and entering . . . accessory to actual bodily harm . . . he'd throw the book at me.'

'Okay, okay. If you want to chicken out . . .'

'I'm not chickening out,' she said indignantly. 'I'll be there. Oh, guess who I saw in Stratford? Penelope de Lavier. She and her partner were getting their new branch ready for the big opening ceremony.' Chris gave a contemptuous grunt as she added, 'I got the distinct impression that Penelope intends to get Mitch to the altar.'

'Perish the thought,' said Chris, with unusual feeling.

'I gather she's not your favourite person.'

'Hard-nosed cow. She got the bread for her bloody shops, her *bowteeks* as she likes to call them, so why can't she lay off? Dittany's the girl for Mitch.'

'I'd like to think so as well, but I wouldn't write the Hon. Pen out of the script just yet.'

'If Mitch marries that upper-class tart,' said Chris, 'it'll be over my dead body.' He sounded as if he meant it.

At midday, Gloria left. Melissa watched the small red car bumping jerkily along the uneven track leading to the road, idly wondering if its cheerfully incompetent driver was ever going to learn clutch control . . . and whether it would be worth contacting her Stanley's auntie with the object of finding out if she had any more specific reasons for doubting the integrity of Vic Bellamy. She decided that it probably would not, closed the front door and made a determined effort to dismiss the whole thing from her mind for at least twenty-four hours. She succeeded to such good effect that by the time she switched off her word processor at five o'clock and crawled wearily into the kitchen to put the kettle on for tea, the plot of *Dancing with Death* had advanced by two red herrings and a dismembered corpse.

At seven o'clock, Kenneth Harris arrived. Once again, she was struck by the subtle change in him. The air of world-weary cynicism that had always seemed to cling round him like a worn garment had fallen away with the superfluous weight; his smile of greeting held none of its former mockery.

'You've got a new car,' she commented as he opened the door of the dark blue Rover. 'Are you pleased with it?'

'I suppose so, but I quite miss the old Ford.'

'Had you had it a long time?'

'Ten years. Isobel used to nag me incessantly to change it. She'll be livid when she finds out I did it the minute we parted.'

The words were spoken with a chuckle, but something in his manner made Melissa ask, 'Did it hurt much – losing Isobel?'

He showed no sign of resenting the question, but he did not reply immediately. At last, he said, 'I suppose no one likes being ditched for someone younger and better-looking, but if you mean, am I still in love with her, the answer's no.' He drew a breath and glanced sideways at her as if about to say something further, but changed his mind. They had reached the outskirts of Stowbridge before he spoke again.

'This place I'm taking you to has only been open since July. A French restaurateur came to the Cotswolds for a holiday, fell in love with the area and decided to stay. He bought an old manor house and called it, would you believe, *Le Vieux Manoir*. They say the food is out of this world.'

'"They" are absolutely right,' said Melissa a couple of hours later. She swallowed the last mouthful of strawberry mousse with redcurrant sauce and laid down her spoon with regret. 'That meal was so good, I wish we could go through it all over again.'

'No reason why we shouldn't,' said Harris, his eyes twinkling in a way she had never seen before. 'How about next Friday?'

'I meant now.'

'If that's a challenge . . .'

She laughed. 'And do irreparable damage to the new, boyish figure?'

'Would you like coffee?'

'Please.'

He gave the order, then leaned forward and planted his elbows on the table. 'Tell me,' he said, in a casual tone that put her on immediate alert. 'What did you mean by that crack about Heyshill Manor? Last night, when I asked where you'd like to eat,' he went on as she hesitated.

'Oh, that.' She did her best to sound equally casual. 'Well, it does have rather unpleasant associations.'

'And yet you've been staying there.'

She kept her eyes on the chocolate mint she was unwrapping and asked, 'Who says I have?'

'One of my officers was driving past yesterday morning and saw you waiting to come out. He mentioned it to me.'

'I wonder why.' She felt vaguely indignant, as if she had been kept under surveillance.

'I'm not sure I ought to tell you this in a public place.' The old mockery had crept back into his smile. 'What he actually said, leaving out the adjectives, was, "It looks as if that crime writer friend of yours is looking into the Foley case for us."'

'Well, of all the cheek!' She was on the point of pretending that she had merely called in at the hotel for mid-morning coffee on her way to Stratford, but decided against it. In certain circumstances, she could lie like a trooper with the best of them, but not to DCI Kenneth Harris, even when he was off duty. It was not so much a matter of scruple, as the impossibility of speaking anything but the truth in the face of his mind-reading gaze.

'I hope you haven't been doing anything foolish,' he said.

'I didn't know there was a "Foley case",' she countered

162

truthfully. 'Last time we spoke, you were careful to avoid suggesting there might be something suspicious about Will's death.'

'I'm still not suggesting that. We haven't had the results of the tests yet.'

'Then what's the problem?'

'If you remember, I warned you the other day that the Richard Mitchells of this world aren't always what they seem.'

Melissa thought of Mitch's insistence on running a clean ship, mentally contrasted it with Vic's suspicious behaviour, and came to a decision. 'Maybe not, and they aren't the only ones,' she said.

'Meaning?'

'Try this one for size. You remember my question about fitting a car with a dummy silencer?' He nodded. 'Know where I got the idea?'

'Surprise me.'

'Vic Bellamy.' She told him the story as far as Stumpy's change of heart, followed by the discovery that the second exhaust pipe had suddenly vanished from Vic's car. When she had finished, he thought for a moment and then said, 'Do you want any more coffee, or shall we go?'

'Let's go.'

'I didn't really mean to talk shop this evening,' he said when they were back in the car and heading for Upper Benbury. 'But as it's come up . . .'

'Well?'

'Do I have your word that what I'm going to tell you won't go any further, Mel?'

It was the first time he had used the contracted form of her name; immediately, it forged a bond between them.

'Of course,' she said.

'The officer I sent to Heyshill Manor to make a routine report on the accident to William Foley is what you might call an eager beaver. He noted that the cellar steps are steep and worn in places, that there was no guard rail across the

163

top and the door had been left unlocked. He also spotted one or two other examples where safety measures seemed a bit slipshod, and added a recommendation that the matter be referred to the Health and Safety Inspectorate.'

'And?'

'I passed the report – with a number of others – to my superintendent. It came back with an instruction to delete all references to a lack of proper safety precautions.'

'I see.' The implication of what he had just told her was enough to confirm what she already suspected: Vic Bellamy had powerful friends. 'It might interest you to know,' she added, 'that there is now a shiny new guard rail at the top of the cellar steps, and an instruction that it must be in place at all times when the door is unlocked.'

'That says it all, doesn't it? A friendly warning instead of a formal summons. No bad publicity, which would be unfortunate though not a disaster, but more important, less chance of the deceased's relatives bringing a successful claim for compensation.'

'I think,' said Melissa in a small voice, 'you're trying to tell me something.'

They had reached Hawthorn Cottage. The brass carriage lantern in the porch spread a pool of yellow light on the gravelled drive. Harris cut the engine and turned to face Melissa.

'Put it this way,' he said. 'It has been hinted that Victor Bellamy may have links with the criminal fraternity, but' – he tapped a forefinger on the steering-wheel by way of emphasis – 'it would take some pretty strong evidence to justify starting an enquiry. If you see what I mean.'

'Do I understand,' she asked, deliberately misunderstanding him, 'that'd you'd like someone to provide you with such evidence?'

'You understand no such thing.' His eyes glittered angrily in the lamplight. 'Don't spoil a pleasant evening Mel. Please, give me your word . . .'

'Oh, Ken.' She put a hand on his arm. 'Can't you tell when

you're having your leg pulled?' She leaned over and kissed him on the cheek. 'It's been lovely – thank you so much.'

'My pleasure.' Very gently, he cupped her face in one hand and kissed her on the mouth. 'Shall we do this again soon?'

'I'd like that.'

She waited while he turned the car round and waved as he drove away. She smiled as she let herself into the cottage, thinking how neatly she had avoided giving any inconvenient promises. And it *had* been a lovely evening.

Chapter Sixteen

Melissa awoke the following morning with the sense of well-being that arises from a pleasant evening, spent in congenial company and followed by a night of restful sleep. She lay for several minutes drowsing in the warmth of the bedclothes, recalling odd snatches of her dinner-table conversation with Ken Harris. For the first time, they had discussed matters far removed from crime and police work, ranging from sport to politics and taking in travel, the environment, organic farming and the funding of the arts on the way.

They had laughed, been serious, exchanged confidences. He had revealed how his youthful ambition to go to university had been frustrated by his father's death and the need to find a job; she had told him how a course in creative writing had revealed a latent talent for crime fiction. '

She smiled to herself, snuggling under her duvet, at the memory of how Ken's lumpy features had softened in sympathy on hearing of the tragedy that had left her with a fatherless son, and of the interest he had shown in Simon's work with an American oil company. Her smile faded a little as she remembered the regret in his voice when he spoke of Isobel's refusal to have children. 'Although it mightn't have been such a good idea,' he had said philosophically. 'Policemen don't always make the best of fathers.' She had swiftly responded, 'I'm sure *you* would have done,' and he had shrugged and changed the subject.

Altogether, Melissa reflected, a very enjoyable evening. It could mark the start of a rewarding relationship. Provided, she warned herself, things didn't get out of hand too quickly, as they had tended to do in the past. She should have learned that lesson by now.

Her mind moved on to the journey home, and thence to tonight's enterprise. Instantly, she was wide awake; her nerves tautened and her brain raced into top gear. What she and Chris were planning was, on the face of it, straightforward enough: a simple case of taking a look inside some rather suspicious premises – well, breaking and entering, if one were to be completely honest, but they did have reasonable cause to believe those premises were being used for something unlawful. Despite Ken Harris's protests, she was pretty certain that firm evidence against Vic Bellamy would not be unwelcome; if the matter was sufficiently serious, his influential connections could hardly protect him against a thorough investigation. On the other hand, if it was something that he could wriggle out of with the help of a clever lawyer, they would have taken the risk for nothing. And there was a considerable risk, she reminded herself . . . perhaps, after all, there was another way of tackling it . . .

'This,' said Melissa aloud as she threw back the duvet and set her feet groping for her slippers, 'is defeatist talk. Wasn't there some old card player who used to say, "When in doubt, win the trick"? That's what we'll do, win the trick. With a bit of luck, we'll win the rubber as well.'

In this positive frame of mind, she went downstairs. It was a pleasant morning, overcast but mild with only a light breeze. After breakfast, feeling the need for fresh air and exercise, she spent an hour in the garden, raking up fallen leaves and transferring them to the compost heap that Iris insisted she maintain. She was interrupted by the warble of the telephone.

Dittany was calling from Stowbridge library. 'That book you wanted about medieval witchcraft has come in,' she said.

'Oh, great. I'll call in and pick it up. What time do you close today?'

'Twelve o'clock.'

There was a flatness in the girl's voice that made Melissa ask, 'Is something wrong?'

'Why do you ask?'

'You sound a bit low.'

'I'm all right.'

'I'll see you presently, then.' Melissa put down the phone and went upstairs to change.

When she reached the library, she found Dittany seated in front of the microfiche viewer. Eric Pollard was bending over her, one hand on the table, speaking in a low voice. Dittany, her lips pressed together and her eyes fixed on the screen, shook her head. He put a hand on her arm and appeared to be pleading, but she flung it off and mouthed 'No' at him. Simultaneously, they saw Melissa approaching. Dittany switched off the machine and stood up to greet her; Eric, looking flushed and angry, brushed past with a curt nod.

'Have I come at an awkward moment?' asked Melissa.

'No, it's all right. I'll get your book.' Her face was pale, there were sooty smudges round her eyes and her smile, as she stamped the book and handed it over, was forced and lacking in animation.

'You don't look well,' said Melissa. 'Are you sure there's nothing wrong?'

Dittany drooped like a flower deprived of water. 'In a way there is,' she admitted.

'Would it help to talk about it?'

The girl fiddled with the electronic scanner. 'I don't want to bore you with my problems.'

'What are you doing this afternoon?'

'Nothing.'

Melissa had the feeling that tears were not far away. 'Come and have lunch with me,' she suggested. 'It won't be anything fancy, just some soup and cheese . . .'

Dittany's manner brightened a shade. 'I'd like that, thank you so much!'

They arranged to meet at the entrance to the car park.

When Melissa reached it after a visit to the supermarket and a prolonged browse in a bookshop, Dittany was already there. Apart from offering to help with the laden carrier-bags, she hardly said a word. They agreed that she would follow Melissa and she returned to her own car.

It was peak time for the morning shoppers to go home and Melissa had to wait for two or three minutes with her engine running while a stream of cars passed, most on their way to the exit, but a few looking for somewhere to park. Last in the line was the blue Renault.

It swung into an empty space close to where Dittany was parked and a middle-aged woman in a tweed suit got out, locked the door and headed for the footpath leading to the town centre. Without hesitation, her heart thumping with excitement, Melissa switched off the ignition, leapt out of the Golf and rushed across to speak to Dittany.

'You see that metallic blue car over there?' she said urgently. 'I have to find out who it belongs to. I can't explain now – just wait here.' Ignoring the girl's look of bewilderment, she hurried off in pursuit of the driver of the Renault.

The path led to a stone staircase and thence to a tunnel under the railway. By the time Melissa reached the top step, the woman was at the bottom and all but lost among crowds coming in the opposite direction. Almost deliberately, it seemed to Melissa, they fanned out across the width of the tunnel so that she had to thread her way between them, muttering excuses as she dodged push-chairs and bumped against bags of shopping.

At the far end, a second stairway emerged into a modern shopping mall, air-conditioned and temperature-controlled under a domed glass roof. In the centre was a circular atrium with a fountain surrounded by potted shrubs. A wrought-iron spiral staircase led to a balcony café, from which subdued chatter and a rattle of cutlery floated down. Young people in sweatshirts and jeans stood around in groups smoking cigarettes, scampering children were being pursued by harassed, scolding mothers, families hurried along or drifted in and out of shops clutching parcels – but nowhere could Melissa see the woman she was following. She stood staring round, gnawing her lower lip in frustration, when someone greeted her by name. She turned and found herself face to face with Lady Charlotte Heighton.

'Mrs Craig, how very nice to see you,' she said in her precise, pedantic voice. 'It was such a pity you were unable to attend our event last night.'

'How did it go?'

'Extremely well. We sold three model gowns and a number of separates.'

'That's good,' Melissa said politely, inwardly fuming at being thus hindered.

'Yes, an excellent result, was it not?' Lady Charlotte's small mouth, which in repose had a pinched look as if she were sucking a particularly sour piece of lemon, curved in a satisfied smile. 'I am sure the Stratford branch will prove an enormous success, thanks to Mr Mitchell's invaluable support. He and Penelope make a delightful couple, do you not agree?' The smile wavered and a frown puckered the smooth brow. 'Are you looking for someone?'

Melissa became aware that her gaze had been darting in all directions while the other woman was speaking. 'Please excuse me,' she said. 'I spotted a friend a few minutes ago and I wanted to speak to her, but I seem to have lost her.'

'How unfortunate. It happens so easily in a crowd, does it not? I do hope you find your friend.' With a gracious smile, Lady Charlotte went on her way.

With little hope now of any success, Melissa walked the length of the arcade, glancing in every shop as she passed, but everywhere she drew a blank. Ruefully, she retraced her steps; as she skirted the ornamental pool, she happened to glance upwards and her gloom vanished at the sight of the woman in the tweed suit descending the staircase from the café. Reaching the bottom, she made for the far exit, with Melissa following at a discreet distance. In a very short time, they reached a line of glass doors which gave on to the High Street in the old part of the town.

The woman turned left and crossed over. Her pace slackened; she paused once or twice to look in shop windows. Once she glanced round, as if checking to see if she was being followed, but Melissa, who had played this game before, had stayed on the opposite side. Eventually, she turned up a short alley leading to the churchyard, and entered a shop. Melissa waited for several minutes; when the woman did not emerge, she decided to investigate more closely.

The fascia-board above the shop bore the name 'Antony Purvis' in Gothic capitals and below it 'Antiques and Works of Art'. The centrepiece of the window display was an easel bearing a seascape in oils, mounted in an ornately carved and gilded frame. The maritime theme was echoed by a few smaller paintings of ships and a pair of bronze mermaids. A framed notice in one corner invited the passer-by to enter and browse with no obligation. Melissa pushed open the door and went in.

A man in a green corduroy suit was standing beside a desk talking to the woman Melissa had followed. She had removed her jacket and was evidently an employee, for in response to something he said, she replied, 'I have it here, Mr Purvis,' took a file from a drawer and extracted a letter which she handed to him. He studied it for a few moments, nodded and returned it saying, 'Thank you, Mrs Wilson,' before coming to greet Melissa.

'Good morning,' he said with a pleasant smile. 'Do you have any particular interest, or would you prefer to look round at your leisure? Our main gallery is upstairs.' With a slightly affected gesture he indicated a staircase in the corner.

His appearance was striking, almost theatrical. His collar-length grey hair fell in symmetrical waves on either side of aquiline features. When speaking, he inclined his head to one side and held the tips of his long, tapering fingers lightly

171

pressed together – rather like an actor playing a clergyman, Melissa thought.

'As a matter of fact,' she began. 'I was wondering . . . that is, I went to an exhibition in London a few months ago and I was very struck by some pictures by a French artist . . . nineteenth century, I think . . . I'm afraid I've forgotten his name. They were interiors . . . one was called *Le Goûter* and there was another of a girl making a bed . . .' She was ad-libbing, saying the first thing that came into her head, aware that she knew very little of what she was talking about and wishing she had studied more closely the catalogue Iris had shown her. 'I think the second one was called *La Chambre à Coucher*,' she continued, becoming a trifle desperate.

While speaking, Melissa had a feeling that Mrs Wilson was uneasy. Her colour had risen slightly and she began rummaging in a desk drawer – almost, it seemed, as if she was trying to hide her face.

Mr Purvis's smile lost none of its urbanity; on the contrary, as Melissa floundered on, it deepened to the point of condescension. 'Ah, yes,' he said smoothly when her store of improvisation ran out, 'would this be the exhibition at Butchers' Gallery last March?'

'I, er, don't remember exactly when it was . . .'

'I think you are probably referring to André Ducasse, sadly neglected during his lifetime and only recently accorded the recognition his work deserves. I am afraid all his known paintings have been snapped up by galleries or private collectors. They may occasionally be seen in exhibitions but very rarely come on to the market. If you admire his style, there are one or two canvasses upstairs which might appeal to you.'

Melissa was about to make an excuse and leave, then decided it would be prudent to keep up the pretence a little longer. She allowed Mr Purvis to escort her to the upper floor and made what she hoped were intelligent comments about the paintings he showed her.

'They're very interesting . . . perhaps I'll come back in a day or two and have another look at them,' she said. 'I must go now, I have an appointment . . . thank you so much for your help.'

Mr Purvis escorted her to the door and held it open for her. 'I look forward to seeing you again,' he said politely as she made her escape. She hurried back to the car park, where Dittany was still patiently waiting.

'Sorry to be so long,' she panted. 'That car . . . I've seen it before, driven by different people. At least I know now where to find one of them.' She glanced across to where the blue Renault had been left; the space was now occupied by a battered Ford Cortina. 'I don't suppose you happened to notice who drove it away?'

'I'm afraid not. Was it important?'

'I'm not sure. I think it may have something to do with what's going on at Heyshill Manor.'

'Really?' For the first time that morning, Dittany showed signs of animation. 'What makes you think so?'

'I'll tell you when we get home.'

When they reached Hawthorn Cottage, Melissa led the way to the kitchen and unloaded her shopping on the table. 'I don't know about you, but I could use a drink,' she said. 'How about a glass of wine?'

'Not when I'm driving,' said Dittany firmly. She accepted a glass of fruit juice and Melissa bustled about, putting things away. She put soup on the stove to heat and set out plates and cutlery.

'So what was all the excitement about the car?' asked Dittany.

Melissa took her time over slicing bread and unwrapping cheese, trying to decide how much she should reveal. 'It's all a bit vague at present,' she said. 'Chris and I have to do a bit more nosing around. We're not saying anything to Mitch just yet because we're not sure if we're on the right track. If I tell you, please don't mention it to him, will you?'

'I'm not likely to have the opportunity,' said Dittany glumly.

'Whatever do you mean?'

'I haven't seen him since Tuesday. We were supposed to be going out this evening but he rang last night and called it off.'

'Did he say why?'

'He was in Stratford yesterday for the opening ceremony at the new branch of Dizzy Heights and it seems the Honourable Penelope had organised a surprise theatre party for this evening. She sprang it on him in front of the people from the press – said it was to say "Thank you" for showing confidence in her business. He told me he didn't feel he could get out of it.'

'No, I don't suppose he could,' said Melissa. 'I saw her and her partner on Thursday in Stratford. They were talking then about tickets for the theatre and they spoke as if Mitch was to be in the party.'

'And he was in London with her on Wednesday night,' Dittany went on. 'He said it was a business dinner but . . .' She was looking sorry for herself again; she had taken out a handkerchief and was twisting it between her fingers, biting her lips and blinking as if trying to avoid the need to use it. 'She's determined to have him, I know she is.'

'Well, he's quite a catch and you can't blame a girl for trying,' Melissa pointed out, making her tone deliberately flippant although secretly she shared Dittany's doubts. 'But seriously, I'm sure you're more his type than she is . . . and so is Chris.'

'What makes you say that?' The threat of tears seemed to have receded for the moment. 'Did he say so?'

'He did. And he says he has no intention of allowing Mitch to fall into the Hon. Pen's clutches, so cheer up and come and have some lunch.'

'I don't want to be a wimp, but I was *so* looking forward to this evening . . .'

174

'I'm sure he was too. These things happen. High-powered tycoons like Mitch are always having to rush around to meetings and functions and boring parties.'

'That's what Eric keeps telling me. He spends all his time trying to convince me that I'll never stand the pace, and Mitch will get tired of me anyway.'

'Eric's pretty keen on you, isn't he?'

'I'm afraid so. He's a nice guy, but he's so *intense*. He wanted a commitment after only a couple of dates. I told him to back off but he's very persistent.' Dittany heaved a sigh. 'He says life in the fast lane soon gets boring.'

'I'm sure it's very exciting if you can take it – and put up with the snags. I remember when my son was at school, the headmaster was always banging on about taking the rough with the smooth.'

'Your son? I didn't know . . .'

One topic led to another, and it was over an hour later that Dittany said she really must be going, and in the same breath reminded Melissa that she had not yet explained her interest in the blue Renault or her pursuit of its driver.

'I think, on reflection,' said Melissa, 'I'd rather not say any more just yet – there may be nothing in it.'

But I'll bet there is, she said to herself as she watched her guest drive away. She was by now certain that the blue Renault, as well as Vic's own car, was being used to carry something both valuable and illegal. In a few hours, with any luck, she would know exactly what it was.

Chris rang during the afternoon to confirm their time and place of meeting. He listened in silence to her eager account of the incident that had led her to the premises of Antony Purvis. When she had finished, he dampened her spirits by remarking that it was interesting but didn't add much to what they already knew, and she hung up feeling deflated and almost ready to believe that even the evening's expedition would probably turn out to be a waste of time.

175

A short while later, she received a second call which made her think again.

'Just checking you're home and everything's okay,' said Iris.

'I came back on Thursday afternoon, and everything's fine.'

'Binkie all right?'

'Fast asleep on my bed.'

'Aah, bless him. Give him a kiss from muvver,' cooed Iris.

Melissa cringed, but countered with, 'How about you? Are you having a successful trip?'

'Very rewarding. Lots of contacts. Been to several galleries.'

'That's good. When are you coming home?'

'Tomorrow. Heard something yesterday that might interest you.'

'Oh?'

'Remember those reproduction paintings by Ducasse – the ones Kim Bellamy uses as door signs?'

'You mean, *La Chambre à Coucher* and so on?'

'And *Le Goûter* and *Le Salon*. Series of three.'

'What about them?'

'Loaned by a private collector in New York for an exhibition at Butchers' Gallery last March. Minor Post-Impressionists. Showed you the catalogue, remember?'

'I remember.'

'Never got back home.'

'What do you mean?'

'Crated up for shipment when the exhibition closed. Van hijacked and later found empty. Police reckon they were pinched to order.'

'And never recovered?'

'Seems not.'

'What an odd coincidence.' Remembering Mrs Wilson's reaction to her enquiry about the same paintings in Antony Purvis's gallery, Melissa's brain was busy with new possibilities. 'Would you have any idea how much they're worth?'

'Quite a lot. Not much of his stuff around. Last one I heard of went well into six figures at Christie's.'

'So for a series of three we could be talking about something like half a million?'

'Or more. Well, see you tomorrow.'

Iris hung up and Melissa sat down to decide if there was any significance in what she had just heard. There was no obvious reason to suspect a connection between the Bellamys and the theft of the paintings; there must be several hundred people besides Kim who had taken a fancy to them at the exhibition and bought reproductions. But, on the other hand, Mrs Wilson had appeared disconcerted when, quite off the top of her head as a pretext for entering Antony Purvis's gallery, Melissa had enquired about them. And Mrs Wilson had been driving the blue Renault. Which Melissa had seen before in slightly odd circumstances . . . and which had at least once spent some time in a garage very close to Heyshill Manor. A garage that Melissa and Chris were planning to break into in a few hours' time.

Chapter Seventeen

Chris backed the Jaguar through an open field gate a short distance from the hotel, on the opposite side of the road. He cut the engine and switched off the lights.

'Got your bearings?' he asked.

Melissa peered through the windscreen. 'I think,' she said after a moment's hesitation, 'we're about halfway between the hotel and the entrance to the quarry. The track runs at a sharp angle from the road; it's pretty well invisible as you drive past on that side.'

What remained of the moon was hidden beneath a heavy blanket of cloud. To their left, the hotel sign shone through the trees like a bright beacon beckoning to the passing traveller; to their right, the land on either side of the road was an undulating chequer-board of black and grey, relieved here and there by the light from a distant dwelling. The occasional car sped past, headlamps sweeping aside the darkness, receding taillights glowing like sparks in a dying fire.

'Is there some kind of barrier across the entrance?' asked Chris.

'Just an ordinary farm gate. It was open last time I was here – I suppose the driver of the Renault left it ready to come out. She was only in the garage for a short time.'

'It might be fastened with a chain. I'll take this, just in case.' He fumbled beneath his seat.

'What is it?'

'Bolt cutter. Easier than climbing about in the dark.' He made to open his door.

'Just a minute.' Melissa caught at his arm. 'We don't want to leave any traces of our visit.'

'What's it matter as long as they don't catch us?'

'It'll make them extra careful, maybe suspend operations for a while. Look,' she went on as he seemed unconvinced, 'all we're after tonight is proof that the garage is being used for something illegal.'

'Suppose we catch Vic Bellamy in there? We might get him to talk.'

It took her a moment to grasp his implication; when she did, she was appalled. 'There's to be no more rough stuff, do you understand? This isn't a commando raid, it's an intelligence-gathering operation. If we see anyone, we keep out of sight; if we find anything, we leave it where it is.' She could feel her nerves becoming taut, heard her voice growing harsher and more urgent.

Chris did not reply. She could sense his disappointment and frustration and almost sympathised; the notion of catching Vic red-handed with a sackful of stolen property and marching him off in triumph to the nearest police station was preposterous, but not without attraction. It was also impractical, highly dangerous and, even if successful, would bring the wrath of Ken Harris crashing round her ears like thunderbolts from Valhalla.

'There's more to this than you realise,' she said, as Chris remained silent. 'I can't explain, but if you don't give me your word, I'm pulling out . . . now.'

There was a pause before he muttered, 'If you say so,' and put the bolt cutter back.

Melissa could hear Khan moving around behind her, as if anxious to be up and doing. Chris was drumming his fingers on the steering-wheel; the rhythm seemed to keep time with the pounding of her heart.

'Okay,' he said at last. 'Let's get on with it. Mind how you go. I won't use the torch till we're off the road. If you see a car coming, duck out of sight. We don't want some clever dick telling the fuzz he's seen someone acting suspiciously.'

It crossed her mind to point out that there was nothing

particularly suspicious about a couple taking their dog for a walk, but she kept quiet. Chris was evidently feeling sore at being baulked in his plans for making a citizen's arrest and there was no point in unnecessary arguments.

They waited until the road was clear in both directions, then sprinted across and ran the fifty yards or so that she had calculated would take them to the track entrance, but she could see no sign of it. Her eyes had still not adjusted to the darkness; even Chris, clad like herself in black, was almost invisible.

'I think we must have gone past it,' she whispered.

'Maybe this guy'll show us.' In the distance, two pinpricks of light had appeared, rapidly growing in size and intensity. Melissa felt herself grabbed and pulled behind a tree. She cowered against the trunk as the car approached, headlamps blazing, heading straight towards them. Half blinded, for one terror-stricken moment she thought some drunken driver was about to run them down. She had forgotten the bend in the road; reaching it, the car swung away, receded and vanished.

'You're right, we had gone past.' Chris set off, back the way they had come. He had remained calm, taking advantage of the car's lights to determine their position; all she had done was cover her eyes and pray. She was going to pieces, she shouldn't have agreed to this, it wasn't too late to back out and tell Chris to go ahead on his own. Then she reminded herself of the treatment meted out to Stumpy. Even though she had played no active part in the violence, she could not entirely escape responsibility for what he had suffered. She owed it to him to do something to bring the perpetrators to justice. Gritting her teeth, she stumbled along behind Chris.

They found the entrance; within a few strides they came to a bank that shielded them from the road. There was barely enough light to distinguish the track itself from the tangle of undergrowth on either side. Chris switched on his torch, masked as before. The yellowish gleam picked out the heavy metal gate. It was open.

'Looks as if something's going on,' he muttered, switching off the torch. 'Keep to the edge of the track and be ready to duck behind the bushes.'

He crept forward, stealthily, pausing every two or three strides. Melissa could just make out his shape against the grey background of the quarry wall. Khan was keeping close; now and again she felt his body brush against her legs. They must be nearly there.

A few more steps and Chris came to an abrupt halt. A hairline of light betrayed the position of the garage door, only a few metres away. He reached out, drew Melissa towards him and put his lips close to her ear.

'Where's the best place to hide?' he whispered.

'There are some bushes . . . but you'll have to shine the torch or we'll never find them.'

'Too risky.'

'Then, close up against the wall, to the right of the door. I remember a clump of elder – we can get behind that.'

'You lead the way. Get a move on, I think they're coming out.' While they were speaking, the thin streak of light had disappeared and from inside the garage came the sound of a car door slamming. Trusting blindly to Providence, Melissa dashed forward; by a miracle, her outstretched hands encountered the ivy-covered wall. She inched sideways, groping, until they closed over rough branches. Blindly feeling her way, arms raised to protect her face from the invisible curtain of foliage, she caught her foot in a trail of bramble and stumbled, striking her shoulder against solid rock. She leaned against the wall with her eyes closed, waiting for the pain to subside, while her heart hammered in her chest like a demented woodpecker trying to get out.

'You okay?' whispered Chris as he eased himself into position beside her.

'Just about.'

'Don't move a muscle. Khan, stay.'

A succession of sounds indicated the garage door opening,

a car starting up, moving forward and stopping, followed by the garage door being quietly closed. Then a slight figure came into view, carrying a torch.

'Looks like a woman,' breathed Chris. 'Is it Kim?'

'Could be. Too dark to tell.'

Without lights, the car crept forward at a snail's pace, the woman walking ahead with the torch to guide it. In a few seconds, they had both vanished; soon after came a faint, metallic clang as the gate was closed and the noise of the engine faded as the car was driven away.

'We'll wait a bit, in case she comes back,' said Chris.

The minutes dragged by. Finally he said, 'She's been gone five minutes. Let's chance it,' and left their hiding-place, leaving Melissa to make her own way. She joined him in front of the garage door and found him examining it by the dim light of his masked torch.

'Piece of cake,' he said. 'Hold this.' He took from his pocket a bunch of small metal keys and, while Melissa shone the light on the lock, tried several before finding one that fitted. 'Okay, stand clear.'

The bottom of the door swung upwards. Holding it at shoulder level, Chris signalled to Melissa to duck underneath. Stationing Khan in the shadows with the command, 'Guard,' he followed her inside and eased the door downwards until the latch clicked shut.

He unmasked the torch and began a systematic, clockwise examination of the interior: first the floor, then the walls and finally the ceiling. He repeated the operation in reverse order, then a third time; with each successive sweep the beam moved faster and more erratically, reflecting the growing frustration of the searcher. Finally his hand fell to his side; in the ring of light thrown upwards from the bare concrete floor, the two sleuths exchanged glances of utter dejection.

Against the wall facing the door stood a set of shelves containing a small assortment of items a mechanic might use: spanners, an oil-can, an inspection lamp, a pair of heavy gloves and a heap of clean rag. On the floor beside it was a flat wooden pallet, mounted on castors. A set of overalls hung from a nail driven into the brick wall and beneath it was a scuffed pair of men's shoes. Otherwise, the place was empty.

'Shit!' said Chris. 'All that for nothing.'

Melissa shook her head in disbelief. 'It doesn't make sense,' she said.

'Huh!' Whether it made sense or not, Chris was clearly ready to admit failure. 'Might as well pack it in,' he said morosely.

'No, wait a minute.' From the moment she realised that nothing was stored in the garage, Melissa had begun to consider other possibilities. 'Chris, if you wanted to hide something worth thousands, maybe tens of thousands of pounds, would you keep it in here?'

'Why not? It's safe enough . . . out of the way . . .'

'And a doddle to break into,' she pointed out. 'All it took was a bunch of skeleton keys and a little know-how.'

'Yeah, well . . . there isn't anything, is there?'

'No, but we're pretty sure there has been at some time, aren't we? Where did it come from?'

'Must be kept somewhere else.'

'Then why isn't it collected from somewhere else?'

Chris shrugged. 'Search me.' He made a move towards the door but Melissa stayed where she was. Her mind had flown back to her walk with Mrs Clifford when, from their vantage point on the opposite side of the quarry, the two of them had deduced that the cloisters of the old priory originally extended beneath what was now the Bellamys' garden. The fact that all but the part now used as a cellar had been bricked up long ago, probably because it was unsafe, did not rule out the possiblity of a passage between the quarry garage and the existing building. It might have been unearthed during the renovations carried out by the previous owner, but never pointed out to Mitch when he bought the place.

The more she thought about it, the more feasible it seemed.

183

If someone had been using the passage when Dandie strayed on to the Bellamys' lawn, he might have sensed their movements. The closing of the garage door would be likely to set up vibrations in a confined space, easily detectable by a dog's keen ears. It was certainly a more likely explanation than the presence of ghosts. But if there was a passage, there had to be an entrance.

Chris was becoming restive. 'What're we hanging around for?' he demanded.

'Be quiet a moment, I'm thinking.'

'Oh, pardon me.'

'That pallet,' she said, ignoring the sarcasm in his voice. 'What do you suppose it's for?'

'To work under the car,' said Chris, in the manner a teacher might adopt before a class of five-year-olds. 'You lift it up on the jack, lie on the pallet . . .'

'I had figured that out.' Melissa kept her tone even. 'What I'm getting at is, how much car maintenance could you do with a couple of spanners and an oil-can?'

Chris scratched his chin. 'Not a lot,' he admitted.

'Exactly. No one's done any major car repairs in this garage; if they had, there'd be oil stains on the floor and loads more equipment. Doesn't that suggest anything?'

He shook his head. 'Search me,' he repeated.

'How do you suppose Vic – or whoever does it – inserts whatever it is into that gadget Stumpy fitted?'

Comprehension dawned. 'Of course, he'd have to get underneath the car.'

'Right. That's one question answered. Now why, I wonder, do they need so much shelving for half a dozen items? That thing must be at least six feet high.'

'Just happened to have it, I suppose.'

'I don't think so. Shine the light over here, will you? I want to take a closer look.'

The unit was constructed of painted metal, reinforced at the back and sides with solid panels, the whole mounted on

184

heavy-duty castors. Marks on the floor suggested that it had at some time been rolled or dragged to one side.

Melissa tugged at the front uprights, but the structure had a solid feel, as if it was screwed to the wall. She began groping among the things on the shelves; behind the pile of rags, she found a knurled nut and at the other end of the same shelf, concealed by a can of oil, was another. With a hand that trembled, she grasped one and gave it an anticlockwise twist. It turned easily.

'What the hell are you playing at?' demanded Chris.

'You'll see in a minute. Undo that other nut.'

'If you say so.'

He stood the torch on the floor and did as she asked, but she could tell from his manner that he considered the exercise a complete waste of time.

The nuts came away, leaving two bolts protruding through holes in the rear panel. Melissa tugged again at the framework; this time it wobbled slightly, but still did not budge. She glanced at Chris; the light, shining upwards on his pug-like features, gave an almost satanic quality to his expression.

'Stop smirking and give me a hand,' she said crossly.

With a shrug, he obeyed. After an initial resistance, the heavy structure rolled forward. When it was clear of the bolts they dragged it sideways, uncovering a heavy metal door.

'Well, bugger me,' said Chris. 'How did you work that one out?'

Melissa tapped her forehead. 'By using ze little grey cells,' she said sweetly.

'You what?'

'Oh, never mind.'

The door had a metal bar for a handle; Melissa grasped it and pressed it downwards, but it would not move. She tried pushing it upwards, with the same result. Chris, looking smug, silently jabbed a finger towards something that in her triumph she had missed – a small panel sunk into the brickwork at right angles to the door and bearing the digits zero to nine.

'And for your next trick . . .' he taunted her. 'You'll need a crystal ball to figure this one out.' His tone had a hint of mockery but she sensed that his disappointment was as keen as her own.

'The last time I saw one of these was in a hotel in France,' she said thoughtfully. 'It was on a small safe; there was one in every room. You had to make up your own six-digit combination and preset it.'

'What happened if you forgot the combination?'

'I did what most people do – used my own phone number to make sure I wouldn't.' A spark of hope flickered. 'I wonder if that's what's been done here.'

'You going to come back with a telephone directory?'

'I mean,' she said crushingly, 'perhaps they've used the number of the hotel. Do you know it?'

'Got it here.' He pulled out a notebook and held it to the light. 'It's 325400.'

'Right. Shine the torch over here, please.'

She punched in the digits; each one emitted an electronic bleep, but when she tried the handle it stayed firmly in place. She bit her lip in disappointment.

'I suppose it was too much to hope for – it would have been a bit daft to use such an obvious number. We could be here for a week and not hit on the right combination. At least,' she added philosophically, 'we can be sure there's something hidden in there. We'd better put everything back.'

They began to lug the shelving into place when Chris said, 'Try Vic Bellamy's private number – it's ex-directory.'

Melissa rolled her eyes to the ceiling. 'Now he tells me! Okay, what is it?'

He thumbed through his notebook again. '329133.'

Holding her breath, she tried again. As she depressed the final 3, there was a buzz and a faint click. She grabbed at the handle as if afraid it would vanish before her eyes and pulled it down. The heavy door swung open.

Chapter Eighteen

The first thing that struck them was the rise in temperature. In the garage, they had shivered; in here, the absence of chill made it feel almost warm. Some kind of floor covering deadened the sound of their feet. Chris swung the torch to and fro as they made their tour of exploration, treading slowly, almost holding their breath as if tiptoeing round a sleeping giant.

'My God,' breathed Melissa. 'I can't believe I'm seeing this.'

They were indeed in another part of the crypt. The torchlight revealed a double line of four-sided, whitewashed pillars, identical to those in the cellar and dividing the space into three aisles that ran longitudinally from the entrance. The slowly moving beam revealed that on every visible face of every pillar hung at least one and in some cases two or three paintings, many of them quite small; the walls were hung with larger pictures, some in antique gilded frames. Most were in oils, but there were a few water-colours; the subjects ranged from portraits, still-life studies and interiors to landscapes, street scenes and religious themes. Several, Melissa recognised as the work of famous artists; each one, she suspected, had formed part of a recently raided collection.

Along the centre aisle was a glass-topped showcase containing enough plunder to fill the treasure chest of a pirate in a fairy tale. As the torchlight glittered on gold and silver jewellery, ornaments and artefacts studded with precious stones, all neatly arranged, she murmured dazedly, 'There's a fortune here.'

'Vic Bellamy must run some racket to pay for this lot,' commented Chris. 'Wonder if he charges admission.'

Melissa gaped at him. 'Chris, don't you understand? This *is* the racket. I'll bet you a year's royalties that every piece and every picture is hot.'

'You reckon?' He rubbed his hands in glee. 'Cor, so we've cracked it! Wait till Mitch hears – he'll crucify Vic!'

'He'll do no such thing. This is a matter for the police, Interpol too, if Vic's been smuggling stuff out of the country in that false silencer.'

'It ain't big enough to hold that.' Chris nodded towards a painting of the Nativity, considerably larger than the rest.

'It might be, if it was taken out of the frame and rolled up, although I guess the gang have got more than one method of shifting their loot.' At the word 'gang', a chilly wave of apprehension ran through Melissa's body. 'We'd better get out of here,' she said. 'That electronic lock could be wired up to some sort of alarm signal.'

'Bloody hell, I never thought of that.' Chris was on his way back to the garage before she had finished speaking and she sprinted after him. They closed the door behind them, heard the buzz and click as the lock was activated, grabbed the shelving unit and shoved it back into position. In silence, with thumping hearts, they screwed back the knurled nuts, cursing when the threads failed to engage at the first attempt, hurriedly replacing the items that had hidden them.

'Let's hope there isn't a reception committee outside,' muttered Melissa. Her mouth was dry and her heart felt as if it would leap out of her throat as Chris slowly raised the outer door.

'Don't worry. Khan would have let us know,' he whispered.

'I hope to God you're right.'

There was no one there. Chris gave a soft whistle and the black shape came padding silently out of the shadows.

'On your way,' he hissed in Melissa's ear. 'If you hear anyone coming, make for cover, fall flat and cover your face.'

They were almost in sight of the gate when a flash of lights and the sound of an approaching car made them stop short.

'Hide!' said Chris in an urgent whisper but Melissa had already plunged into the undergrowth at the side of the track. She missed her footing and choked back a cry of alarm as she toppled sideways, landing heavily but unhurt in a dry ditch with Khan at her side. It was lighter now; the cloud had thinned a little and she had a momentary view of the soles of Chris's boots a yard from her nose before burying her face on her folded arms.

The car had stopped a short distance away, but they could still hear the engine running. There was a grating sound as the metal gate was unlocked and then it came on again in a rush, the wheels passing within a couple of metres of their hiding-place, flinging up loose gravel that fell in a gritty shower over them as it swept by. Moments later came the sound of the garage door being lifted. Melissa held her breath as the seconds ticked away; hearing a movement, she raised her head to see Chris peering over the edge of the ditch, cautiously parting the bushes. Then came a faint metallic clang as the door closed.

'They've gone inside. Run for it!' Chris leapt to his feet and led the way; Melissa scrambled up and raced after him. With Khan at their heels, they tore along the track, through the open gate and on towards the road. They reached it as a stream of cars approached from both directions; each second that they had to wait for an opportunity to cross seemed like an eternity. They ran like hares to where the Jaguar stood, half hidden in the field entrance, and all but fell inside. The engine roared as Chris sent the powerful car streaking away as if they were competing in a rally. It was several minutes before he spoke.

'Two men. One could have been Vic, but I didn't really recognise either of them.' After a pause, he added, 'One had a gun.'

'A gun?' In the act of massaging her bruised shoulder, Melissa stopped and shuddered. The villains in her books

189

usually carried guns, but she had never encountered them in real life and had no wish to. 'Are you sure?'

'Sure I'm sure.'

Once again, he fell silent, concentrating on the road. Every few seconds he glanced in his mirror, but there was no sign of pursuit. Melissa's pulse rate had almost returned to normal when the unexpected warble of the car phone sent it soaring again.

'Yeah?' Chris listened for a moment before saying, 'Sorry, boss. Me and Melissa have been kinda busy.' Another pause, during which she could hear faint, staccato barks coming from the receiver. 'Tell you later. I'll drop Melissa off and be with you in about forty minutes.' Another bark. 'Yeah, sure.' He handed Melissa the instrument. 'The boss'd like a word.'

She barely had time to get the receiver to her ear before he started speaking. 'Mel? What's been going on?'

'I'd rather not talk on the phone, if you don't mind. Where are you?'

'Having supper at some bloody awful restaurant in Stratford. Pen organised a theatre party. Shakespeare.' He made no effort to conceal the fact that he had not enjoyed the evening. She made a mental note to pass the news on to Dittany at the earliest opportunity, but for the moment, other matters were paramount.

'Can anyone overhear you?' she asked.

'No. You got something to report?' Excitement sent his voice rocketing up the scale.

'Mitch, listen carefully. When you go back to your friends, don't give the slightest hint that anything unusual's happened. Act absolutely naturally. All you've done is make a routine call to Chris, okay?'

'Sure, but . . .'

'We're on to something big.'

'Right, listen, Chris is coming to pick me up.' She pictured him, eyes laser-bright, thinking on his feet. 'You come too.

We'll drop Pen and her mates at their hotel, then we can talk on the way home.'

'Not a good idea. How would you explain me to the others?'

'That's a point. So when do we talk?'

'Tomorrow morning?'

'Stuff that, I wanna know right away. Why don't Chris 'n' me come back to your place tonight?'

Melissa glanced at the instrument panel; it took her a second or two to locate the clock among the array of dials. It was almost eleven. Hard to believe that all that action had been crowded into less than an hour. She looked out of the window and saw that already they were on the outskirts of Cheltenham. She might as well agree straight away as be badgered into it.

'All right. I'm nearly home now. You could be at Hawthorn Cottage soon after midnight.'

'Great. See you then.'

'Remember what I said – not a word, not even a hint, to anyone.'

'No, ma'am. See you later.' From being successively irritable, impatient and domineering, his tone suddenly dripped with honey. He had got his own way.

'Are you telling me I've got to let that bastard carry on running me hotel as if nothing's happened?' Hands in pockets, Mitch paced to and fro in Melissa's sitting-room like the proverbial caged animal. 'The man's a crook, he should be banged up . . .'

'You have no means of proving that Vic's involved in this,' reiterated Melissa for the umpteenth time. 'Everything I've told you so far is circumstantial and no policeman would arrest him on what we have to tell. You can't sack him without good reason. In any case, the last thing we want is for him to think anyone's on to him.'

'He'll have guessed by now that someone's been inside his Aladdin's cave.'

'He can't be sure. Chris and I left everything as we found it, so with any luck he'll assume it was a gremlin that set off his alarm system. It's not unusual, but he might change the combination, just to be on the safe side.'

'There must be some way we can get him.'

'Not us, the police.'

'But you said the fuzz won't touch him.'

'I said, he's got influential friends who can protect him from being pushed around on mere suspicion. When I tell Ken Harris what I've seen tonight, he'll take it seriously, I can promise you that – but he'll do things his way.'

'So what do you want me to do?'

'Absolutely nothing. Business as usual. There's a very sophisticated organisation running this lot and I doubt if Vic Bellamy is the brains behind it. It could be anyone; that's why it's vital to keep all this strictly to ourselves.'

'I guess you're right,' Mitch admitted grudgingly. Then his face broke into an unexpected grin. 'Perhaps it's the Hon. Pen. I'll bet half her clients are crooks – what a lark if she turns out to be the arch-villain!'

Melissa smiled. 'Stranger things have happened.'

'It beats me why there's no way into that hidden gallery from the hotel. Are you sure there isn't another door anywhere?'

'We didn't see one. The only way would be through the cellar, and they couldn't run the risk of its being spotted by someone working down there. They've got electricity, though – there's air-conditioning and lighting. It probably runs off one of the power points the other side of the wall.'

'And you didn't recognise either of the men who nearly caught you?'

'One may have been Vic, but we don't know for certain. We've no idea who the other could have been.'

'There's Des, the security bloke.'

'Did you employ him?'

'Nah. He came with the place.'

192

'You didn't vet him?'

'Never thought of it.' Mitch stopped pacing and stood on the hearthrug, chewing his lip. 'And what about poor old Will Foley? We still don't know how he died.'

'They haven't released the results of the tests yet,' said Melissa wearily. It was gone one o'clock in the morning, her shoulder was sore and it had been, one way and the other, an eventful day. 'Look, Mitch, Chris and I have told you everything that's happened, everything we've seen and heard. I've called my friend in the CID but all I got was his answering machine. As soon as he gets the message, he'll call back – I've told him it's urgent. Once I've spoken to him, he's bound to want to talk to you.'

'Yeah, well, I'll be around till Monday evening, then I'm off to New York for a couple of days. Like you said, it's got to be business as usual.'

There was another silence. Mitch stared moodily at the floor. Chris sat in an armchair with his arms folded, his face expressionless. Melissa stifled a yawn and began gathering up empty coffee-cups. Khan, stretched out beside her chair, lifted his head and followed her with his eyes.

'I suppose we'd better be going,' said Mitch. 'It doesn't look as if your copper's going to call back tonight.'

'No,' agreed Melissa, thinking that it was just as well. She was not looking forward to confessing her escapade to Ken Harris and the last thing she wanted was to do it before witnesses.

Mitch picked up Chris's coat and threw it across to him, then put on his own. Chris took the car keys from his pocket and made for the door. 'Khan, heel,' he commanded.

The dog sat up, looked first at Melissa and then at Chris. He gave a soft whine, but stayed where he was.

'C'me on, don't sod me about.' Chris snapped his fingers. Reluctantly, Khan got to his feet, followed as far as the front door and stopped, whining again.

'What's up with him?' Mitch grasped the studded leather

193

collar and tugged. Khan resisted, sitting back on his haunches.

'He doesn't seem to want to go home,' said Melissa, trying not to sound impatient, wishing they would all leave and allow her to go to bed.

Khan most certainly did not want to go home. They managed to coax him outside, but when Chris held open the rear door of the car he backed away. He stood for a moment with pricked ears, then put his nose to the ground and began running to and fro, growling softly.

'Something's upset him. Maybe there's a prowler around,' said Mitch. 'You're pretty isolated here, Mel. Don't you ever get jumpy?'

'I'm not the nervous type, and anyway I normally have Iris next door.' She tried to sound unconcerned, but the dog's strange behaviour was beginning to make her feel uneasy.

'Tell you what, why don't we leave him with you for tonight? He seems to want to stay.'

'Thanks, I'd like that.' Until that moment, she had been unwilling to admit, even to herself, that she was growing more edgy by the minute. It was irrational and idiotic, probably caused by the excitement of the evening combined with sheer exhaustion, but none the less disturbing.

'That's settled, then.' They all went back indoors while Chris gave Melissa instructions on feeding. She assured him that there was meat in the freezer and that the village shop, which opened on Sunday mornings, had a good supply of dog biscuits. At last, the men departed, leaving her free to lock up.

'There's going to be fireworks when Binkie shows up in the morning and sees you,' Melissa informed her new companion. 'And I can't wait to see Iris's face. Now, where are you going to sleep?'

Khan seemed in no hurry to sleep anywhere. He accompanied her while she checked all the windows and doors and turned off the downstairs lights, sniffing round every room as if he were the gas-man checking for leaks. Melissa, yearning for her bed, was becoming impatient.

'Come on, boy, settle down, will you?' She started up the stairs but the dog did not follow. Instead, he stood by the front door, ears pricked, hackles raised. 'What is it, boy?' she whispered. 'Is there someone out there?'

Khan began scratching at the door, whining softly. Melissa could hear nothing, but the dog's teeth were bared in a snarl and a soft growl rumbled in his throat. Hardly daring to breathe, she stood still and listened.

For several seconds there was silence, followed by faint sounds as if someone was tiptoeing along the grass verge that bordered the drive to the cottages. A ripple of fear ran through her. She thought of what had happened to Stumpy's caravan and the ripple built up into a wave, threatening to turn into blind panic.

The sounds came closer, then stopped. Her groping fingers found the torch that she kept in readiness against possible power failures; she must act swiftly, catch whoever was out there off guard. Muttering, 'Go for it, Khan,' she switched on the torch and flung open the door.

She heard a gasp of alarm as the beam fell on a helmeted figure in jeans and bomber jacket, holding in one hand something that glinted in the light. Then Khan sprang; there was a yell of mingled pain and alarm and, with a thud and a tinkle of breaking glass, the intruder landed flat on his back, one arm firmly clamped between the nutcracker jaws, the other making futile efforts to beat the dog off. Fragments of a shattered milk bottle littered the driveway and the pungent odour of petrol hung in the air. From somewhere not far away came the spluttering roar of a motor-bike starting up and driving away at speed.

Melissa shone her torch on the intruder's face. He was a hollow-cheeked youngster with a wispy moustache and untidy locks of mousy hair straggling beneath the helmet.

'What's the game?' she demanded.

The youth screwed up his eyes, blinking and twisting his head to and fro in his efforts to avoid the powerful beam. 'Call off the dog, miss,' he pleaded. 'I won't give no trouble, honest.'

'He won't hurt you if you lie still. Was that your mate making off on the bike?'

'Yeah, the rat.'

'Who sent you?'

'I dunno what you're talking about.'

'We'll see about that. Was it just the two of you?'

'That's right. Please, miss, call 'im off.'

'Stand up slowly and don't get any ideas about running away or he'll tear your arm off. Khan, leave!' She had no idea if the threat had any substance, but it had the desired effect; as Khan obeyed, the lad struggled to his feet and stood, stock-still and trembling, waiting for orders.

'Right. Inside!' With a gesture of the torch, she marched her prisoner into the kitchen and told him to sit down and remove his helmet and boots.

'What's your name?' she demanded.

'Clegg,' he muttered. He cut a sorry figure in his shabby jeans and cheap jacket; his hands were trembling and his eyes blinked incessantly as if he was trying to dislodge a speck of grit. He was none too clean; already, Melissa was thinking that making him remove the boots had not been a good idea.

'Let's try again. Who told you to fire-bomb my house?'

Clegg's eyes seemed to glaze over; it was as if a shutter had come down. 'Dunno what you're talking about,' he repeated sullenly.

'Okay, you can explain to the police. Khan, guard!' She went to the telephone.

The bell rang several times before a sleepy and disgruntled Ken Harris answered. 'Mel! For God's sake, couldn't it have waited . . . *what*?' She heard a creak and a thud as he leapt out of bed. 'How many?'

'Two. One escaped on a motor-bike. I've got the other here.'

'Are you sure you're okay?' The concern in Harris's voice gave her a momentary, quite unexpected pleasure.

'Don't worry, I'm fine.'

'I'll send a patrol car, and I'll be along myself as quick as I can.'

'No need to bust a gut. He can't get away.' She glanced at her bare-headed, bootless prisoner, still apprehensively eyeing the watchful Khan, and was amazed at how calm she felt. 'Oh, and look out for your tyres. There's broken glass all over the place.'

Chapter Nineteen

'Well, well, Blinker Clegg. Bit off your patch, aren't you?' The uniformed constable's tone held the mild surprise of one meeting an old acquaintance in unexpected circumstances, but there was nothing friendly in his expression as he stared down at Melissa's prisoner.

'Out for a bike ride with me mate, wasn't I?' said Clegg.

'You usually take a bottle of petrol when you go biking, do you?' Beneath the mildness, the voice had a sharper edge. 'Emergency supply, in case you run out on a lonely road?'

'What's all this about petrol?'

'You tell me.'

Clegg shifted on his chair, eyes darting here and there beneath fluttering lids. Khan, now seated protectively at Melissa's side, watched his every movement. She had experienced an anxious moment when the police arrived, wondering if the dog would accept her assurance that they were friends, but he had behaved like a lamb. Now she was sitting as far away from the malodorous Clegg as the small kitchen would allow while Constable Driver put his questions.

Clegg's gaze came to rest on a hole in his left sock.

'Lost our way, hadn't we?' he mumbled. 'Saw the light and came along to ask. Next thing, that bleeding dog had me on the ground.'

'After hitting you with the bottle?' Driver pursed his lips and shook his head. 'Come on, Blinker, you can do better than that.'

'I never had no bottle, honest. There must have been someone else prowling around.'

'You're dead right there. Who was with you?'

'Just a mate.'

'A mate with no name?'

'Met him in a pub, didn't I?'

'You can tell us about him later. Aha, what've you got there, Hodson?' A second officer, who had been searching outside, came in at that moment with a transparent plastic bag in his hand.

'There it is,' he said. 'Primed and ready to throw.'

Driver took the bag, glanced at the contents, sniffed, and then held it out for Melissa to see. 'You know what this is, don't you, Madam?'

She breathed in and swallowed, doing battle with the contortions in her stomach at the whiff of petrol and the sight of the shards of glass, jagged peaks where the base of the bottle had broken off, the neck still intact and plugged with a piece of cloth from which trailed a strip several inches long. The realisation of what a narrow escape she had had was like a punch in the solar plexus.

'If that fuse had been alight when the dog brought him down, all three of you might have copped it,' Hodson said grimly.

'Yes, I know,' she whispered.

He gave her an anxious glance. 'Are you feeling ill, Madam? Can I get you some water?'

'It's all right, thanks, I'll be okay.'

Driver held the bag up to the light, turning it this way and that and peering at the contents as if they were goldfish swimming in a bowl. 'Any chance of finding your prints on this little lot, Blinker?' he asked.

'I keep telling you . . .'

'Save it. I'm arresting you on suspicion of loitering near private property with intent to commit arson . . . and possibly murder.'

At the word 'murder', Clegg looked up at him in terror, eyelids madly vibrating, hands clutching the edge of his chair. 'No . . . no!' he gasped. 'You . . . you've got it all wrong. It was only . . . I mean, he promised we weren't going to hurt no one . . .' He broke off and clapped a hand over his mouth, realising that he had said too much.

'I'm sure we're very glad to know that,' said Driver silkily. 'You can tell us who "he" is and exactly what you *were* going to do, down at the station.'

'By the way, there's a nice tyre print in some mud at the end of the drive,' said Hodson. 'Unusual moulding – shouldn't be too difficult to trace.'

'Splendid,' purred Driver. 'We wouldn't want Blinker to take *all* the blame, would we?' He looked down almost benevolently, like a schoolmaster with a penitent pupil, at the sorry figure in front of him. Melissa half expected him to pat Clegg on the head.

The proceedings were interrupted by a growl from Khan, whose keen ears had detected what the others heard moments later – the sound of an approaching car.

'That'll be Chief Inspector Harris,' said Melissa, in response to Driver's questioning glance. 'I was trying to contact him on another matter when . . . this happened. It's all right, Khan – another *friend*,' she added as Hodson went to the door in response to Harris's knock.

The big detective looked weary and unshaven. He greeted Melissa formally, addressing her as Mrs Craig, and immediately took charge, fixing Clegg with his characteristic, unwavering gaze while the two uniformed officers made their report. There was a hard set to his features as he was shown the remains of the bottle, and suppressed anger in his voice as he said, 'Take him down to the station and get what you can out of him. I'll talk to him later, when I've had a chat to Mrs Craig.'

He followed the three men out to the car, still giving instructions. When he came back, Melissa was leaning out of the open window, drawing in gulps of fresh air.

'What was the idea of getting him to take his boots off?' he asked, grinning.

She felt suddenly foolish. 'Er, I suppose, to stop him running away.'

'I think *he*' – Harris nodded towards Khan, relaxed now and happily snoozing in front of the Aga – 'could have taken care of that. You know your trouble, Mel? You read too many detective novels.'

She gave a watery smile, closed the window and slid on to a convenient chair. 'If I did what you're always telling me to do, stick to writing them, this wouldn't have happened, would it? That's just to save you the trouble of saying it,' she added quickly.

His manner was unusually gentle as he said, 'You look all in. Why don't I make a hot drink? I could use one as well.' He was already at the sink, filling the kettle. 'What'll it be – tea or coffee?'

'Tea, please.'

'You were trying to contact me earlier, before your visitor turned up. Were you expecting him?'

'Oh, no. It never entered my head . . . although I should have been more careful, after . . .' This wouldn't do; she must explain things coherently, in the right order.

'Where d'you keep the cups and saucers?'

'In the top cupboard. You'll have to open a fresh bottle of milk.'

'Got them. Right, go on with what you were saying. Come on, Mel,' he said, as she hesitated. 'I know you've got something to tell me. After what?'

'After what happened to Stumpy Dart.'

'Stumpy?' Harris spooned tea into the warmed pot and poured on boiling water. 'You said you thought he'd been warned off, but . . .'

'I'm talking about the second warning. His caravan was burned out some time on Wednesday night or early Thursday morning.'

Harris froze in the act of pouring milk into teacups.

'I don't remember seeing a report.'

'He didn't report it.'

'So how come you know about it?'

'I went to see him on . . . after it happened. It was so sad.'
She had a momentary vision of Stumpy, crushed, bewildered
and terrified as he contemplated the wreckage of his home.
'The van was just a shell.'

'Did he say it had been fire-bombed?'

'Did he hell. He insisted the fire had been caused by an
exploding gas bottle, but I was certain he wasn't telling the
truth. He was scared witless.'

'But not hurt?'

'No. I guess they must have lured him outside first.
I imagine those two jokers who came here tonight were
planning to do the same. It wasn't a murder attempt, just a
warning.'

'Why would they feel a second warning was necessary, I
wonder?' Harris's tone was reflective, but she knew it was all
part of his technique. He was waiting for her to supply the
answer. He put the two cups of tea on the table and sat down
opposite her. 'From what you told me on Friday, he'd already
got the message.'

'Yes, well, I'm afraid I wasn't being exactly straight with
you.'

'I rather gathered that. So now you're going to tell me what
you've been up to, to merit a similar warning.' His voice was
ominously quiet. He shovelled sugar into his tea and stirred
it, slowly and deliberately, not taking his eyes off her for a
second.

She recalled the expression Mitch had used when speaking
of Will Foley: 'like he could see the inside of your skull'. This
was the moment she had been dreading. She picked up her
cup, took a sip of tea, put it down again, looked at her watch,
fidgeted with the spoon – anything to avoid meeting that
unnerving gaze.

'Well?' said Harris, in the patient tone of one who has
unlimited time. 'I'm waiting.'

'You remember I told you I went to see Stumpy Dart about that dummy silencer?' she began.

'I remember.'

'He denied all knowledge of it, but I was sure he wasn't telling the truth, so Chris and I went back to his workshop later that night to look for it. Then Stumpy found us. There was a bit of an argument' – Melissa had made up her mind that she was not going to go into details that might land Chris in trouble – 'but we insisted we only wanted to see it, not take it away, so he agreed to show it to us. He told us all he knew about the man he'd made it for – he swore he hadn't given his name, but we're sure it was Vic. He also mentioned a woman driving a blue Renault that we thought might be Vic's wife, Kim.'

'You've seen Kim in a car like that?'

'I've never actually seen her driving any car, but it seemed logical.'

'All right, I agree everything points to them, but you can't prove any of it, can you?' Harris's voice was dry and matter-of-fact, pointing out the fundamental weakness in her case.

'We can't *prove* anything – that's what I've been trying to get through to Chris. If we'd come up with one piece of real evidence, I'd have been on to you like a shot.'

'But you reckon you found some tonight?'

'Yes.'

'All right. Go on.'

The next part of the story was straightforward and told without interruption: her encounters with Mrs Clifford and the 'ghostly' emanations that had upset Dandie; the walk that had led to the discovery of the quarry garage; the pursuit of the blue Renault and its handover in the multi-storey car park in Stratford-upon-Avon; her subsequent call on Stumpy in the hope that he might recall some details of the car that had accompanied Vic Bellamy and her horror at seeing the wrecked caravan.

At this point, Harris interposed with a question. 'You said

you thought Bellamy or his wife must have listened in on your telephone call to Stumpy and warned him not to tell you anything. How do you suppose Bellamy – if it was Bellamy – found out about your second visit?'

'He must have seen the mud on my shoes, guessed where I'd been and gone back to the workshop himself to find out what had been going on. I suppose Stumpy admitted he'd told us all he knew and it was decided he needed a sharper lesson, to make sure he wouldn't tell anyone else. The police, for example.'

'And later, it was decided to teach Melissa Craig not to poke her nose into what didn't concern her.' Something that might have been anxiety flickered across the impassive features.

Melissa stared down into her empty cup. 'I guess so. Vic must be a pretty ruthless man.'

'Go on with the story – I take it that isn't the end?'

'Not quite.' She told of her second encounter with the blue Renault and her visit to the premises of antique dealer Antony Purvis. He made a few notes and interposed the occasional question, without showing any particular reaction.

'That brings me to tonight. It was real cloak-and-dagger stuff.' She made a conscious attempt to sound light-hearted and risked a half-smile; he responded with a frown and a tightening of the mouth that said, as plainly as words, 'Just get on with it, will you?' He looked exhausted; she felt a pang of guilt, remembering that he must have been out late on another case and that she had dragged him out of bed. She herself had gone through the fatigue barrier; an hour or two ago she had been ready to drop, but now she was alert, the adrenalin flowing strongly as she recalled the episode in the quarry garage.

'There isn't much more,' she said.

As she described the night's adventure, his expression went through a series of changes that she later described to Iris as 'like a pan of stew coming to the boil'. Quickening interest fused into alarm and incredulity as she explained how they had stumbled on the correct combination and opened the concealed door. When she revealed what lay behind it, he sat for several seconds, open-mouthed and speechless. His eyes widened in horror and his normally ruddy features became almost purple as she went on to tell how near they had come to being caught.

'Will you never learn, Melissa?' he exclaimed in a voice thick with emotion. 'You might have been killed!'

'Well, I wasn't, was I?' She felt better now that it was over. 'And I have taken the lid off a big art scam, haven't I? Don't I get even one Brownie point?'

'Brownie point? Of all the nerve . . . !' He thumped the table with his fist, sending the cups dancing on their saucers. They both heard a movement as Khan sat up, alert and watchful.

'I'd keep calm if I were you. He's very protective of me,' said Melissa demurely.

'What you need is protection from yourself,' retorted Harris. He drummed on the table with large, powerful fingers, his lips compressed, his expression grim. 'These people are dangerous and they're playing for big stakes. If you'd been caught in that place, I doubt if you'd have got out alive.'

'You knew about this already?'

'We've known for a while that there's a sophisticated ring of art thieves working the area. Private collections as well as museums and galleries have been looted, antique dealers' shops raided – you read the *Gazette*, you've seen the reports. The stuff's been vanishing into thin air and we reckon a lot of it's been pinched to order and probably goes abroad. We've been making enquiries for months and getting nowhere . . . it's as if there's a conspiracy of silence . . . and you sit there and calmly tell me how *you've* taken the lid off "a big art scam".' In sheer exasperation, he dug his fingers into his scalp and tugged at his thatch of iron-grey hair. 'Melissa, I could shake you!'

'Sorry, did I shoot your fox?' It hadn't been such an ordeal after all; in fact, she was beginning to enjoy herself. 'Shall I make some more tea? Or could you use something stronger?'

'No, thanks. I'll go now and we'll talk again tomorrow. I need time to think this over.' With a wary eye on Khan, he stood up. 'Mel, it looks as if you may have uncovered the lead that's been eluding us, but I'm warning you, keep out of it from now on. For your own safety, first and foremost, but any wrong move now could louse things up. I'll want to talk to you again, and to your Mr Mitchell, to make sure he and this fellow Bright don't get any more clever ideas.'

'Oh, Chris doesn't have ideas – well, not often,' said Melissa reassuringly. 'And I've already warned Mitch not to breathe a word to anyone. He's promised not to, but he's bursting to see you.'

'I expect to give him that pleasure very soon.' At the door, Harris lingered for a moment. 'After tonight, whoever was behind the attack will assume you've told us all you know so there'd be no point in having another go at you. Just the same, if you're scared at being left on your own . . .' She waited for him to finish but he left the remark hanging in the air. For a moment, the official policeman's mask had slipped, revealing a man who was unsure of himself, almost embarrassed.

'I'll be fine,' she assured him. 'I have Khan to look after me.'

'Yes, of course.' It was difficult to say if he was relieved or disappointed. 'I'll give you a call in the morning, after I've interviewed Clegg.'

'I'll be here.' She felt certain he had been on the point of offering to stay with her, and wondered how she would have reacted if he had.

Chapter Twenty

'I want to make it clear at the outset,' said Detective Chief Inspector Harris, 'that nothing, *nothing at all* of this conversation is to be mentioned outside these four walls – not even the fact that it took place. We're up against some very clever people and we want to keep them in the dark as far as we possibly can.'

The walls in question were those of the sitting-room of Mitch's country home. It was Sunday morning; Mrs Wingfield had served coffee and withdrawn to the kitchen to prepare lunch. Melissa sat beside Mitch on a sofa facing the fire and the two dogs lay at their feet. Chris had made for his usual seat in the corner, but Harris, with a great show of affability, had insisted that he move closer to the others. This he did with obvious reluctance; knowing his history, Melissa suspected that he was not entirely at ease in the presence of the law.

As usual, Harris had settled on an upright chair, from which he now surveyed his small audience, a notebook on his knee and a pen in one hand. Observing him, Melissa thought afresh how much better he looked without the surplus pounds. One could never describe him as handsome, of course, but now he'd lost some of that heaviness round the jowls . . . She jerked her mind back to the matter in hand as he reiterated the need for confidentiality and they all nodded vigorously, impatient for him to proceed.

'From what Mrs Craig told me last night, it seems she and Mr Bright may have located the hiding-place of a quantity of stolen property,' he began. 'If that is the case . . .'

'Hang on a minute,' said Mitch. 'Why "if"? There can't be

any doubt about it. I always knew Vic Bellamy was up to no good – I had this gut feeling, didn't I, Chris? – so why don't you just go in and nick him?'

'Mr Mitchell, I accept that there is good reason to suspect Bellamy, and I compliment you on your perspicacity, but it isn't quite as simple as that.' Harris's tone was mild and Melissa was impressed by his diplomacy, but she sensed his irritation at the interruption.

'Okay, so what's the problem?' Mitch demanded.

'In a nutshell, we have no proof at the moment that any of the pictures or other items in that gallery are stolen.'

'Oh, come on. Why would anyone stash stuff away with all that security, if it wasn't hot?'

'Vigilant owners often go to considerable lengths to protect their belongings against thieves.'

'You trying to tell me that's Vic's private collection, and all legit?' Mitch's face registered the incredulous dismay of a pools fan who has filled in a winning line but forgotten to post his coupon.

'You may find this hard to believe, but it could very well be *someone's* private collection, although I doubt if it belongs to Bellamy. There are plenty of eccentric characters in the art world, and some very wealthy ones.'

'Do they go round chucking fire-bombs?'

'Can you prove there's a connection?'

'Oh, for God's sake! Go look for yourself, why don't you? Take an expert who could tell you what's been pinched and what hasn't . . .'

'Mr Mitchell!' For the first time, Harris betrayed a hint of impatience. 'Kindly allow me to point out a few difficulties of which you seem to be unaware. Firstly, to search that garage, we need a warrant. In the circumstances, we'd probably get one but it's by no means certain. Assuming we did, and everything in it was clean, we'd end up with egg on our faces. Of course, if we *were* to find stolen property there – and I'm inclined to agree with you, sir, that it's very likely – the owners would be happy . . . but we wouldn't necessarily be any nearer knowing who's behind the thefts.'

'Arrest Bellamy, then – make him talk.'

'On what charge? There's a little thing called the Police and Criminal Evidence Act. It's not so simple to arrest people on suspicion nowadays.'

Mitch was not going to give up easily. 'How about "inviting him to assist you with your enquiries" – isn't that what you call it?'

'That could very well be counter-productive, by putting him and the people behind him on their guard. In any case, from what Mrs Craig has told us, it might be difficult to establish a direct link between Bellamy and that concealed gallery.' Harris turned to Melissa. 'You did say there's no connecting door with the hotel cellar?'

'I'm almost certain there isn't. Vic went out of his way to let me have a good look round. It was all done as if in response to Mitch – Mr Mitchell's – request to show me the oldest parts of the building, but I can't believe he'd have been so open about it if he had something to hide.'

'Mr Bright, you had a glimpse of the two men who turned up just as you were leaving the quarry. Could you swear that one of them was Bellamy?'

Chris shook his head. 'I said, it could have been him. He was the right build.'

'You claimed one of them had a gun. How well could you see?'

'Got a glimpse of it in the car lights.'

'Then what did you do?'

'Waited till they went inside the garage and ran like buggery – we all did.'

'All?' Harris's forehead crinkled.

'Me, her and him.' Chris gestured at Khan.

'Ah, yes, the dog. So you caught the briefest glimpse of something that in near-darkness *looked* like a gun, but could perhaps have been a torch, or even a two-way radio.'

'Here, whose side are you on?' demanded Mitch.

'I'm trying to point out the flaws in the evidence we have so far, and what any solicitor worth his salt would make of them,' said Harris with what Melissa felt was admirable patience.

'It's what I've been saying all along,' she said quietly, as Mitch sat back looking glum.

'Are you telling me you're just going to sit there and do nothing? After all Mel – Mrs Craig – and Chris have done to uncover this scam?'

'I'm not saying anything of the kind. We have a very promising lead, but from now on we handle things our way. There's to be no more private investigation – understood?'

'Yeah, okay.' Mitch looked marginally happier, although it was plain that he had expected more immediate and more dramatic developments. 'So what happens next?'

'I'd like you to tell me how you came to acquire Heyshill Manor. I understand it belonged to the late Sir Hugo Stoneleigh-Pryor – how soon after his death did the executors of his estate put the property on the market?'

Mitch's mouth spread in a wide, dimpled grin. 'It never came on the open market. I happened to be staying in the hotel when old Sir Whatsit kicked the bucket. I got me spies working straight away, contacted his solicitor and told him I wanted to buy it.'

'I see.'

As if sensing a hint of disapproval in Harris's tone, Mitch was quick to jump to his own defence. 'I know what you're thinking, indecent haste and all that. Let me tell you, Chief Inspector, I didn't build up me empire through hanging about and letting others get in first. I want something, I go after it. I never play dirty though – that's right, innit, Chris?'

'Right,' said Chris.

'I'm sure that's true, sir,' said Harris. 'Please go on.'

'The sole heir to the estate and executor to the will was old

Sir Whatsit's elderly sister. I made me offer, the solicitor passed it on, and she asked to see me.'

'That was unusual, wasn't it?'

'She's an unusual old girl. A bit potty, in fact. She told me the two of them didn't see eye to eye on a few things, and one of them was the colour of blood. He reckoned theirs was bluer than yours or mine.' Mitch's eyes sparkled; he was like a schoolboy imitating his headmaster as he continued in an exaggeratedly 'upper class' accent. ' "Ay was *awfully* fond of may brothah," she says, "but he reahly was the most *fraitful* snob. He'd have simply *hated* the thought of the manah going to someone *common*." ' He rubbed his hands together, chuckling. 'That's why she sold it to me – 'cos me Dad was a coster-monger. Good joke, innit?'

'The lady must have quite a sense of humour,' agreed Harris, without a trace of a smile. 'So there were no hitches – the sale went through smoothly?'

'Not quite. Her solicitor informed mine that someone else was after it, with a better offer. I said I'd match it, but it turned out the old girl wasn't interested – she'd made up her mind to sell to me and that was that. So the other party upped his offer, with the same result.'

'Have you any idea who the other party was?'

'The solicitor wouldn't say, although Mr Medway and I had the impression he was keen for me to back out. Maybe there was something in it for him if he'd been able to persuade me to let go. After the deal was completed, he tried again – said some consortium had put up an offer I'd be mad to refuse, but I told him they could stuff it.'

'Mr Medway is your solicitor?'

'Right.'

'I'd like his address, please.'

'I'll look it out for you. Anything else?'

'If I could have a look at the drawings and surveyors' reports on the building some time . . . ?'

'You can see them now.' Mitch got to his feet, plainly

211

anxious to co-operate in every possible way. 'You've seen them already, Mel – you want to stay here and have more coffee, or a drink?'

'If you don't mind, I'd prefer Mrs Craig to come with us,' said Harris.

'As you like.'

Mitch led the way to his office and spread the documents on the table. On the plan of the cellar, Melissa showed them what she estimated to be the location of the underground gallery.

'I'm pretty sure this is the dividing wall,' she said. 'There's nothing against it this side which could conceal a door.'

Looking at the plan, she suppressed a shudder. It all came rushing back – the shock at seeing the still figure at the foot of the steps, the agonising minutes spent struggling to staunch the flow of blood, the smells, the hum of machinery, the ghostly voices . . .

'What is it?' asked Harris, seeing her start.

'I've just thought . . . remember my telling you how the staff believe the cellar is haunted? I could have sworn I heard something while I was down there that sounded like spooky voices, but I thought afterwards I must have imagined it. Suppose there *was* someone, on the other side of the wall? Maybe Vic encourages the legend, just in case one of the staff happens to be down in the cellar at the same time as there's someone in the gallery?'

Harris thought for a moment. 'If they've got any sense, they'll be careful not to show their clients the goodies at a time when they're liable to be overheard.'

'But as a safety precaution, in case of a slip-up?'

'It's feasible, I suppose.'

'I've remembered something else. When Vic Bellamy came to find out what was going on, he seemed more angry than concerned about how badly Will was hurt. He muttered something about pinching the key while Janice wasn't looking, and "What was he doing, nosing around down there?"'

Harris frowned. 'Are you sure?'

'Of course I'm sure. I remember getting a bit ratty with him.'

'My officer's report didn't mention anything about Foley having taken the key.' Harris scribbled in his notebook. 'He said the staff, and Bellamy himself, were unanimous that he was on the way to the gents and must have gone through the wrong door by mistake.'

'He may have given a visit to the gents as a reason for leaving the bar, but there was no mistake. He meant to search the cellar. That's why he had a torch.'

'The report didn't mention a torch either.'

'It was on the floor, a little way away from where he was lying. It must have rolled there.' Melissa thought for a moment. 'I remember now; after they'd taken Will to the ambulance, Vic came down to clear up. He took it away with the rest of the mess.'

'Why didn't you mention this before?'

'Nobody asked me. Besides, I never gave it a second thought. Remember, I had no inkling at the time that Mitch was suspicious of Vic, and I was feeling pretty shocked.'

'You must have been.' A touch of gentleness broke through Harris's official manner for an instant, barely noticeable but unexpectedly heart-warming. 'It seems that Bellamy suspected Foley of snooping around, but was anxious not to let his suspicions be known.'

'Of course . . . in case of awkward questions about what he might have been looking for,' Mitch broke in.

'Did Foley tell you he was planning to search the cellar, sir?' asked Harris.

'Never said a word. Like I told Mrs Craig, he could be a right sphinx when he wanted to. Y'know, when he died I very nearly came to you lot and said I reckoned there was something fishy about it, but Tanny talked me out of it.'

'Tanny?'

'Dittany. Me girlfriend.'

'How much have you told her about all this?'

'She knows a bit. Nothing about the gallery, or the fire-bomb – I don't want to scare her.'

'I suggest you keep it that way. Remember what I said earlier.'

'Okay. About Will, is there any news yet about the cause of death?' A shadow fell over Mitch's normally cheerful face. 'His daughter keeps phoning me, she's really upset, not being able to arrange the funeral . . .'

'I'm afraid not. These reports can take a couple of weeks to come through. Tell the lady she'll be notified as soon as possible.' Harris closed his notebook and put it in his pocket. 'If I could just have details of your solicitor?'

'Mr Medway? Sure.' Mitch referred to an address book on the secretary's desk. 'Here it is.'

'And perhaps I could take these papers away with me? I'd like to study them more closely.'

'Help yourself.'

'Thank you, sir, you've been most helpful.'

'You'll keep me posted? If there's anything you want any of us to do . . .'

'It may be some time before there are any developments, so I must ask you to be patient. All I want you to do is carry on your business as if nothing had happened. No more amateur sleuthing, is that understood?'

'Yessir, Chief Inspector!' Mitch gave a mock salute. 'That's exactly what Mel – Mrs Craig – said I should do.'

Harris permitted himself a hint of a smile. 'I hope Mrs Craig will practise what she preaches,' he said drily. He assumed a stern expression as he looked from Chris to Melissa, and back again. 'Since no complaints have been made, I shall not be pursuing the matter of illegal entry, but I strongly advise you not to make a habit of it.'

The dogs followed them to the front door and sat on their haunches on the step, one on either side of Mitch as they took

214

their leave. Melissa patted Khan's head. He licked her hand, but made no attempt to follow her to her car.

'He's happy to be home,' she remarked. 'He did a great job last night. Thanks for letting him stay.'

'Glad he was there,' said Mitch.

Before getting into his own car, Harris said to Melissa in a low voice, 'You'll be sure to tell me if you think of anything else that might be relevant?'

'Of course. You'll let me know how things are going, won't you?'

His only response was an enigmatic lift of an eyebrow.

When she reached home, Melissa's spirits lifted at the sight of the vintage Morris Traveller parked outside the door of Elder Cottage. Iris was hauling a battered canvas holdall from the back, while Binkie wound himself round her legs, purring in ecstasy.

Melissa gave her friend a hug. 'Oh, Iris, I'm so glad you're back!'

'Not sorry to be home. Hate London. Can't think why anyone wants to live there.'

'But you've had a good trip?'

'Very good. Got something interesting to tell you. Come in for a drink.'

'Love to.'

'Hope Gloria's kept the place warm. Supposed to check every day.'

'I'm sure she has.'

They sat in the cosy kitchen and sipped home-made dandelion wine while Iris dropped her bombshell.

'Remember those paintings I told you were nicked?' she said.

'The ones Kim Bellamy's got reproductions of?'

'That's right.'

'What about them?'

'No colour reproductions were ever officially made.'

215

'But there must have been, I saw them,' protested Melissa. 'Besides, you showed me the catalogue . . .'

'Only done in black and white. No colour trannies, no postcards.'

'I don't understand. How did Kim get hold of them, then?'

'You tell me.'

'I suppose she could have taken the shots herself, when she visited the exhibition?'

'Unlikely. Rules are very strict – no photography at exhibitions.'

'How did you find this out?'

'Pure chance. Friend had a private show at the same gallery. Called round to see him, he was busy for a moment, got talking to the gallery owner. She was sorting out some post-card reproductions and I asked her which were the ones that were nicked. She showed me the Renoir and a Van Gogh. None by Ducasse.'

'Did you ask her about them?'

'Only casually. She was quite emphatic that they weren't selected for colour reproduction.'

'So how did she account for the ones I saw in the Bellamys' flat?'

'Didn't mention them.' There was an impish sparkle in Iris's keen grey eyes. 'You're the detective – thought I'd tell you first.'

Melissa nibbled thoughtfully on a nut cookie. 'What's the procedure for getting reproductions of paintings for catalogues and postcards and so on?'

'Gallery owner makes a selection from the exhibition items and sends them to a studio that specialises.'

'They're not photographed on the premises?'

'Not normally. Conditions not right.'

'Presumably the negatives and transparencies become the property of the gallery?'

'Yes.'

'And they keep them, so they can reorder?'

'Some are kept in an art library. That way, anyone who cares to pay a fee can use them for book illustrations or calendars or whatever.'

'So maybe Kim got hold of hers that way?'

'Only if it was photographed in colour in the first place. The woman was quite definite it wasn't.'

Melissa's synapses were fairly humming. 'Have you still got your catalogue of that exhibition?' she asked.

'Sure. Want to borrow it?'

'Please.'

Chapter Twenty-One

Melissa left Iris to her unpacking and returned to her own cottage in a state of considerable excitement. She immediately rang Gloria to ask for the address and telephone number of her husband's Auntie Muriel.

'I think she may be able to help me with research for my new novel,' she explained, raising her voice slightly to overcome what sounded like the outbreak of Armageddon in the background. 'You did once tell me she worked as a lady's maid, didn't you?'

'That's right. Ooh my, she'll be that thrilled!' Gloria's voice rose to a squeak. 'She do love to talk about her times with the gentry. She be a bit posh in her ways, like, but she do tell some good stories. I got her address right here, and her phone number.'

Miss Muriel Parkin received Melissa's request in the calm manner of one who has been trained to show surprise at nothing, and extended a cordial invitation to tea that afternoon.

'I shall be pleased to help you in any way I can, Mrs Craig,' she said. Her voice was low-pitched and a shade over-refined. 'Gloria often speaks of you and the books you write. I'm sure they're very good, although' – here she gave an apologetic cough – 'I confess I never read detective novels myself. I always feel there's so much *real* wickedness in the world.'

'That's all right, lots of people feel like that,' Melissa assured her. 'I'll see you this afternoon, then.'

In contrast to the cheerfully extrovert Gloria, with her loud laugh, somewhat garish taste in clothes and sense of humour as broad as her hips, Miss Parkin was a quietly dressed woman of sixty or so with the genteel manner of an Edwardian governess. Melissa tried to picture her at the family gatherings which Gloria often described in hilarious detail, and found it difficult.

'It's very good of you to spare me your time,' she said as she followed her hostess into the sitting-room of the tiny bungalow.

'Not at all. I love to talk about the old days.' Miss Parkin gave a little sigh and patted her faded blonde hair, which was dressed in old-fashioned curls like the Queen's. 'Things were so much *nicer* then, I always think. Please take a seat while I make the tea – the kettle has just boiled.'

She went out, quickly and yet without apparent haste. Melissa sat down in a wing chair, upholstered in crimson velvet to match the curtains, and glanced round. She was struck by the contrast between this small, neat room and Gloria's clutter of ill-matched modern furniture and gaudy knick-knacks. Here, everything was traditional in style, the few ornaments of good quality and carefully placed. There were two bookcases and a glass-fronted cabinet displaying a collection of porcelain figurines. On the plain walls – Miss Parkin did not share her young relatives' flamboyant taste in wallpaper – were a few good pictures. Some photographs in silver frames stood on a table under the window, among them a portrait of a lady in court dress, posed beside a potted palm against a background of elaborate draperies. Melissa went over to examine it more closely, just as her hostess re-entered with a tray of bone china tea-things.

'Ah, I see you're admiring Lady Sophia.' She set down the tray, picked up the photograph and handed it to Melissa with an affectionate smile. 'Beautiful, wasn't she? Now that,' she pointed to another picture, 'is her daughter, the Honourable Deirdre, in the dress she wore for her coming-out ball. She was so excited, I had quite a job to get her to stand still while I dressed her. She wasn't presented, of course – they did away with all that after the war. Such a pity, I always thought.'

'You must find working at Heyshill Manor a big change from what you were used to,' said Melissa.

'I didn't intend to work after I retired, but with inflation, my pension doesn't go so far.' Miss Parkin's smile held no trace of self-pity. 'My nephew very generously offered to make me an allowance, but I value my independence. And I did find it rather lonely here on my own, especially after spending part of the year in London. I simply *loved* London. There was so much to do in my free time: concerts, theatres, art galleries . . . especially the art galleries.'

'You enjoy looking at pictures?'

'Oh, yes. Lady Sophia owned some wonderful paintings and she very kindly taught me a little about them. You see that one there?' She indicated a study of roses in a silver bowl which hung above the mantelpiece. 'Lady Sophia left me that in her will and I get so much pleasure from looking at it. It's not particularly valuable, of course, but it is my most treasured possession.'

'I believe Mr and Mrs Bellamy are art lovers too,' said Melissa casually, after she had admired the picture.

There was a brief silence while Miss Parkin poured tea and offered an assortment of home-made cakes and scones. Then she said, 'I'm not sure what you mean by "art *lovers*". They have what seems to me a rather *vulgar* attitude towards it.'

Her manner had undergone a subtle change. Melissa had the impression that she did not consider her present employers deserving of the same respect as Lady Sophia and her family. She nodded and smiled to encourage further confidences, which were soon forthcoming.

'Do you know,' Miss Parkin continued, her nose wrinkled in distaste, 'they actually have a reproduction of a lovely Renoir nude on the bathroom door!'

'Yes, I know, I've seen it. I must say, I thought it was a bit naff.'

'Quite so.' Melissa had the impression that the sentiment was approved, but not the adjective. 'I dare say you noticed that every door in the flat has "an appropriate picture", as Mrs Bellamy calls it.' Miss Parkin let out a trill of scornful laughter. 'I don't *say* anything, of course – it's not my place – but I can't imagine what gave her the notion. As a matter of fact, I did rather a dreadful thing last Thursday.' A sudden, mischievous smile made her kinship with the rumbustious Parkins entirely credible.

'When you broke the glass on the Ducasse *Salle à Manger*, you mean?' said Melissa.

Miss Parkin's eyes widened. 'How did you know it was a Ducasse?'

'Gloria said it was the one on the dining-room door. I saw it when Mrs Bellamy took me to her flat to clean up, after the accident to Mr Foley.'

'Ah yes, what a tragedy that was. But' – here a note of admiration crept into Miss Parkin's voice – 'I'm surprised . . . no, *impressed*, I should say, that you recognised it as a Ducasse. He isn't terribly well-known.'

'It was on loan to an exhibition in London recently.'

'Oh, I do so miss going to London galleries,' sighed Miss Parkin. 'I simply can't afford it these days.'

'I dare say that's where Mr and Mrs Bellamy saw the Ducasse paintings,' Melissa suggested.

Miss Parkin's lip curled. 'The nearest *they've* ever been to an art gallery is probably a peep-show on a pier at the seaside,' she said disdainfully. 'I can't *imagine* where they might have seen it. Would you like some more tea?'

'Thank you.' Melissa held out her cup. 'Was Mrs Bellamy very cross about the broken picture?'

Miss Parkin's laughter trilled out anew. 'She wasn't there when it happened, and so far as I know, she hasn't even noticed.' Her pale eyes sparkled with an impish glee. 'I found a Dutch interior in the spare bedroom and hung it up in its place. I've taken the broken one to be repaired.' She refilled their cups and offered more cakes. 'Now, tell me how I can help you with your novel.'

Melissa took out her notebook and a list of questions, prepared somewhat hastily in the cause of authenticity. Despite the fact that they were merely a subterfuge, they elicited such a wealth of anecdote and description of people and places, often related with a wicked sense of humour and an occasional slippage of the veneer of decorum, that the time flew past unnoticed. When the ormolu clock on the mantelpiece – doubtless another legacy from a wealthy employer – struck five, Melissa had already made up her mind to set her next murder mystery in pre-war London. Almost, she had forgotten the real reason for her visit.

'It's been absolutely riveting,' she said as she prepared to leave. 'Thank you so much.'

'Not at all – I've thoroughly enjoyed our chat. Perhaps you'll come again?'

'I'd love to. By the way, could you tell me where you took the picture to be mended? I have one or two that need reframing.'

'Mr Dodson, in Stowbridge. His work is excellent. He repaired this for me.' She caressed the frame of the rose-bowl study with a small, ringless hand. 'He's an old-fashioned craftsman who appreciates good pictures. Not like these places where they do all the work by machinery and don't know the difference between a cheap modern daub and an old master.'

'Would you mind giving me his address?'

'Of course. You can take it from the receipt for Mrs Bellamy's picture.' Miss Parkin fetched a slip of paper from a drawer and handed it to Melissa. 'He's very busy at the moment; he said he couldn't have it ready before Wednesday at the earliest.' Her lips twitched. 'It will be interesting to know if Mrs Bellamy misses it before then.'

Melissa looked up from copying Mr Dodson's address, to which she surreptitiously added the date and number on the docket. 'I get the impression that you have no great opinion of the Bellamys,' she said.

Miss Parkin cleared her throat. 'They aren't exactly the

type of person I would choose to work for,' she admitted. 'I've been accustomed to the *genuinely* well-to-do, you understand, not the *nouveaux riches*. One wonders sometimes how such people acquire their money.' She pursed her lips and gave a knowing nod. 'Not always entirely honestly, I fancy.'

'Are you suggesting that the Bellamys are criminals?' Melissa was suddenly hopeful of learning something significant. Miss Parkin, however, appeared to feel that she had gone too far, and hurriedly backtracked.

'Oh, dear me, no . . . at least, it's just that . . . well, one reads so often about the tricks these so-called business people get up to. There was a case in the paper recently of a managing director, a most highly respected man, so they said, who was sent to prison for stealing money from his firm's pension fund. No person of *real* quality would stoop so low.'

'I'm sure you're right,' Melissa agreed politely. It was clear that Miss Parkin's assertion, reported by Gloria, that Vic Bellamy was a crook, was no more than what Mitch would describe as a 'gut feeling'. It was interesting, but of no practical use. However, the picture might very well be. She took leave of Miss Parkin and hurried home, eager to pass on the results of her visit to DCI Harris.

'I think I can help you with your enquiries,' she told him when he answered the phone.

'Oh? What enquiries?'

'Into the Bellamy case.'

There was a silence. Then he said, in his oily sandpaper voice, 'I thought we agreed there was to be no more amateur sleuthing.'

'I know we did, but this is something I stumbled on by chance – or rather, Iris did.'

'Iris? Surely, Mel, you haven't been gossiping with that old biddy, after what I told you?'

'I haven't revealed anything confidential, and please don't refer to my best friend as an old biddy,' she retorted. 'You said there was no proper evidence of Vic Bellamy's involvement with anything illegal, and I happen to have found some, that's all. If you aren't interested . . .'

'Of course I'm interested,' he said impatiently. 'Stop playing games, Mel. What's this about?'

'I'm not telling you over the phone.' She was determined to make the most of her small triumph. 'Why don't you come round for a drink?'

'I'm in my gardening clothes, and I haven't eaten yet.'

'Then go and change, and come to supper. Chilli con carne from the freezer, not exactly cordon bleu, but . . .'

'Thank you.' He sounded mollified. 'Give me time to get cleaned up, then.'

He arrived an hour later, freshly shaved and casually dressed in slacks and a brown knitted sweater that gave him the appearance of an outsize teddy bear. He had a bottle of Rioja tucked under one arm.

'A Spanish wine seemed appropriate with the chilli,' he remarked as he followed her into the kitchen. 'Where do you keep your corkscrew?'

'In that drawer, and the glasses are in the cupboard on your left.'

He filled two goblets and handed her one. 'Cheers!'

'*Santé!*' She took a mouthful and nodded in appreciation. 'Mm, nice. I hope you don't mind eating in the kitchen.'

'It's where I always eat when I'm at home on my own.'

'Me too. The Bellamys as well – I have it on the best authority.'

'Oh?'

'My cleaning lady's husband's aunt, Miss Muriel Parkin. That's who I've been to see this afternoon.'

He listened without interruption while she told her story. When she had finished, she fetched Iris's catalogue and pointed out the relevant pictures. 'The owner of Butchers' Gallery will confirm all those paintings vanished on the way back to their owners, and that colour reproductions were never made of these three. All you have to do is get Mr Dodson to hand over the one that came from the Bellamys' flat and . . .'

'Thank you, Melissa. I do know a little about detective work.'

'Sorry. I got a bit carried away. But do try and get it back by Wednesday or poor Miss Parkin might lose her job.'

'I can't guarantee that, and it might have been better if you'd told me about the broken picture as soon as you realised its significance, instead of rushing off to make enquiries on your own. I warned you not to say anything that might arouse suspicion or start gossip.'

'But I didn't. Miss Parkin has no idea there's anything dodgy about the picture, or that I've got any particular interest in it. In fact, if you'd sent PC Plod down to question her, she'd have been far more likely to spread the story around. As it is, she won't give it a second thought – I think you should be very grateful to me!' Melissa turned on her most disarming smile; after a moment, his stern expression relaxed and he smiled back.

'All right, you win. You're forgiven, provided the chilli comes up to scratch.'

After Harris left, having given a somewhat guarded undertaking to 'keep in touch', Melissa thrust what she had mentally dubbed 'Operation Aladdin' to the back of her mind. Her novel was approaching a crucial stage; her celebrated sleuth, Nathan Latimer, was faced with a knotty problem which was causing his creator considerable difficulty. For the next two days, she spent so much time in her study that Iris, concerned at her non-appearance, called round to drag her out for a walk, insisting that she needed exercise and fresh air.

Wednesday brought the usual visit from Gloria, bursting with news as she took off her jacket and assembled her cleaning materials.

'Auntie Muriel's been found out!' she informed Melissa. 'Monday morning, soon as she went up to the flat, Mrs B.

pounced on her, wanting to know where her dining-room picture had gone.'

'Oh dear, was she very cross?'

'Not so much cross, Auntie Muriel said, more like scared it were stolen. When Auntie explained what had happened – ever so apologetic, she were – Mrs B. seemed that relieved, she never told her off nor nothing. Then she asked for the ticket and said Auntie M. weren't to worry, she'd collect it herself and pay for it.'

'That was very kind of her.'

'That's what I said, but Auntie M. said, when one of the kitchen staff breaks anything, they gets their wages stopped. She thought it were a bit fishy.'

'I wonder why?' said Melissa.

Gloria shrugged, picked up the vacuum cleaner and headed for the sitting-room. 'Search me. Auntie Muriel's got a funny way of thinking sometimes. She enjoyed talking to you, by the way, thinks you're a real lady.'

'Oh, thank you. I enjoyed it too.'

The minute Gloria had finished her morning's work and left, Melissa put in a call to DCI Harris. He received the latest intelligence with a flattering interest.

'That's a great help, Mel, thank you,' he said.

'Did you contact the gallery in London?'

'I did.'

'And?'

'Our enquiries are proceeding.'

'Can't you tell me any more than that?'

'Not at the moment.'

'I'll be in Stowbridge tomorrow – it's my day at college. Why don't we meet at the Grey Goose for lunch?'

'So that you can ply me with drink to make me talk? I know your wicked ways.' He gave a gravelly chuckle. 'All right, it's a date – but don't bank on prising anything out of me. Our enquiries are at a delicate stage.'

*

'So, what's new?' asked Melissa as she joined Harris at the bar of the Grey Goose.

'All in good time. What will you have to drink – a St Clements?' She nodded and he gave the order. 'What about food?'

'A chicken sandwich, please.'

He carried their drinks to a corner table. Melissa repeated her question. 'Did you go to London?'

'I did.'

'And the gallery owner confirmed what I said?'

'Of course.'

'I'll bet she was excited when you told her what I'd seen.'

'Stop fishing, Mel. Ah, thank you.' A waiter put plates of sandwiches on the table between them. Harris held up his empty glass. 'Get me a refill, will you?'

Melissa tried again. 'Did you check on the blue Renault?'

'Naturally.'

'But you aren't going to tell me who it belongs to?'

'No.'

'Someone I know? Oh, all right,' she said hastily as she caught his eye. 'But you might at least tell me what to look out for, next time I go to Heyshill Manor.'

'You're going there again? Why, for God's sake?'

'To Mitch's birthday party on the thirty-first and the performance of *Innocent Blood Avenged*. It's Hallowe'en – I wonder if Battling Bess will put in an appearance. Why don't you come too? I'm sure Mitch will invite you if I ask him.'

'I'll think about it.' Harris finished his sandwiches and took a pull from his second pint. 'As a matter of fact, I'm sending Sergeant Waters there this afternoon, to question the staff about a different matter altogether.'

'What's that?'

'William Foley's death. As you were there when the accident happened, I'd like to ask you one or two questions as well.'

'Go ahead.'

Harris lowered his voice. 'The result of the autopsy came through yesterday.'

'And?'

He leaned forward. 'You can keep this to yourself for the moment – in fact, I shouldn't really be telling you, but I know I can trust you – the pathologist found heroin in the bloodstream. It points to a substantial overdose.'

Melissa shook her head in bewilderment. 'I don't understand it,' she said. 'He was completely anti-drugs of any kind.'

'That's what his daughter says. She got very angry at the mere suggestion. The report confirms there's no sign of addiction or regular use, so what we have to do is find out when and how it got into him. Or, what seems more likely, how someone else got it into him.'

'You mean, you believe he was murdered?' Melissa put down the second half of her sandwich, her appetite suddenly diminished.

'It's very much on the cards.'

'How soon before death do they reckon he took it?'

'Half an hour at the most. He'd had one or two drinks, which would have speeded things up.'

'So he must have taken it at the hotel, during the rehearsal.'

'It looks like it. That's why we have to question everyone who was there, and I'm starting with you. How did you come to be on the scene so soon after the accident?'

'Will was needed on stage. They said he was in the bar, and I wanted to talk to Janice – the bar manager – so I offered to take the message.'

'Was he there?'

'No, but he had been.' Melissa thought for a moment, reliving the scene. 'As I remember, Janice said he'd left a few minutes earlier.'

'Who else was in the bar?'

'A party of hotel guests . . . they went out after a few minutes to have their dinner. There was Janice, and Kevin, her young assistant . . . and Vic Bellamy was sitting on a stool, having a drink. We exchanged a few words and then he left as well.'

'What did you do then?'

'I stayed on to talk to Janice. She was telling me all about the ghosts. Scared the pants off young Kev.' Melissa smiled at the recollection. 'Let's see, what happened next? Chris Bright came in, wanting to know where Will had got to. He still hadn't gone back to the rehearsal. Then some other people came in and ordered drinks, and the draught beer had run out so Janice sent Kevin down to the cellar to change the barrels. He didn't want to go – she'd put the wind up him with her ghost stories – but he went in the end. Half a minute later he was back, having found Will. I was nearest to the door, so I went with him, and saw . . .'

'Must have been a shock.' Harris put a large, reddish hand on hers and she allowed it to remain there, grateful for its comforting warmth. 'You said something the other day about the cellar key.'

'It's kept hanging on a nail in the bar. When Kevin went to get it, it wasn't there.' She repeated her account of Vic Bellamy's reactions while they were in the cellar together. 'Ken, you remember Mitch talked of suspecting "something fishy" about Will's death?'

'I remember. Perhaps I didn't take it seriously enough, but of course, the report from the path lab hadn't come through then. Have you any idea what he was driving at?'

'He told me he believed Vic Bellamy had a hand in it somehow, but he had nothing at all to go on except one of his famous "gut feelings". It's another reason why he asked me to stay at the hotel and nose around.'

'I'll have something to say to him about that. How dare he put you at risk!' Harris's colour deepened with anger.

'I'm the one you should be cross with,' she said humbly. 'I didn't have to agree to it.'

His expression softened. His hand was still on hers and he began gently tracing circles on the back of it with his forefinger. 'I'm beginning to think it's a waste of time getting cross with you,' he said.

'Ken, do you think Vic had anything to do with Will's death?'

He released her hand, his face thoughtful. 'After all you've told me, he has to be a suspect, but we're up against means and motive.'

'Surely, the motive's obvious. He was afraid Foley was about to expose him.'

'But, according to you, he seemed surprised to think he'd been nosing about down there.'

'And according to your man's report, he subsequently suggested he'd opened the cellar door by mistake.'

Harris shook his head. 'People do sometimes change their ideas on what happened, after reflection. Not that I'm prepared to accept his version without corroboration . . . but look at it this way. If Bellamy, or one of his associates, wanted to do away with Foley, why do it on their own doorstep, and why choose such an unlikely method? It's not as if they were dealing with a known user whose supply they could contaminate with a fatal dose. Still, until we can eliminate him, he stays on the list of suspects. In fact, until we start probing more deeply into Foley's background, he *is* the list of suspects!' He drained his glass and stood up. 'Sorry, Mel, I have to be going.'

He held the door of her car while she got in. 'I take it you've had no more late-night visits?' he said.

'You mean, from the likes of Clegg? No, thank goodness. What did you get out of him, by the way?'

'Nothing much. He's well known to us as a no-hope gofer who'll do anything for fifty quid. We traced the bike owner's last known address, but he's gone missing. He's the one we need to find.'

'Ken, you will keep me in touch with developments?'

He gave a lop-sided grin and said, 'Drive carefully, Mel.' He closed the car door, waved and strode away, leaving her

230

to drive home in a state of mingled frustration and perplexity.

The following evening Melissa cooked a farewell supper for Iris, who was leaving in the morning for France. She looked peaky and harassed, and got up to leave soon after nine o'clock, saying she needed an early night. 'Haven't been sleeping too well lately,' she admitted.

'You've been overdoing it,' Melissa chided her, remembering the trips to London and the painting course she had been preparing.

'Tell me something I don't know. Everything's come at once the last fortnight.'

'Aren't you drinking your camomile tea?'

'Hasn't been doing the trick lately.'

'Dittany's got some herbal capsules she swears by. Shall I ring and ask her what they're called – you could get some tomorrow.'

'No, thanks. Not into drugs, even herbal ones.'

'That's what . . .' Just in time, Melissa bit back the words that might have led to a betrayal of confidence.

Iris frowned. 'What's what?'

'Nothing – just a thought.' It was too mild a term to express the notion that had erupted in her brain but she managed to conceal her agitation. 'I'll pop round in the morning to see you off,' she said as Iris put on her coat.

The minute the door closed behind her, Melissa flew to the telephone to call Ken Harris.

'What is it, Mel? You sound excited.'

'Ken, I think I know how Will Foley was killed . . . and I'm terribly afraid, unless we do something about it, there'll be another death.'

Chapter Twenty-Two

The night of the thirty-first of October was clear, frosty and still, the sky a moonless dome on which numberless stars glittered like chips of ice. In the darkness, the lights of Heyshill Manor Hotel shone out with more than their usual brilliance.

Ken Harris parked the Rover and switched off the engine.

'Wait here a minute,' he said and strolled over to the exit. He stood for a moment, his hands in his pockets, apparently watching the passing traffic. Melissa saw the driver's window of a nearby car roll down and a hand holding a cigarette briefly appear, as if tapping ash on to the ground. Then the window was closed and Harris came striding back, his feet crunching on the gravel. He opened the passenger door of the Rover for Melissa to get out.

'Right, let's get this show on the road,' he said. 'I hope to God we pull it off – if it goes wrong, the powers that be will feed me to the lions.' He took her arm and ushered her towards the door.

Her head was full of questions but she knew better than to ask them. He had given her a few terse instructions and made it clear that he had told her all she needed to know. She would have to wait for the rest.

Other cars were arriving, bringing Mitch's birthday guests – sleek and prosperous-looking men with cashmere overcoats over their dinner suits and expensively clothed and bejewelled women at their side. Among them, she recognised some of the so-called 'captains of industry' with whom Mitch had become acquainted in the course of building his business empire. She wondered what they really thought of the 'barrow-boy millionaire'.

Until that moment she had been reasonably confident in her off-the-peg designer outfit; now, seeing the fur wraps, model gowns and general air of opulence, she felt outclassed. She glanced at Harris, unfamiliar but surprisingly distinguished in evening dress. He seemed to read her thoughts.

'You look great,' he assured her.

As they approached the front door, it was opened with a flourish by a sinister, cloaked figure with a deathly white face and a livid scar on one cheek, its shirt-front liberally bedaubed with 'Kensington Gore'.

'Welcome to the Haunted Manor!' it intoned, rubbing its hands together and emitting a spine-chilling laugh. 'Your host and hostess await you in the Blue Room.'

'Whoever's that?' whispered Melissa as they moved in the direction the apparition was pointing.

'DC Baxter,' he whispered back. 'Plays the Demon King every year in his village pantomime.'

They found themselves in a low-beamed room, illuminated by bluish lamps which cast an unearthly glow on the faces of the guests. Across one wall was stretched a banner bearing a flight of witches on broomsticks, surrounded by bats and assorted demons.

'The art department at the Tech must have been busy,' commented Melissa. 'It's quite effective, don't you think?'

Mitch came forward to greet them, a shade flamboyant in his frilled evening shirt and satin cummerbund. At his side was the Honourable Penelope, a picture of elegance in a sheath of satin with a double rope of pearls glistening round her neck. There was no doubt, thought Melissa as he planted a hearty kiss on her cheek, that even in the unflattering light they made a handsome, if oddly assorted couple.

'Mitch, Penelope, I'd like you to meet Ken Harris,' she said. 'Ken, may I introduce Richard Mitchell, our host, and Penelope de Lavier.'

'It's a great pleasure to meet you both,' said Harris. 'And so kind of you to invite me to your birthday celebrations, Mr

Mitchell.' He allowed his gaze to rest admiringly on Penelope for a moment before bending over her hand and kissing it. 'I'm looking forward to Mel's début as a playwright.'

'No need to be formal,' said Mitch cordially, playing his part to perfection. 'I'm Mitch, and this is Pen . . . and we'll call you Ken, won't we, Pen?' He guffawed. 'Pen and Ken . . . could be a pair of cartoon characters!' It was plain he was in high spirits. 'Go and grab yourselves a glass of champers.'

'I thought you'd be busy backstage,' said Melissa, as she and Penelope pecked the air in the general direction of one another's faces.

'Charlie's taken over the props, leaving me free to act as hostess for Mitch,' explained Penelope, her smile a glow of self-satisfaction. 'It's something I've recently begun doing, and he *does* so appreciate it.' *And I intend to carry on doing it*, said the smile, as its owner turned to greet the next arrivals.

'You don't have to overdo the charm,' Melissa hissed, as she and Harris moved out of earshot.

He grinned. 'It's all part of the act – I'm supposed to be a Eurocrat, remember? We have to know all the social graces.'

They collected their glasses of champagne from a young waiter wearing plastic horns on his temples and a forked tail coiled round one arm. He said something in a low voice to Harris, who nodded imperceptibly before turning away.

The room was crowded with chattering guests, many of whom appeared to be acquainted. Melissa caught sight of a stout man in dangerously tight trousers talking to Lady Charlotte, who was wearing a plain but doubtless inordinately expensive black dress with voluminous sleeves. Evidently she had already discharged her preliminary duties as props manager for the evening's entertainment.

Melissa and Harris found themselves buttonholed by an eager young man with a pale wisp of a wife. With little or no encouragement, he launched into an account of how he had pulled off a complex deal with a company in Tennessee. Melissa responded by saying that her son worked for a company in Texas, whereupon there ensued a somewhat aimless conversation about motels, fast food joints and driving on interstate highways. The young man was so impressed with his own achievements and experience of America that it did not occur to him to enquire what Harris did for a living, which Melissa felt was just as well, although she was confident he had done his homework.

It was a relief when Detective Constable Baxter, the ghoulish effect of his disguise enhanced by the eerie lighting, appeared in the doorway, struck a resounding note on a large brass gong and in sepulchral tones summoned the guests to dinner. To much laughter and cries of simulated disgust, he recited a menu – devised, no doubt, by their host – consisting of toad's tongue soup, roasted viper with bat sauce and devilled kidneys, washed down with vintage hemlock. It was plain he was thoroughly enjoying himself.

The actual food – served by waitresses in conical black hats, their features disguised with hooked noses and blackened teeth – was excellent. The champagne flowed, the conversation was unflagging. Mitch sat at the head of the table between the Honourable Penelope de Lavier and the Lady Charlotte Heighton, the two aristocratic women whose comparatively modest business had leapt into prominence on the news of his investment in it. Their smiles were silent shouts of triumph; they chatted to him, chatted across him, laughed and joked with their other neighbours. They might have been competition entrants who had won a night out with a celebrity. For these winners, however, this was no once-in-a-lifetime experience. They had a proprietorial air towards their prize, as if confident that one of them would soon be staking her permanent claim. Melissa thought of Dittany, eating supper with the rest of the cast of *Innocent Blood Avenged* in another room, and despite Chris's confident assertion, her misgivings returned.

The coffee was served, curls of smoke from expensive cigars began drifting overhead, someone banged on the table for silence and Mitch rose to his feet. He gave a brief and witty speech of welcome, delivered in a racy Cockney manner with the occasional *risqué* aside which brought appreciative guffaws from some members of the audience but a touch of frost to the smiles of the ladies at his side.

He then announced that the curtain would go up on the entertainment in fifteen minutes and people began discarding their napkins and pushing back their chairs. The women reached for their handbags; Charlotte said something to Penelope behind Mitch's back and left the table. Melissa, seated opposite Harris, noticed one of the waitresses lean across his shoulder as if to refill his wine-glass. He put a hand over it and glanced up at her with a barely detectable movement of the head. She put down the bottle and left the room. Melissa's pulse began to accelerate as she and Harris joined in the move from the dining-room to the Priory Suite. The drama was about to begin.

Like the room they had first entered, the Conference Room had been given a Hallowe'en atmosphere, with subdued lighting and some rather grisly pictures featuring skulls, gibbets and corpses. The guests, by now in the mellowest of humours and prepared to laugh, shiver or scream as circumstances demanded, settled into their seats. From behind the heavy black curtains that had been rigged up across the platform, a tinkling piano struck up a few bars of 'With her Head Tucked Underneath her Arm'. As Mitch stepped out and bowed, a pair of skeletal hands appeared and placed the table of props at his elbow, evoking gleeful gasps of mock horror.

Mitch was in fine form. He delivered the opening couplets that Melissa had written for him, did the business with the poison bottle, the gun and the rope, and finally thrust the stage knife at his own chest – a gesture which, despite the absence of Kensington Gore, had a most realistic effect and evoked some gratifying screams from the more nervous members of the audience. He then proceeded to recite a further stanza of his own:

We hope our masque will not turn out a bore
And at the sight of blood upon the floor
Be not alarmed! The trick could not be neater –
'Tis but stage blood, at twenty quid a litre.

'S'matter of fact, it's dearer'n that, but twenty-two quid wouldn't scan,' he explained, and vanished amid laughter and applause. The skeletal hands removed the table, Mitch returned to his seat in the front row, the curtains parted and the play began.

Recognising that the audience's attention span was bound to be limited, Melissa had written the piece in five short scenes, with an interval after the third. The first was between the heroine – played by Dittany – and her personal maid, the former consulting the latter as to which of her several suitors she should marry. The maid then left her sleeping mistress to confide to the audience her love for Tom Stannard, the gamekeeper, and her belief that his failure to ask for her hand was due to his lack of money. To a resounding chorus of 'Aaah!', and a poignant rendering of 'Hearts and Flowers' on the piano, she made her exit, wringing her hands in despair.

In Scene Two, Mendelssohn's 'Spring Song' heralded the entrance of Tom Stannard and the housemaid, Susan Patch. Strolling hand in hand and gazing into one another's eyes, they exchanged vows of eternal love. The pianist skilfully transposed the melody into a minor key as Susan, amid titters and expressions of mock disapproval, confessed that she would soon bear his child. Without money, how were they to marry and give the baby a name? They agreed to appeal to their wealthy mistress for help. As they made their exit, they were followed with exaggerated stealth by the two villains, whose presence they studiously ignored despite thunderous rolls on the piano and shouted warnings from the body of the house.

By this time, everyone was thoroughly fired up and entering into the spirit of the thing. Even Melissa, despite her awareness that drama and possible danger were not far away, found herself carried along by the general enthusiasm. Charlotte, her duties over for the moment, emerged from backstage and perched on the window seat as the curtains parted for Scene Three. She, too, appeared to be relishing the fun. Only Ken Harris, seated beside Melissa at the end of the row, seemed unable to relax. He joined in the laughter, but now and again he glanced at his watch and she knew his mind was elsewhere.

The scene opened with the criminals, who had tracked the lovers to the house of their wealthy employer, overheard discussing the details of their dastardly plot. In spite of her preoccupation, Melissa found herself hissing with the best of them. The action moved to its bloodthirsty climax: the villains entered the bedroom where the heroine lay sleeping; she awoke and challenged them; to the crashing opening chords of the 'Hammerklavier' sonata, Eric Pollard, in the rôle of Sam Snatchit, raised his arm to strike the fatal blow. Dittany's scream of terror as the knife descended changed to a thoroughly convincing groan; her hands clutched at the handle, she writhed in agony and the groan became a dying gurgle. The music changed to a *marche funèbre*, Kensington Gore flowed in a realistic tide over the front of her nightdress as, to well-deserved applause, the curtains closed. The substitute props manager, looking well pleased with the effects, stood and joined in the clapping before disappearing backstage. Without a word, Harris got up and followed, with Melissa at his heels.

The producer and those members of the cast who had not appeared in Scene Three were making their way into the kitchen-turned-greenroom for the interval, showing every sign of delight at the way the show was going. On stage, Dittany was wiping her hands and the property knife with a rag and chatting to her 'murderer' and his accomplice, while the stage hands shifted furniture around them. On the other side of the curtains, Mitch could be heard announcing the interval.

DC Baxter, who had been doubling as the accompanist, was standing beside the piano. Melissa caught the exchange of glances that passed between him and Harris, and saw him nod in the direction of someone standing behind her. She swung round to see Charlotte staring at Dittany in apparent shock and disbelief. Harris walked over to her.

'What is wrong, Madam?' he asked. The question was spoken quietly but there was something menacing in the way his bulky frame towered over hers.

She shook her head, pulling herself together with an obvious effort. 'Just a slight giddiness . . . the heat, I expect,' she said. She picked up a script that someone had left on the edge of the stage and fanned herself.

'Perhaps you'd better sit down.' He took her arm. 'I'll get you some water.'

'I assure you, I am perfectly all right,' she said, shaking her arm free. She had recovered her poise and was looking at him with the expression of an outraged duchess. 'Who are you? What are you doing here?'

He took out his identification card and held it in front of her. 'Detective Chief Inspector Harris of the Gloucestershire County Constabulary,' he announced. Her mouth fell open and then closed again; her eyes grew wary. Heads turned and the room became quiet. 'I'm here to investigate some very serious crimes. Ah, thank you, Baxter.' Harris took the plastic bag that the young officer, who had removed his 'Demon King' make-up, handed over. 'I'm sure you know what this is, Madam,' he said, holding it under Charlotte's nose.

She gave the bag a cursory glance. 'It appears to be a kitchen knife,' she said, with an air of disdain.

'It *is* a kitchen knife,' said Harris smoothly. 'And it is sharp enough to kill. In fact, it was *intended* to kill.' He paused for a moment to allow the implication to sink in. By now, the atmosphere was electric; horrified glances were exchanged, cups of coffee left untouched on the table. 'Perhaps, Madam,' he continued, 'you can explain how this very dangerous weapon came to be substituted for the property knife used in this production.'

Charlotte met his gaze without flinching. 'I have absolutely no idea what you are talking about,' she declared. She might have been talking to an insurance salesman; had the conversation been taking place on the telephone, Melissa thought, she would have hung up without more ado.

'And I suppose you have no idea where the property knife is hidden?'

'What *are* you talking about, Chief Inspector? It was used on stage a few minutes ago – that young woman has it in her hand.' She inclined her head towards Dittany, who was standing on the fringe of the group, frowning in perplexity. At that moment, Mitch came bounding into the room.

'Tanny, you were marvellous!' he exclaimed. With outstretched arms he went to enfold her in a full frontal embrace, but she held him away and pointed to the sticky mess on her gown. He laughed and slid an arm round her shoulders. Then he caught sight of Harris and the ring of serious faces around him, and his smile faded. 'Something wrong?' he asked.

'Mr Mitchell, I am so glad you are here,' said Charlotte. 'Will you kindly instruct these *policemen*' – the acidity injected into the word was enough to turn litmus paper bright scarlet – 'to stop asking foolish and distressing questions.'

'Policemen?' Mitch appeared to hesitate. 'What . . . ?'

'It's all right, they know who I am,' said Harris. 'I'm glad you're here, sir. Perhaps you can tell me exactly what you did with the property knife, after you finished speaking the Prologue.'

'After I did meself in with it?' Mitch's eyes twinkled at the recollection and he gave Dittany's shoulder a squeeze. 'Did all right, didn't I, doll?' She gave him an adoring smile and for the moment he appeared to forget the question.

'After you finished speaking your lines, what did you do with the knife, sir?' repeated Harris patiently.

Mitch frowned, as if trying to remember. 'Put it back on the table, I suppose. Pen – that is, Charlie – was looking after the props.'

'You didn't return the knife to its sheath?'

'Nah, that's Props' job. What's up, Charlie, you look peaky.' His concerned glance met with a frigid stare.

'Lady Charlotte was just answering a few questions,' said Harris. 'Perhaps, Madam, you will tell us exactly what you did after Mr Mitchell's Prologue.'

'What do you suppose I did? I took away the table – everyone in the room saw me do that – and I put the knife back into its sheath, ready for Scene Three.'

'The property knife, or this one?' Harris held up the bag; his eyes searched hers, but she met them without flinching.

'The property knife, of course. What are you suggesting?' Her chin tilted skywards. 'Really, this is absolutely preposterous – I shall complain to the Chief Constable.'

'That is your privilege, Madam.' Harris turned to his junior officer. 'Baxter, you were sitting at the piano throughout, weren't you?'

'That's right, sir.'

'Could you see the props table all the time?'

'Yessir.'

'How many people went near it, or touched it, after this lady brought it off the stage at the end of the Prologue?'

'Just one, sir.'

'And that was . . . ?'

'Me, sir.'

'And what did you do?'

'I checked the knife that was lying on the table in its sheath. It was that one.' He pointed to the plastic bag that Harris was still holding. 'I removed it from the sheath and replaced it with the second property knife you gave me earlier this evening, sir, and put the real one in the bag, as instructed.'

'Well done, Baxter,' said Harris. 'You thwarted a deliberate attempt to bring about the death of Miss Blair.'

To a chorus of astounded gasps, everyone looked from Charlotte to Dittany and back again. Mitch took Dittany in his arms and held her close, heedless of the damage to his shirtfront. Harris turned to Charlotte; she stared back at him in a brief show of defiance before her eyes dropped. Her face was bloodless.

'What did you do with the original property knife?' he demanded.

'I have absolutely nothing to say. I wish to see my lawyer,' she replied tonelessly.

'You can call him from the station,' said Harris. 'I'm detaining you for further questioning. DC Baxter and PC Peck' – he indicated the 'waitress', who had shed her disguise and entered the room unobserved – 'will escort you.' He glanced at his watch. 'I think the interval is up, Mr Mitchell. The show must go on, mustn't it?'

'If you say so. Sure you're okay, Tanny?'

'Of course I am, but you're a mess.' Dittany jabbed a finger at his shirtfront, stained scarlet from contact with her gown. 'You'll have to do some ad-libbing to explain that.'

'Leave it to me!' He kissed her forehead, then went over to where Charlotte stood, stone-faced, between the two young officers. 'Why, for God's sake?' he asked. 'What had Tanny done to you?'

Her only response was a look of blistering scorn. 'Get her out of here before I forget meself,' he muttered, and went to join the rest of the cast assembling for Act Two.

'Is that it?' whispered Melissa as she and Harris made their way back to their seats.

He shook his head. 'It's only the beginning. Listen.' Faintly, through the double-glazed windows, came the sound of police sirens. 'Sounds like Operation Aladdin has begun as well – I'll see you later.' He bolted from the room as the lights began to dim.

'What beats me,' said Mitch, 'is how Harris knew Charlie was planning to switch the knives.'

'He didn't know for certain,' said Melissa, 'but after we'd spent ages talking it round, it seemed the obvious thing to do.'

242

'But how did she do it?' asked Dittany. 'Where did she get the real knife — and what did she do with the property knife she exchanged it for?'

'She had the real knife inside her sleeve, tucked into a couple of elastic bands round her arm. She was clever enough not to keep the property knife on her person after the switch, though. She hid that in Eric Pollard's duffel bag. Everyone knew he was madly jealous of Dittany's relationship with Mitch, so I guess she thought he'd be accused of committing a *crime passionnel*.'

'How unspeakably wicked!' said Dittany in a low voice.

The four of them — Dittany, Melissa, Mitch and Chris — were comfortably installed in Mitch's sitting-room, after enjoying more of Mrs Wingfield's cooking. Attila was sprawled in front of the fire and Khan had taken up his usual place at Melissa's feet.

'So what's the full story, Mel?' demanded Mitch.

'I don't know the full story yet,' she admitted. 'All I can get out of Ken Harris is that "exhaustive enquiries are continuing" — and I don't think the pun was intentional,' she added, remembering Stumpy's contribution to the affair.

'Coppers know how to keep their mouths shut when it suits 'em,' commented Mitch. 'Like poor old Will. Did that harpy do for him as well?'

'Yes, but unintentionally. The heroin was in doctored capsules that she planted in the bottle in Dittany's handbag. It was sheer chance that those were the ones Dittany gave to Will.'

'That means I killed him! Oh no, I can't bear it!' Dittany covered her eyes and burst into tears. Mitch put an arm round her and she sobbed on his shoulder for several minutes.

'It wasn't your fault, sweetheart,' he said, stroking her hair. 'If it hadn't been Will, it would have been you. But I still don't understand why Charlie wanted to kill Tanny.'

'To stop you marrying her. I don't understand why at the moment, but it seems Charlotte was behind the scheme for

243

you to marry Penelope. In fact, once we'd figured out how Will had died, our first thought was that Penelope had planted the doctored capsules herself.'

'Pen a killer?' Mitch burst out laughing. 'Do me a favour – she's too soft to tread on a spider. All that toffee-nosed, Queen's-Garden-Party stuff is just her way. In fact, I might have thought about it ... until I met Tanny.' He looked fondly down at the silken head still leaning on his shoulder.

Dittany sat up and put away her handkerchief. 'Tell us how you found out about it,' she said.

'Just a bit of inspired guesswork. Something my friend Iris said reminded me that you had given Will some of your capsules but said you didn't know if he'd taken them. It occurred to me that he might have slipped them into his pocket and taken them later. The forensic people examined the jacket he was wearing and found traces of heroin that could have leaked out of them. Then a witness said he'd seen Will in the gents at the hotel earlier that evening, swallowing capsules with a glass of water. We know what happened after that.'

There was silence for a while. Then Mitch said, 'So how did you figure out the business with the knife?'

'Once Ken Harris knew about the capsules, he was sure the killer would try again. Dittany had no possible motive for killing Will, so it was clear that she was the intended victim. The stabbing scene in the play looked an obvious opportunity – it would be a simple matter to switch the knives. He didn't let me in on the details beforehand, but he told me afterwards that he and DC Baxter had a musical signal worked out – if he played the "Hammerklavier" instead of the piece they'd been using at rehearsals, it meant the switch had taken place.'

'You mean, Baxter was there to keep an eye on things and do the necessary if the knives were switched?'

'And PC Peck. The young waiter with the horns and tail is a police officer as well.'

Mitch's eyes widened and he gave Dittany a squeeze. 'Just think of that, doll – you had your own personal detectives looking after you. I'll have to call you Princess from now on! Of course,' he turned back to Melissa, 'I knew something was up when Harris took charge of the arrangements. He told me to close the hotel for the night and give the Bellamys the evening off.' He scratched his head, evidently still somewhat bemused by the way things had turned out. 'I had some cock and bull yarn ready in case Vic cut up rough, but he seemed quite chuffed about it. Said he thought it was very considerate of me!'

'I'll bet he was chuffed. It meant – or he thought it meant – there was even less chance than usual of the gang being spotted bringing in the spoils of that night's break-in.'

'How did Harris know there was going to be a break-in that night?'

'One of his men had had a tip-off, but the informant didn't know where it was going to take place. The police took a gamble that the stuff would be delivered to the quarry, and it paid off. There's a report in this evening's *Gazette*.'

'Have we got it, Chris?'

'Mrs W. takes it. She likes to do the crossword.'

'Get it, will you?'

Chris went out and returned with the local paper. On the front page, under the headline POLICE SWOOP ON HIDDEN ART HOARD, the report read: 'After a tip-off, police last night raided a disused quarry to the north of Cheltenham and recovered a quantity of stolen property, including paintings, silver and jewellery. Four men and two women are being questioned in connection with a number of burglaries in various parts of the county. Further arrests are expected.'

'Strewth!' said Mitch when he had read it. 'I wonder who else is in it.'

'I tried to get Ken to tell me, but he wouldn't say a word beyond what I've told you. We'll have to wait till the case comes to court.'

Chapter Twenty-Three

It was several months before the case came to court, and when it did, it sent shock waves throughout Gloucestershire and the neighbouring counties. Several of the most respected members of the community stood revealed as parties to a criminal conspiracy, the magnitude, complexity and sheer effrontery of which left honest citizens, as they read the accounts of each day's revelations, spluttering with mingled outrage and disbelief over their breakfast toast and marmalade.

During a period of several years, art treasures to the value of hundreds of thousands of pounds had been spirited away from their owners and stored in a secret gallery, there to be offered for sale. Prospective buyers had to meet only two basic conditions – an abundance of ready cash and a total absence of scruple. Since most of the purchase money was itself the result of illicit dealings, principally in drugs, these conditions presented few problems.

At the centre of the intricate network that had developed over almost ten years, controlling every aspect of acquisition and distribution, ruthlessly dealing with omissions and misdemeanours, sat Lady Charlotte Heighton. The woman whose wild and scandalous behaviour in the sixties had shocked society and delighted the gossip columnists, had outwardly mended her ways. After disappearing from the public eye for a period, she re-emerged as the budding entrepreneur who had sought – and eventually obtained – the backing of business tycoon Richard Mitchell.

The trial was almost over when Iris arrived home from her winter sojourn in Provence. The day after her return she marched round to Hawthorn Cottage to demand an explanation of the highly-coloured and garbled tales that Gloria had brought with her that morning.

'I've kept all the reports for you to read,' said Melissa. 'Most of it's been a revelation to me.'

'Don't pretend you didn't know what was going on.'

'Not all of it. Honestly!' Melissa insisted as Iris sniffed in disbelief.

'All right.' Iris settled down in Melissa's kitchen, planted her elbows on the table and fixed her friend with beady eyes. 'Tell about the revelations. Had the feeling you were on to something before I left. Too busy with my own thing to ask questions.'

'Thank goodness for that. At least, now it's over, I can tell without causing you loss of sleep.' Briefly, leaving out all references to her narrow escapes, Melissa recounted the events that had culminated in the attempt on Dittany's life and the arrest of the principal culprits. Iris's eyes grew steadily wider and her eyebrows stretched to her hairline as the story unfolded.

'Amazing!' was all she could say at first. Then came the inevitable question. 'How did it all start?'

'If you read the reports, you'll know as much as I do.'

'Can't be bothered to plod through all that lot.' Iris brushed aside the sheaf of newspaper cuttings with an impatient movement of one hand. 'You tell,' she commanded.

'I'll try, but it's unbelievably involved. It seems Charlie acquired some pretty dubious friends during her wilder days and some of them were into drugs on a large scale. Those characters are always on the look-out for ways of laundering their cash, and antiques and old masters are prime favourites. Apart from their value, possession of an original Rembrandt or two does carry a certain cachet. Charlie also had friends in the art world, not all of them very particular about where they got their wares. She started in quite a small way, putting potential customers in touch with suppliers.'

'And then?'

'Like Topsy, it just growed. By this time, she had launched her first Dizzy Heights branch and some of her customers were wives or mistresses of wealthy crooks. She soon smelled out potential customers for old masters. The demand increased to the extent that she and her associates needed help with the logistics. Through the grapevine she heard of Vic Bellamy.'

Iris's eyes nearly popped out of her head. 'The manager at Heyshill Manor?'

'Right. When Charlie Heighton first met him, he was running a pub near Witney and Kim was his bar manager. He was also a high-class fence who'd managed to avoid police attention, and he was only too ready to sign up with her. The business expanded and they were on the look-out for new premises when Sir Hugo Stoneleigh-Pryor decided to convert Heyshill Manor into a luxury hotel. And guess who got the principal contract? One of Charlie's customers, an outwardly respectable architect who was making a mint on the side by kidding gullible clients that planning consents cost money. His surveyor – another crook whose racket was to charge exorbitant sums for unnecessary work – came across the bricked-up part of the crypt. Word got back that here was the perfect store for the loot.'

'Did Sir Hugo realise what was going on?' asked Iris.

'Almost certainly, but he probably drew a fat fee for pretending not to. His main interests were hunting and high living, and so long as the hotel made money, he let them get on with it. They brought Vic in as manager – by this time Kim had conned a wedding ring out of him – and the set-up was perfect. They rigged the crypt up as a gallery where the richest and most trustworthy clients could come and make a choice. They even produced a catalogue for those who for whatever reason couldn't attend in person.'

Iris gave a soft whistle. 'So that's how Kim got her prints.'

'Exactly. Once the originals were sold on, the gang had no

248

further use for them. Incidentally, it was you who put us on to that – you and Gloria's Stanley's Auntie Muriel.'

Iris smirked. 'Clever me! Do I get a commendation?'

'An unofficial one, maybe. I made Ken Harris promise to keep our names out of it, and he said he'd do his best.'

'So Lady Charlotte was the mastermind?'

'That's right. Incidentally, it was on her orders that Vic sent the likes of Clegg and his partner to issue "warnings" to anyone who stepped out of line.'

'What about the Hon. Pen? Where did she come in?'

'Charlie took her on as a partner in the boutique because she had fashion flair and the right looks and background. Penelope was very much under her thumb, and later she was to come in very useful – or so Charlie thought. When Sir Hugo died so unexpectedly and the gang lost control of the hotel, they had to do some very quick thinking. Fortunately, Mitch allowed Vic to stay on as manager – at the time, of course, he had no suspicions and was glad of Vic's expertise. But they knew his reputation for straight dealing and guessed that if he got wind of what was going on in one of his businesses, he'd put the boot in right away. But if he were to marry Penelope . . . even he would hardly shop his own wife.'

'And then Dittany happened along. That must have been a blow.'

'It was. And by this time, Mitch had his suspicions of Vic and they got wind of that as well. Charlie must have hit the panic button at this point – trying to kill Dittany wasn't the smartest thing she'd ever done.'

'She ought to get life for that.'

'That'll be the subject of a separate trial. Ken doesn't think they'll be able to pin Will Foley's death on her, though – there isn't enough evidence.'

'Pity. How did the police get on to Lady C.?'

Melissa preened herself. 'I put them on to her. She was the driver – and the owner – of the blue Renault. She'd put the goods in the car, drive to a prearranged place and meet her contact to hand over the keys. The contact would pick up the car to make the delivery, and there'd be a similar arrangement to hand it back.'

'Sounds a bit complicated.'

'Not really. The important thing, as far as Charlie saw it, was for her to avoid being spotted actually handing over the ill-gotten loot. When I met her in the shopping arcade that day, she'd just arranged for Mrs Wilson to pick up an early Constable for a customer of Antony Purvis.'

'Purvis? The Stowbridge art dealer?' Iris looked shocked. 'He's a local councillor. Can't trust anyone nowadays.'

After the trial, which ended in the conviction of the culprits on a long list of charges, Ken Harris took Melissa Craig to dinner at *Le Vieux Manoir*.

'I see the Hon. Pen got off with a suspended sentence,' she commented as they tucked into *moules marinière*. 'Was she really so dominated by Charlotte Heighton that she had to go along with everything she was told to do?'

'That's what her Counsel pleaded, and the court accepted,' he replied in a detached tone.

'I gather you don't believe it?'

'Did she strike you as someone who could be that easily led?'

'Frankly, no, but Dittany Blair is more charitable than we are. She wants Mitch to keep her on as fashion adviser at Dizzy Heights.'

Harris looked up from his plate in astonishment. 'He won't agree to that, surely?'

'I don't think so for a moment, and I told her so,' said Melissa emphatically. 'When it comes to his business reputation, he doesn't compromise an inch. That's something Dittany will have to accept if she's to have any future with him.'

Harris paused in the act of mopping up the sauce from the *moules* with a piece of French bread and looked thoughtful. 'Do you think she will – have a future, that is?' he asked.

Melissa shrugged. 'Time will tell. I advised her not to rush into any long-term commitment until she knows him a bit better. Incidentally, Iris is cock-a-hoop – he's commissioned her to do a painting of Heyshill Manor.'

'He's going to carry on running it?'

'Of course. He's put in a new manager and is turning the gallery into a function room for private parties. It'll be ideal for discos – the kids can turn up the decibels as high as they want without disturbing the hotel guests.'

'So all's well that ends well?'

'You could say that.'

After dinner, he drove her back to Hawthorn Cottage.

'Coming in for coffee?' she said, but before he could reply, his pocket pager started bleeping.

'I'll come in and use your phone, if I may,' he said, with a resigned sigh. 'I'll take a rain check on the coffee.'

BETTY ROWLANDS

OVER THE EDGE

Landscape with Still Life . . .

The summer school art students gazed in awe at the view across the gorge, where the foaming river rushed headlong towards the distant Mediterranean. Above their heads, a lazily circling red kite. Below them, six hundred feet down . . . still life.

Unnaturally still.

Exclamations of wonder turned to gasps of horror at the sight of the man lying sprawled on a rocky ledge just above the water. All too obviously dead.

On the face of it, a tragic accident. But the discovery, days later, of a second body in almost the identical spot changed assumptions of accident to suspicions of murder. And Melissa Craig, researching into the strange and violent history of the area, is drawn yet again into a present-day mystery.

'Melissa Craig . . . is an engaging, human heroine'
Financial Times

HODDER AND STOUGHTON PAPERBACKS

BETTY ROWLANDS

A LITTLE GENTLE SLEUTHING

Melissa Craig earns her living from crime.

A detective story writer desperate for some peace and quiet, she has bought and renovated a Cotswold cottage. But even as she moves in, among the usual chaos of builders and removal men, a series of frantic wrong-number phone calls brings a first disturbing note.

Then her next-door neighbour – a strong advocate of vegetarianism and organic food – unearths a corpse while digging for leaf mould in the woods.

Urged on by an engaging young journalist, Melissa turns her literary talents to real-life detection and, beneath the rural idyll, uncovers a bizarre underworld of villainy, conspiracy and despair . . .

'A fine new heroine'

Scotland on Sunday

'A splendidly lively debut . . . Good plotting, well-crafted writing and believable characterisation'

Publishing News

HODDER AND STOUGHTON PAPERBACKS

BETTY ROWLANDS

FINISHING TOUCH

This woman simply had to be her next victim!

Working out how to kill her would have to come later, Melissa Craig thought vengefully. Just as soon as she was able to get back to writing the well-overdue next thriller.

Meanwhile the woman twittered away, with her silly prejudices and utter insensitivity to the fact that there had been a real murder.

A girl was dead. Someone Melissa had first seen mutilated in effigy. A knife plunged into her portrait and sliced viciously downwards from throat to stomach while the Art College Award Show audience gasped with horror at such aesthetic vandalism.

But this time the knife had cut into flesh, not canvas. Flesh and blood.

And someone Melissa had grown rather fond of was the prime suspect . . .

'Gently old fashioned whodunnit, riddled with lurking anguish'

The Times

HODDER AND STOUGHTON PAPERBACKS